PENGUIN BOOKS

THE STORMWATCHER

Graham Joyce is the author of *Dreamside* and *House of Lost Dreams*, as well as the British Fantasy Award winnnig *Dark Sister*, *Requiem* and *The Tooth Fairy*. *Requiem* and *The Tooth Fairy* are published by Signet. His novels have been widely translated.

His first novel was written on the Greek island of Lesbos, where he lived for a year before travelling in the Middle East, and it was while visiting Jerusalem that he was inspired to write *Requiem*. He is the son of a miner, and it was his childhood in a Warwickshire colliery village that formed the backdrop for *The Tooth Fairy*. Graham Joyce now lives in Leicester with his wife and daughter, and divides his time between writing and lecturing in Creative Writing at Nottingham Trent University.

GRAHAM JOYCE

———————

THE STORMWATCHER

PENGUIN BOOKS

PENGUIN BOOKS

Published by the Penguin Group
Penguin Books Ltd, 27 Wrights Lane, London W8 5TZ, England
Penguin Putnam Inc., 375 Hudson Street, New York, New York 10014, USA
Penguin Books Australia Ltd, Ringwood, Victoria, Australia
Penguin Books Canada Ltd, 10 Alcorn Avenue, Toronto, Ontario, Canada M4V 3B2
Penguin Books (NZ) Ltd, 182–190 Wairau Road, Auckland 10, New Zealand

Penguin Books Ltd, Registered Offices: Harmondsworth, Middlesex, England

First published in Penguin Books 1998
3 5 7 9 10 8 6 4 2

Printed in England by Clays Ltd, St Ives plc

To my daughter, Ella Josephine

So many thanks owed to so many people, but especially to Luigi Bonomi for superb editorial input and crafty advice; Elizabeth Bland for brilliant eye-control; Derek Johnston for insight and for showing me the Creative Walk; Mark Chadbourn for hot tips; Chris Manby for photos; Nick Royle for cool Guides; Quentin Willson for wheels advice and the Bordeaux raid; Michael Moorcock, Iain Banks and Jonathan Carrol for kind words; to the October Project and the lovely BFS; and also to Helen Willson, Sue Johnsen and Anne, Pete, Jessie and Chloe Williams for being dazzling holiday companions nothing like the people described in this book

Prologue

All motion in the atmosphere is caused by the unequal heating, by the sun, of different parts of the planet. Heat is constantly seeking to exchange, between the warm tropics and the cold polar regions. This causes the movement of air, winds, changes in air pressure, temperature fluctuations, clouds, precipitation of rain and snow.

Everything we call weather.

Going round and round in an endless effort to settle and even out that which can never be settled or evened out.

I

'Look through the face, Jessie. Through the face and beyond. Then you will really begin to see.'

With no idea of what it was she was supposed to see there, Jessie stared into the oval mirror. The dressing-table in which the mirror was framed, a heavy, mellowed mahogany piece of bedroom furniture, was over a hundred years old, and the silver of the glass was mottled yellow. The metal amalgam was failing and the mirror was foxed. Too many people, Jessie thought, have looked hard into this mirror.

'See what? What will I see?'

Jessie's self-appointed tutor stepped behind her, a shadow in the poor light of a dark room in a failing mirror, placing a cool pair of hands over Jessie's eyes. 'That's for you to find out. If I told you, it would spoil the surprise.'

Adults are strange, Jessie thought. The hands fell to her shoulders and she shifted her head slightly. Instantly her eleven-year-old face winced in anticipation of the reproach.

'I've told you that you mustn't move! Not an inch. Not even a flicker. It won't work if you fidget and move about.'

The rebuke, floating to Jessie on sour breath, felt unnecessarily sharp. Truth was she was getting a little bored with staring into the mirror, and so was relieved when the call to supper came from the kitchen directly below. She turned to look up at her instructor. The hands fell away from her shoulders, and a brief nod gave her permission to get down from the stool in order to go downstairs to join the others.

But her instructor pressed an elegant and manicured white hand on Jessie's breastbone before allowing her to escape.

'Remember, it's our secret, Jess. Telling is undoing. Remember?'

Jessie nodded before slipping away. She didn't need reminding. When she took her place downstairs only her younger sister Beth had beaten her to the table.

'This all looks beautiful!' Matt enthused as he sat down and tore a chunk of baguette for himself.

'Then wait for everyone else to get seated,' said Chrissie, trying to find room on the table to place an enormous wooden bowl of salad.

'Sorry.' Matt pulled the half-chewed hunk of bread from his mouth, offering it to the kids, who both said, 'Ugh!'

'Don't worry,' said Sabine who, everyone knew, preferred to stand on ceremony. 'We can't wait all night.' There was a certain rigid order in which she liked things to be done, and they were all having to learn it. One, candles to be lit in advance of the first bottom brushing the first seat; two, breadbasket to be shared round before anyone lifted a knife or deranged the cutlery; whereupon, three, someone, preferably one of the men, might pour the wine. Then, and only then, could one cheerfully, and with a compulsory sparkle in the eye, wish the company *bon appétit*, and since Sabine was the only French person among them, she should not be the one to do so. Nothing had ever been *said* about this definitive ritual sequence, but then Sabine had an extraordinary ability to make her wishes known without using words to secure them. Now here she was, as James took the last but one place at the table, saying that it all didn't matter.

'Grace,' said Beth, who was seven and enjoying it. She looked disapprovingly round the table. 'Someone should say grace.'

'Quite right.' Rachel, arriving last at the table, sat down and folded her hands together. Her dark hair gleamed wet, and her skin, pink from a hot shower, seemed to advertise the jewel-bright blue-green tattoo she sported on either biceps. 'You say grace for us, Beth.'

Sabine straightened her back and James scratched his head.

Chrissie bit a fingernail, while Matt looked wholly vacant. 'We thank thee, Lord,' Beth whispered proudly, eyelids fluttering, 'for these thy wholesome gifts and pray that we might – STOP KICKING ME, JESS! MUM, TELL HER TO STOP KICKING ME!'

'Jessie!' Sabine warned her daughter.

'I'm not,' Jessie lied pointlessly.

'– for these thy wholesome gifts and pray that we might come to know thee more with every passing day.' Beth opened her eyes and looked shyly from one to other of the adult company.

'It's the Christadelphians,' Sabine said by way of apology. 'She's been going to their Friday-night youth club.'

Matt thought the Christadelphians, whatever they were, sounded creepy and said so. Chrissie asked him what he would know about any of it.

'Anyway,' Jessie said. 'I'm hungry, so *bon appétit.*'

Everyone responded with a breezy chorus, the breadbasket was passed, wine glasses clinked pleasingly in the still, chalk-dusted, early-evening air. From the villa's vine-canopied terrace, the land rolled away in a grassy incline until it levelled at a field of almost house-high corn. Beyond the corn sprawled a hag-toothed outcrop of powdery, weathered limestone, and beyond that the hills climbed again into the distance. Dusk took on an ultraviolet tone, so that the white rocks stood out like faintly illuminated headstones. Twilight roosted on the tower of the dovecote and over the out-buildings of the converted farmhouse, bringing with it the muddy and dimly narcotic odours of the nearby river Lot. In this light a glass of wine raised in toast looked blue-red, and the bright silverware reflected back a plane of mercurial shadow. Anyone watching in secret from behind the limestone crags would have seen a single halo of candlelight struggling to hold back the mustered forms of the encroaching evening, within which protection five adults and two children bent over their meal.

'I'm relaxed,' said Matt. 'I feel relaxed.'

'It's only the second day,' said Chrissie. 'Don't feel too relaxed.'

'Better to be relaxed after the second day than only on the second-to-last day,' Sabine observed.

'That's obvious.' James refilled his glass. 'You always like to state the obvious.'

'And you might fill other people's glasses before you fill your own.' Sabine looked to Chrissie. 'My husband would keep silent for a week rather than say something which is less than blindingly original.'

'Sometimes I wish Matt would keep quiet for a week.'

'Stop arguing, children,' said Rachel, who had no partner to fault.

Beth suddenly laid down her knife and fork. 'I don't like the room we're in. It's creepy,' she said, borrowing Matt's word.

'What's creepy about it?' Rachel wanted to know.

'Noises,' said Jessie. 'It's got noises.'

Jessie and Beth had been given the room under the converted barn. The ancient, beeswaxed floorboards were bowed precariously and creaked mightily. If a breeze picked up, the heavy wooden window shutters rattled hard. The room had a cold spot.

'It's the owl,' Sabine explained to the others. 'A barn owl nests above them. When it comes back from its night flights it clatters over their heads.'

'An owl!' said Rachel. 'I wish I had an owl above my room.'

Jessie's eyes opened with admiration at Rachel, who seemed unafraid of anything. But Beth, disgusted, added, 'And there are mice under the floorboards.'

'You can change with me if you like,' Rachel offered.

'Don't spoil them,' James said severely.

'We are here for a fortnight, James. If they're not comfortable . . .'

'We let them choose the damn rooms. If they have another, they'll find something wrong with that in two days. You don't dance round 'em.'

But it was all bluster, and everyone knew the decision had

already been made. Tomorrow Jessie and Beth would swap rooms with Rachel.

'We could have an owl watch!' shouted Matt.

Rachel was in. 'Yes. Oh, yes.'

'What's an owl watch?' Jessie wanted to know.

'When you stay up late. Really late. Sitting under the stars. And you drink lots of wine – but not in your case. And you watch for the owl. It's white, and soundless, and it moves through the night like a ghost.'

'What do you do after you've seen it?'

Matt considered for a moment. 'You become a one-feather owl watcher. Then if you see another one, you become a two-feather owl watcher. And you go through life, counting, until you become a seventy-feather watcher.'

He's making it up, thought Jessie. *Making it up. How much is made up, and how much is not?* 'And then?'

'I don't know. Only seventy-feather owl watchers know what happens. And they won't tell anyone.'

'Ignore him,' said Chrissie.'

'Believe what you want. It's true.'

Sabine, Matt and James were old friends, but Sabine still had to ask, 'Where does he dream up all this stuff?'

'He's still a child,' Chrissie said. 'That's where he gets it from.'

But Jessie and Beth were persuaded. Beth was already a true believer, and Jessie needed to be. 'Can we have an owl watch, Daddy?'

James sank a measure of wine in one swallow, setting his glass back on the table before leaning towards his children. He regarded them with a rheumy, alcoholic eye. 'Maybe. Now, if you've finished, it's bedtime for both of you.'

Beth went round the table, kissing the adults goodnight in turn. Jessie remained in her seat, pretending to be mesmerized by a candle flame. She was fixed, an effigy, staring dead ahead at the flickering light.

'Jessie,' said Sabine.

'Come on, Jess,' said her father.

The other adults became paralysed, faces averted from Jessie, not wanting to be recruited into the challenge. But each of them was wondering: *is this how it starts?* Though none of them had ever actually experienced any of Jessie's displays, each of them had heard distressing tales either from James or Sabine or from both. The silence at the table was invaded by the sound of cicadas swarming in the grass.

'Are you going to bed?' James asked in a reasonable voice.

Jessie wet her thumb and forefinger with her tongue and snuffed out a candle flame. 'O K.' She rose from her seat like a sleepwalker, kissed her mother and father, and followed Beth to bed.

Matt lit a cigarette. 'I thought we were going to have one of Jessie's "moments" there.'

'We all did.' James filched one of Matt's cigarettes.

Chrissie observed that Jessie had been good as gold since they'd arrived, and Matt agreed. Sabine pointed out that they were only on Day Two, whereupon James made the word 'fuck' sound only like a sharp exhalation of breath. Rachel expressed the view that while they were here they should all assume responsibility for Jessie – and Beth, come to that – and share some of the load with James and Sabine.

'I wouldn't wish that on any of you,' James said, managing to make it sound as if he wasn't joking.

'We can take the kids off your hands a bit,' Matt said, being the least likely of the available adults to do so, 'to give you and Sabine a bit more time together.'

James startled everyone by standing up. 'I'm off to bed. I don't feel too good.'

After he'd gone, the cicadas thrashed in the grass, the candle flame guttered but stayed alight. 'Is James all right?' Chrissie asked Sabine.

'You mean when he's not drunk or stoned?' Sabine suddenly let tiredness collapse her face. Mauve shadows stuck to the small pouches under her eyes. 'He's been complaining about feeling unwell for months now. He won't talk to me about it or see anyone. He just complains and goes to bed. Like that. You know something? We all really need this holiday.'

It had been James's idea, originally, to take this holiday together. In truth, he had his own agenda for wanting other people around him, in that the presence of others reduced the simmering heat of the family cauldron. Sabine, in turn, had leapt at the opportunity. She welcomed the idea of others helping her, not with the burden of Jessie but with the burden of James. Then James had changed his mind, dragged his feet, and then was ebullient about the idea all over again, suggesting that Rachel be added to the company. A former employee at James's ad agency, she had recently been giving Jessie and Beth piano lessons. The lessons need not be interrupted, James pointed out, if they could find a *gîte* with a piano. Sabine wasn't sure, in the same way she'd never been sure about Rachel's suitability as a music teacher for her girls. But, James pointed out, she was recovering from yet another relationship which had exploded in her face, and the charitable thing to do would be to invite her, and apart from that everyone, meaning Matt and Chrissie, who in truth had never expressed an opinion about Rachel either way, thought well of her.

'So, Sabine,' Matt said, patently changing the subject, 'how does it feel to be back in your own country?'

'It feels good. And especially to be here with all of you.'

'God, it's hot,' Chrissie said, fanning herself with a placemat. 'How about a swim? Let's all take our clothes off and jump in the pool.'

'What, me on my own with three women?' said Matt.

'We won't look,' said Rachel, peeling off her white vest, and she was first in.

2

Every morning a mist. A dense, damp mist hanging like thick muslin drawn across the landscape, penetrated only by the outline forms of the strongest trees and the sharpest limestone crags. And yet the foreground remained clear and sunny and bright, as if the mist unrolling towards them like a bolt of draper's cloth had stopped thirty metres from the house. But, despite the heat of the morning, the damp invaded the house. It swelled and cracked the timber shutters; it glued wooden drawers and made them stick tight; it dampened sheets; it teased knee and elbow joints and tormented old bone fractures.

'Is this normal for the Dordogne?' Jessie heard Rachel ask. And Chrissie ask. And Matt ask. 'This mist. Is it normal?'

Her mother was expected to be an expert on all matters French, from folk customs to meteorology, but her answer every time was, 'Don't ask me. I'm from the north.'

'Perfectly normal.' James knew no more about it than any of the others, though he had been to the region before, twice. Any idle comment about the weather might be interpreted by James as a criticism of his choice of holiday venue.

And indeed the mist was not at all unusual for that district of the Périgord – or the Dordogne, as the British persist in calling it – lying as it does between the wide banks of the Lot and the meanders of the Dordogne itself. Every morning the engine-like progress of the yellow sun rolled the moisture of the land into a ball of grey floss; and by mid-morning the job was done and all mist burned off. The sky once again was the blue of heraldry. It was August, and the land had already delivered before the holidaymakers had arrived. Nuggets of corn had ripened and gleamed on the cob; figs plumped and split on the branch; plums fell and burst open on the ground. It made them feel somehow posthumous.

It was into these blue skies that Jessie gazed, watching the last of the disappearing mists. Her eyes seemed to reflect the pattern of the skies.

'That's a good trick,' said her instructor. 'How do you do that?'

Trick? 'Do what?'

'Make your eyes change colour like that. A moment ago they were grey like a sticky paste. Now they're like cornflowers.'

'I was just looking at the sky.'

'That's not what I meant, Jess. I meant, where do you go when your eyes glaze over like that? In your mind, where do you go and what do you see?'

Jessie shrugged. 'Nowhere. Nothing.'

'You were going to be wicked at the table last night, weren't you? When your father told you to go to bed. You decided not to. Can you always decide?'

Jessie looked pained. 'Can I go and swim now?'

Jessie's instructor regarded her steadily. 'Yes. But first let me ask if you looked in the mirror this morning.'

'Yes.'

'A full twenty minutes?'

'It was hard. Beth kept coming in and out and asking me what I was doing.' It was true. The task was more demanding than it seemed. Just finding a few moments alone was difficult in a house full of people.

'You'll just have to ignore Beth. It's not going to work if you don't do it properly. You won't see anything. Try again this evening, when everyone is busy. I'll aim to keep Beth away from you. Now go and swim.'

Jessie peeled away, paused briefly on the edge of the pool, dived and shrieked as she hit the cold water. A keen swimmer, she had already developed a fine style and an impressive speed. After a moment she was joined in the water by Matt and then by Rachel.

Sabine and Chrissie came down to relax on sunloungers. James was still in bed.

Everyone was concerned about Jessie. Jessie the golden child, Jessie the starred one, physically mature beyond her eleven years, clever beyond reproach, poised on the brink of womanhood. Jessie with her father's blue eyes and her mother's wonderful sallow skin; Jessie with her hair the colour of honey and fire and a careless, almost dirty laugh that came from neither parent; Jessie with a wayward streak, a dropped stitch in what should have been the flawless weave, the bug in the otherwise perfect programme.

What a flaw. What a bug. Jessie was inclined to take walks. She could go missing for hours at a time, and had done since she was three years old. She was disposed to swim in places not designated for bathing, such as dangerous reservoirs and lethal quarry pits and in the spaces between canal locks. She was inclined to take off her clothes in inappropriate places, such as in supermarkets near the bakery section, or in the High Street on the town's Carnival Day, or in the churchyard at a cousin's wedding.

'Why did you do it, Jessie? Tell us why.'

'It was the smell of the fresh-baked bread.'

'Why, Jessie? Why?'

'It was when they started throwing confetti.'

She also had a bizarre and frustrating trait of asking people their name, even though she knew the answer, even though she had known the person in question for several years, and even though, at occasional times of stress, that person was her school-teacher, or even her mother or her father. The trait might exhibit itself several times a day or not for a month or two. It always seemed to arrive apropos of nothing:

'Goodnight, God bless, and what's your name?'

'Well, as I told you last night and last week and the week before last week, I'm your father.'

'Yes, yes.'

'Can I stay up and watch television and what's your name?'

'For Christ's sake, Jessie! I mean, for Christ's sake!'

'Yes, yes.'

Naturally, Jessie had been looked at. She'd been looked at on the National Health by a child psychologist who made James angry by refusing to tell him what he wanted to hear. The psychologist said that, on the face of it, there was nothing wrong with Jessie.

'What do you mean "on the face of it"? For Christ's sake, either there is something wrong with her or there isn't.'

'Do you always get angry so easily at home?'

'Oh, clever. Very clever. And I thought this was about Jessie's behaviour. Silly me.'

'My husband doesn't mean to be rude.' Sabine was accustomed, in her dealings with doctors, tax inspectors, council officials, bankers and hi-fi salesmen, to smoothing ruffled feathers behind him.

'All I mean is that there is a context for these things. I've given her a battery of tests. Jessie's response to all the standard questions and stimuli are perfectly normal. In fact she's well above average intelligence and shows a surprising degree of emotional maturity. What I haven't been able to detect are the trigger points for these examples of disturbing behaviour.'

But James didn't want context, and he didn't want trigger points. He wanted to know what was wrong with Jessie. He wanted someone to identify for him, clearly, that the blue wire had inadvertently been connected to the green fuse, and he was prepared to pay privately and handsomely for someone who could.

'The problem is neuro-physiological,' he was reassured by a much older and uncommonly genial specialist, who poured a fine malt into heavy lead-crystal tumblers. 'It's caused by a chemical imbalance exacerbated by the hormonal rush the poor thing is experiencing just now –'

'This started long before puberty,' Sabine put in.

James held up his hand to her. 'Let the doctor finish, darling.'

'Your wife is correct, but I'd expect the condition to stabilize. There are drugs we can prescribe in the short term. I mean, we wouldn't want to be surprised in Sainsbury's again, now, would we?'

Sabine didn't like the idea of drugs and said so. James argued science, progress and the chemical solution, characterizing Sabine's objections as superstitious.

'It's nothing to do with superstition, it's just that –'

'ADD,' the specialist interrupted. 'Your daughter suffers from a variant of what we've come to call Attention Deficit Disorder.'

'The National Health doctor dismissed that diagnosis,' said Sabine.

'Well,' the specialist smiled, 'they do tend to skimp on the tests.'

So the drug Ritalin was prescribed and seemed to work. It also seemed to incline Jessie towards apathy, to banish the sheen from her eye, to inflict her with constipation and to give her nightmares. Sabine felt that the visit to the specialist had done little more than equip them with an obscure phrase and that the only person who felt better after the consultation was James. She reduced the dose without telling her husband.

This covert action caused no problem for Jessie for three months. Then one Saturday afternoon she returned from swimming in a highly excitable state, asking if it was all right to go to Brighton with her boyfriend.

'With who?' said James.

'My boyfriend. I met him at the swimming baths.'

Flustered, James called Sabine. He'd hoped for at least another two or three years before this question raised its inevitable head. 'You mean, his parents want to take you to Brighton?'

'No, he wants to take me.'

'To Brighton? How?'

'On his bike.'

'Bike?'

'Motorbike. He's waiting outside.'

James hurried to the window. Through the leaded glass he saw, at the bottom of their driveway, a young motorcyclist in racing leathers sitting astride his idling machine and smoking a cigarette. He held a crash helmet under one arm and was staring moodily into the gutter. James stormed to the door, almost wrenching it from its hinges, and marched down the driveway. The young man had one earring and a severe case of acne. He stamped out his cigarette in the road when he saw James approaching.

'She's eleven.' James barked. 'ELEVEN!'

Without a word, the young biker refitted his helmet and accelerated away. When James returned to the house Jessie was thrashing, kicking and screaming, fighting to break free of Sabine's grip. A teaplate, a cup and a wine glass lay broken on the kitchen floor. James had to help Sabine restrain his daughter. He pushed her on to the sofa and held her until he felt the fit subside. Unnoticed, Beth cleared up the breakages with a dustpan and brush. Eventually Jessie pulled away and went to her room.

'That talk,' James said to Sabine. '*The* talk. It's time you had that talk with your daughter. In fact, it's clearly long overdue.'

Sabine took a deep breath. 'Come on, Beth. You may as well hear all this stuff too.'

Sabine knocked quietly on Jessie's bedroom door. Jessie, snuffling, let them in. James brought up a tray of tea and biscuits and left them to it. Beth listened with wide, appalled eyes. Jessie wore the expression of someone who was being ticked off. Sabine laid out the facts of life as honestly and plainly as she could, avoiding moral censure but arguing for the sanctity of, and special place for, sexuality in a loving relationship. Then she asked if there were any questions.

'What's necrophilia?' Jessie wanted to know.

Sabine put her hands together under her chin, began to speak and then said, 'Beth, will you go and fetch your father?'

Matt came dripping from the swimming pool, beads of moisture gleaming on his hirsute body. He flopped like a seal on to one of the sunloungers.

'And then,' Sabine was telling Chrissie. 'She wanted to know about anal sex, oral sex, bondage, God knows what. I couldn't believe it.'

'Did you tell her?' Chrissie asked.

'Some things, some no.'

'I think,' Rachel said, also dripping pool water, 'the best policy is to be honest about everything.'

'Everything?' Sabine asked. 'You can't be candid with an eleven-year-old about Golden Rain.'

'Surely we have to,' Rachel argued, going unheard.

'What's Golden Rain?' said Matt. 'Second thoughts, I think I know.'

'Exactly. But where is she getting all this stuff from? Who's telling her all these things?'

All eyes turned to look at Jessie, who cut a beautiful, stylish front crawl through the shimmering water of the pool.

3

Each afternoon a sleep, a siesta, dozing under the hot, hot engine of the sun, sprawled close to the baked earth where even lizards crawl under rocks, sweating even under shade, sleeping off the meticulously prepared lunch and the carefully chosen local wine. A good time to slip away. A good time, while everyone dreamed.

Getting the nod from her instructor, Jessie eased away unnoticed, padding silently through the dust and the parched grass up to the house. The house was a place of still shadow. To enter was like slipping into another kind of pool. Shadows stirred and rippled, moved through the kitchen like a wave, lapped at the foot of the stairs. The wooden stairs creaked.

In the bedroom Jessie perched on her stool before the mirror and looked. Her instructor sat on the bed, watching her carefully.

'That's it, Jess, stay perfectly still. It's a good time. They're all out there, dreaming. Can you feel them dreaming? Can you feel their dreams trying to get in? Each dream is a living creature, did you know that?'

Jessie continued to mirror-stare as her instructor stretched out on the bed, unafraid, it seemed to Jessie, of being caught. And even if someone came, what were they doing? *Talking*. That's what her instructor had told her. *We'll say we were talking.*

'Can you feel the weather changing, Jess? Oh, yes – you may not be aware but it's changing. Stirring. These are the last great days of the summer. The fanfare of the dying season. Perhaps you haven't noticed, but a vast wheel has turned. A wheel so enormous you can't see it before your eyes. Maybe you've observed the mists, how they've thickened in the mornings. We will have to watch the weather now. Very closely. Things are moving. Things are in the saddle.'

Jessie didn't understand all of the things her mentor said to her. Many of them were puzzling and obscure. But she listened carefully, attending to every last syllable. And she did exactly as instructed. She gazed at herself in the mirror. She practised the art of unblinking. She had made a study of every pore of her un-blemished face, of each freckle hatched either side of her nose by the sun, until her instructor had told her to use the mottled rust flowerings of the foxed mirror to gaze *through* and *beyond* the glass until a shadow, a grey light, formed around her features and –

'Hey! Something happened!'

'What?' Her instructor sat up. 'What did you see?'

'A tiny blue spark. It came from the corner of my eye and jumped across the mirror. A bright-blue spark. No, grey-blue.'

'Good.' Her instructor examined her wristwatch. 'That's enough. A good start. You must keep it up. This is only the beginning. Now we should go down and rejoin the others before we're missed.'

'Was someone moving around last night?' Sabine poured tea. Rachel had brewed a pot while the others dozed.

'These are coffee cups,' James complained. 'Don't we have tea cups?'

'Don't be so pedantic,' said Matt.

Beth wanted to know what pedantic meant.

'It means making fine scholarly points,' said James, 'so Matt is using the word quite wrongly, which I hope you never do. He means fastidious, don't you, Matt?'

'Apparently.'

'It was me,' said Chrissie to Sabine. 'I couldn't sleep. I got up and made some coffee – in a tea cup, I'm afraid. The dawn was just breaking. I sat and watched the sun rise, and then I went back to bed.'

'Chrissie is like Lady Macbeth,' said Matt. 'I married Lady Macbeth.'

Chrissie looked hurt. 'What does the dawn look like?' Rachel said, changing the subject quickly.

'Strange. A bit disturbing, really. The sky had a pink smear to it, and the mist was hanging across the valley in shreds. Like spectres coming out of the forest.'

'I've got some good sleeping pills,' Sabine offered, and Rachel laughed. 'What is it?' Sabine wanted to know.

'Nothing.'

'Tell me.'

'Well,' Rachel began, 'here is Chrissie, describing something strange and beautiful, a dawn which none of us have seen, and you offer her a sleeping pill.'

'So? I don't get it.'

'It's nothing,' Rachel said, already regretting her explanation. 'Just my quirky sense of humour.'

'You think it's strange and beautiful,' Sabine said stiffly, 'to suffer from insomnia, unable to sleep, tired half to death, wandering the house in the middle of the night out of desperation?'

'I wasn't quite that bad.' Chrissie laughed.

'No,' Sabine said, gathering up the cups and saucers. 'But perhaps your husband isn't quite as *fastidious* or as *pedantic* as mine.'

They watched Sabine's back as she hurried towards the house. 'Don't worry, Rachel.' James forced a smile. 'It's me she's mad with, not you.'

And you're mad with me, thought Jessie.

No one asked James why Sabine might be mad with him. They were afraid he might tell them.

'I hadn't even finished my tea,' said Matt.

That afternoon they made a small excursion to a *crêperie*, where they indulged a taste for beautiful and exotic pancakes. Jessie and Beth irritated James by preferring to travel in Matt's Ford Ka rather than their father's Mercedes-Benz. 'Yes, you can go in Matt's bubble-car if you really have to,' said James.

'It isn't a bubble-car, silly,' said Jess.

At the *crêperie* Beth and Matt were in such high spirits they both managed to get chocolate and ice-cream not only on their faces but also on their knees. Sabine gave Beth a ticking-off, but Matt got away without censure. Jessie wolfed her pancake and blew instead of sucked the straw in her milkshake. When the bill arrived, James whipped out a platinum-tipped pen and unleashed complicated sums all over a napkin.

'Just split it,' suggested Matt.

'You had fruit, ice-cream *and* maple syrup. An extra twelve francs.'

'But you had a second coffee,' Sabine pointed out.

'Six francs, then, subtracted from twelve, but Chrissie also had another coffee and –'

'Just divide it seven ways,' Rachel said.

'And,' Sabine pointed out, 'the girls had the souvenir badges.'

'Free. So that leaves fourteen francs for the –'

'They were only free,' Sabine sounded exhausted, 'if you had the extra-large helping of ice-cream.'

'For Christ's sake,' said Matt, throwing a few folded bills on to the table. 'Let me pay for the lot. My treat.'

'No fear,' said James, dividing and subtracting rapidly to the last half-franc, 'I know your game.'

'What game?' Matt was indignant.

'Forget it,' said Chrissie. 'Just give him the money.'

'Take that money back,' James said, peeling a note from the wad, 'and give me another three francs fifty. Rachel, is this yours? You want ten francs back. Wait, let's not forget the tip. Let's say for each person another . . .'

Eventually they all went outside while James settled with the waiter. 'What game?' Matt said again. No one answered. Everyone seemed suddenly drained and depressed.

That evening, suspecting that he'd offended his wife and possibly everyone else by spending the first two days of the holiday in a surly, uncooperative mood, James judged that a correct ratio of happiness might be restored by organizing a barbecue. It was what he did at the agency when morale was low or a major contract had been lost. Or even when one had been won. James was a great believer in the Office Beano. Everyone got pissed together and ended the evening in either a pointless clinch with a fanciable colleague or a senseless altercation with an office rival, said what they'd got to say and turned up the next day ready to quit or get on with their work. As a management style it had its theorists.

'A barbecue. Great,' said Matt who, with Chrissie, was dispatched to restock the wine.

'Good idea,' said Rachel, who was entrusted to return from the *boucher* with suitable strips of red beef for the griddle.

Leaving only the immediate family to endure the tyranny of the perfectionist, the purist who saw it as his life's work to give to other people nothing less than the very best that the world might offer.

'Don't bring back any more of that number nine,' James told Matt. 'In fact, forget that local stuff altogether. I have a feeling they sell more than they grow. Go to the second *cave*, the one behind the post office, and get the special reserve *vin du patron* in the second dump bin on the right –'

'Yeh, yeh, yeh.' Matt and Chrissie sped away, wheels spinning a cloud of dust.

'Nice lean cuts, Rachel. Ask him what kind of beef. We don't want Charolet. And he does a beautiful garlic-and-leek sausage, but check the skin. I'm suspicious about the synthetic skin –'

'Leave it to me, James.' Rachel climbed on her bicycle and rang the bell twice, though the road in front was empty.

James flung himself into barbecue preparation. Jessie and Beth were summoned from the pool and pressed into service. Sabine was assigned a subordinate role as James's knife shredded onion on the chopping board. 'Sauce. I'll give these people a sauce to die for.'

Sabine gently pressed a hand on his forearm, halting the progress of the knife. She kissed him lightly. 'Don't get in a state. It's only a barbecue.'

The furious chopping was resumed. 'State? Who's in a state? We're not in a state, are we, girls? You always mistake enthusiasm for a state, Sabine. Out of excitement comes creativity. And what's wrong with trying to give people the best? If I want to give these people the best, is that a bad thing?'

'No, I –'

'These people always settle for less than they're capable of. You can see that. I just want them to see we don't have to do that.'

'"These people" you keep referring to are our friends. And if we are going to survive the full two weeks together here, you're going to have to make some allowances.'

'So what are you saying?'

'I'm saying, just don't get in a state.'

'Listen to your mother's English,' James said loudly to the girls. 'It lets her down at times like these. What she calls a state we call enthusiasm. Don't we?'

'Yes,' said Beth.

'We're such enthusiastic people,' Jessie said drily. James stopped chopping, set down his knife, and gave Jessie the Look.

When Matt returned he was delegated to light the charcoal and exercise a small pair of bellows. Chrissie was put on salad duty. Rachel, having the girls help her lay the table, showed them how to fold the napkins coronet-style. Rushing out of the kitchen some moments later, Sabine told the girls to fold the napkins properly. 'This isn't a steak house,' she said sourly.

The girls looked at Rachel, and Sabine, realizing instantly, apologized.

'It's all right,' said Rachel. 'They do look a bit silly.'

'Please don't change them.' Flustered, Sabine returned to the kitchen, where there was some noisy dispute about the wine.

'Footwash!' shouted James. 'He's come back with footwash!'

Chrissie looked up apologetically. 'He said it was cheap.'

'Matt! What the hell is this stuff? MATT!'

Matt came in with blackened fingers and a broad smile. 'Dirt-cheap. And a whole crate of it for the price of just one bottle of that other stuff.'

Chrissie shot a warning look at Matt. Sabine looked pleadingly at James, whose spring was coiling visibly.

'But it's undrinkable!'

Matt poured himself a glass and tipped it back in one. He smacked his lips. 'Wonderful, *dahling*.' The children laughed. Matt dunked his charcoal fingers in Chrissie's salad bowl before dashing back to his bellows. James looked crestfallen. Chrissie crawled back under her salad. Sabine prodded at something simmering on the stove.

The barbecue went ahead, but not before James had decided when the steaks were ready. James had five categories of rare steak. He shook his head sadly and muttered over the condition of the sizzling cuts of beef. Matt cheerfully left him to it.

The meal proceeded with toasts to the many cooks. It was jolly. It was fun. The cheap red wine loosened tongues. Sabine was witty, decorous, charming. Chrissie got the giggles and recounted anecdotes from when she and Matt had lived in Paris. James chewed his steak carefully and winced – but only very slightly – at each mouthful of wine. The two girls loved being allowed to stay up like this and attended carefully to every word spoken by the adults at the table. Only Rachel, ever watchful, seemed to notice how frequently Jessie stole a glance at her father. It occurred to Rachel that Jessie was keeping a weather-eye.

After the children had gone to bed, Matt produced his smoking paraphernalia and expertly built a joint. It was something he could do with one hand. This skill had been available twenty years ago when James had first encountered Matt at university in the Seventies. If Sabine disapproved, she said nothing, merely passing the lighted joint on to Rachel, who held on to the thing longer than was sociable. Sabine only looked up when Chrissie in her turn passed it to James. The minute sigh vented between her lips would have passed unnoticed had not James challenged it.

'What?'

'Nothing.'

'Honestly.'

'It makes you depressed,' protested Sabine. 'You know yourself that it does. Depressed and paranoid.'

'If it didn't before,' James croaked before exhaling, 'it will now.'

'You know perfectly well what I mean.'

'Leave him alone,' said Matt. 'James has every reason to be paranoid.' Matt, at least, laughed loudly at this.

They lapsed into silence, listening to the relentless chorus of cicadas rising from the dark land. Sabine was the first to get up. Rachel helped her clear the plates from the table. James was the next to leave, followed by Chrissie.

'Don't be too long,' Chrissie said, kissing Matt. 'Don't sit up all night.'

'I'll be along soon,' Matt assured her.

The yellow candlelight painted the honey-coloured stone of the farmhouse. Matt sat alone on the vine-covered patio. He refilled his glass and rolled himself another smoke. A huge moth with wings like leather nosedived out of the blackness directly into the candle flame and was consumed. The flame crackled, the light guttered out. Matt sat in the darkness for a while, listening to the cicadas.

He heard a strange thing in the unceasing chittering out there in the black landscape. Beneath the obvious rhythm of the cicadas it was possible to detect a second pulse, a counter-rhythm set up as if by another team of cicadas. And behind that second beat, there lay another and, within that, another, as if each pulse subdivided a million times. It was possible to get lost journeying through the audial complexity.

Then something happened which made Matt feel very afraid. The cicadas stopped. Their chittering ceased entirely, as if on a given signal. Matt's ears pricked up. A primitive ripple of fear chased along his skin. Silence, pure silence, invaded. Then the cicadas, mysteriously and one by one, started up again, filling the valley at a new pitch. Matt let out a sigh. He realized that, although it had only been for a few seconds, he had been holding his breath against the silence. He had to scrape away the remains of incinerated bugs before relighting the candle. The yellow light now cast a sickly pallor on the stone walls.

The cicadas suddenly stopped again. Something breathed from out of the dark field. Then the cicadas started up again, at a faster beat it seemed, and more excited. Within the smoke and the vapours of the night, Matt was spooking himself. He collected up his gear and went inside, leaving the single candle burning and a half-finished glass of red wine on the table.

4

Chrissie, it was said, was sex on legs. This was said often but only by men. Women usually reserved different words for her. But when Chrissie invited Rachel to take a walk into the nearby village, the phrase also occurred to Rachel. But then Rachel was not one of those women who feel angry at the inappropriately flirtatious behaviour of other women; or who condemn the overt, girlish signalling which most females learn to repress when they are fifteen years old; or who instantly feel uncomfortable when made to stand on the smoking rim of a sexual volcano.

Rachel sat on the wall waiting for Chrissie, the stone under her bottom warmed by the sun, the jasmine and the winding honeysuckle still dewy from another morning mist. When Chrissie appeared in a white cotton dress Rachel felt a sudden and startling pull in her belly. *Is this what men feel?* she thought, and her cheeks flamed.

Chrissie's white dress bared her shoulders, invited speculation over her breasts and stopped short at mid-thigh. Her dark hair was tied back in a simple pony-tail, and she wore gold sandals that laced around her calves. There was about her more than a hint of luscious Olympian venery. Rachel, in her T-shirt and blue jeans, felt mortal.

'Is it going to work out, do you think?' Rachel asked after they'd put a little way between themselves and the house. The road on either side was closed in by twelve-foot-high corn heavy with ripe cobs. There was no traffic and they walked in the middle of the road.

'I don't know. There's a lot going on.'

'Two weeks to get through.'

'One day at a time.'

'I think it will be fine. If James could just relax a little bit.'

Chrissie stopped in the road. 'What are you talking about?'

Rachel flushed. 'About whether we can survive two weeks together under one roof.' She was embarrassed now. Chrissie's mind had clearly been elsewhere.

They walked again. 'I see what you mean,' said Chrissie. 'I suppose if everyone drinks enough it will be fine. But you're right about James – too quick to get a bug up his arse.'

'Hmm.'

'Do you think he's a good fuck?'

Rachel, who knew, said, 'I've no idea.' She looked at Chrissie, aware that Chrissie was trying to shock rather than test her. 'Do you?'

'No, I think he'd be a lousy lay. Too uptight.'

'Is that how you judge men? On whether or not they might be a good lay?'

It was Chrissie's turn to look at Rachel. 'No, it's not how I judge them. But it's the first thing that crosses my mind whenever I meet a new man.'

'Really?'

'Yes, really. Does that make me a bad person?'

'No. But it's just so . . .'

'And then when I've met them, I have to know if I could. I mean, if I wanted to. Not that I would in all cases, you understand. I just have to know if I *could*, if I wanted.'

And when Chrissie said she had to know, she meant exactly that. Over the years her judgement on the issue had become twenty–twenty. On meeting a new man, in any situation or in any context, she simply turned up the heat until eye-contact held for a moment more than necessary or a simple gesture or word confirmed for her that she indeed could, if she wanted. Challenge over, the matter would generally be dropped.

Rachel found herself trying to look at Chrissie obliquely as they walked along the road. There were other things about her. The woman had history. Rachel liked people with history.

'Look!' Chrissie said suddenly.

The cornfield had given way to open meadow. Brambles grew in a tangled hedgerow. Chrissie was already diving into the thicket, her arm outstretched. She seemed merely to have to tickle the fat, juicy blackberry for it to fall into her hand. She pressed it into her mouth and reached for more. Rachel watched, fascinated, as Chrissie's lips took on a purple stain. 'Got anything to carry them in? We should take some home. Before the devil spits on them.'

Rachel produced a bag. Chrissie scratched herself to get at the glittering fruit. Rachel admired the way she pressed her long legs into the brambles to reach for the best, her white cotton knickers revealed as she stretched. The air was heady, seductive with the odour of blackberry. Together they collected half a kilo before walking on with murderers' fingers.

In the village they bought postcards and enjoyed the admiring glances of the local Frenchmen. They ordered coffee at a pavement café, where the waiter sweltered charm. 'French men,' Chrissie observed, 'are not afraid to make their interest known.'

'The same is said of French women.'

'Yes. We're all fucking Puritans.'

The waiter came out and apologized for the delay. The power had gone down. 'An electrical storm, *mesdames*. It will only be a few moments.'

'He likes you,' said Chrissie.

'Sod off.'

'It's true. He's taken a shine. His moustache is twitching.'

They talked girl-talk. They laughed easily together, but Chrissie's eyes would stray often and at anyone's approach. Rachel found herself involuntarily copying this reflex. They talked about the children.

'Jessie's going to be a beauty, isn't she? And she's so open to influence.'

'What do you mean?' Rachel said.

'Oh, I can't tell. It's something about her that reminds me of myself.'

Rachel looked thoughtful. 'She certainly sees more than people realize.' She then asked Chrissie how long she and Matt had been together and how they'd met.

Chrissie seemed to respond willingly but without answering the questions. Then she declared that Matt was a man who found it difficult to show affection. 'I'm thinking of getting a new one before my body goes to seed. Like the blackberries. Before the devil spits on me.' Chrissie smiled. 'Rachel, you have to know when I'm joking.'

Rachel, not usually slow on the uptake, felt confused and rushed into reciprocating with some information about herself. She admitted feeling that James and Sabine had invited her along because they felt sorry for her. Chrissie nodded sympathetically but made no effort to deny this was the case. At least she gave no indication of any knowledge of the affair with James. While it was clear that Sabine knew nothing, Rachel was less certain about Chrissie and Matt. Rachel then explained her recent parting with a long-term boyfriend. Chrissie was interested and asked questions. Inevitably she asked Rachel if her ex-lover had been any good in the sack.

'Not especially.'

'So, then, he had to go.'

Rachel suddenly bridled. 'That's bullshit. There's a lot more to it than that.'

Chrissie retreated quickly. 'You're right. Sometimes I sicken myself by the stupid things I say.'

Puzzled, Rachel looked hard at Chrissie. The tough-bitch posture was tissue-thin, and she saw for the first time the fragile china doll beneath. Chrissie's vulnerability softened her. 'Let's pay the bill and go.'

Between the village and the converted farmhouse stood an old church. It was a low building with a steeply pitched roof of dark, mud-coloured tiles and a bell tower. The old brick was the colour of rotting parchment, and the air of decay about the building was made more sinister by the presence of five dense, poisonous cypress trees growing like stiff arrowheads from the dry earth of the neglected walled graveyard.

They wandered between the gravestones, fascinated but disquieted by the Gallic habit of posting photographs of the dead. The church was locked. A vast keyhole suggested that only a large wrought-iron key would open it. Rachel bent and squinted through the keyhole without being able to see much.

'Have you ever fucked in a churchyard?'

Rachel got up from the door. 'Are you spending the day trying to shock me? Because it's getting boring.'

'No, honestly. I'm just curious.' It was true. Chrissie wasn't trying to shock. She was genuinely interested in finding out how far other people's experience matched her own. She already regretted having said anything. The consequences of the things she said never struck her until the words were out.

But now it was Rachel who was curious. She had her own history to measure. 'I'm sure you're going to tell me about it.'

'No. It was a long time ago. Forget I said it.'

'Chrissie!'

'It was back in the days when I had to break all the rules. Childish, really. Let's go. Churches give me the creeps.'

Chrissie hurried out of the graveyard and pressed on to the house. When they got back, everyone was lying around the pool. Chrissie kissed Matt fully on the lips before waving the bag of blackberries in the air. 'Blackberries as big as your bollocks!' she laughed. Then she remembered the presence of the girls. She put her hand over her mouth. 'Sorry!' she moaned.

Rachel changed into her swimsuit and wondered how long the summer would hold out before the devil spat.

5

'Where's James?' someone wanted to know. Jessie looked round for someone else to answer. After a long period of silence, in which the sun appeared to shift in the sky, Sabine sighed and adjusted her sunglasses on the bridge of her nose. 'He's still in bed.'

'In bed at noon?' said Matt. 'Can't have that. I'm going to rouse him.'

'Leave him,' Sabine advised. 'He won't thank you.'

But Matt wasn't having it. He bounded up to the house and into the master bedroom. The room was shuttered and dark. It carried a smell like mushrooms, like fungus, maybe dry rot festering beneath the floorboards. James huddled under his bedcovers. Matt's instinct was to jump on his old friend, like a five-year-old. Instead he loosened the wooden shutters. They opened with a crack and daylight spilled into the room, almost hissing as it impacted against fetid dark.

James groaned.

'What's going on?' said Matt.

James rolled over and blinked at him. 'What do you mean?'

'This is the third day, and ever since we arrived you've been acting like you can't stand to be here. What is it? You got a girlfriend at home? Is that it?'

'No.'

'You won't talk with anyone. You make faces any time someone else speaks. You spend the days in bed.'

'Leave me, Matt. I'll be up in a while.'

'I'd like to know if you're going to be this shitty for the full two weeks. Not that I'd do anything about it. Just so I'd be able to forget it. Christ, this room stinks.'

'I'm sick, Matt.'

Matt looked at James. 'Hungover?'

'No, not hungover. I'm sick. I'm ill.'

'You want a doctor?'

'I've had a doctor. At home. Listen to me. I'm ill. Don't say anything about this to Sabine. She doesn't know.'

'What are we talking about?'

James sat up in bed. His eyes were bloodshot and his face was pallid. 'I really don't want to say any more just yet. But I might need you to help me through this holiday.'

Matt's boyish cockiness evaporated. 'Can I get you a coffee?'

'That would be good. I'll be up in a moment.'

Matt left him to it. In the kitchen he measured the rich coffee thoughtfully. He felt uncomfortable. He didn't know whether James was genuinely ill or whether he'd just been tricked into indulging him for the rest of the holiday.

'Can you feel it? Can you sense it anywhere in your body?'

Jessie sat on the dry grass, not sure if she could feel anything in particular. The house lay some way up the hill, at her back. Her instructor sat behind her, gently kneading her shoulders.

'Look up, Jessie. What do you see?'

'Blue, blue sky.'

'Anything else?'

'No. Just blue sky.'

'Look for tiny, hairline cracks in the blue, Jessie. Minute silver sparks like the one you saw leaping out of the mirror. They last for only a split second, but they are there. There has been an electrical storm nearby, and it's coming our way. And even if you can't see it, you should be able to feel it.'

'Where?'

'In your skin. In your blood pressure. In your brain waves. We don't trust the human body nearly enough. People have forgotten how to read it. All these things are affected by a storm. As are people's sex drive. My guess is that you were conceived after a storm.'

'How do you know that?'

'People feel good after a storm. The air is charged. It's cleaned. It's full of negative ions. And the thunder and lightning leave vapours behind them that make you feel terrific. That's what everyone needs up at the house. A good storm. And some of them need it more than others, and quickly, I'd say.'

'Who needs it the most?'

'That's not for me to say. But look! Don't you think the sky has changed colour since we first sat down? Just a little?'

Jessie looked. It was difficult to see how the sky had changed at all. Perhaps it had deepened a shade; perhaps there was a little more water in it than there had been moments earlier. At times she had doubts about her instructor. But then a sliver of mercurial light broke from a sudden cleft in the unrelenting blue, like a hare chased from the thicket by a dog, and it was gone, instantaneously.

'Hey! I saw something!' She turned wide-eyed to her instructor. Everything her instructor told her was true.

'Good. And did you feel it? A prickle in your skin? Did your heart skip half a beat?'

Jessie rubbed her arm, uncertain.

'Don't worry about all that,' her instructor said kindly. 'You'll learn to recognize these things with practice. Now then, shall we drive into town and pick up your photographs?'

James thwacked a badminton shuttlecock back and forth to Rachel in desultory fashion, a grudging concession to having fun. Fun, he'd been told, was what he wasn't having enough of. James could eat and drink with enthusiasm – if he'd chosen and prepared everything himself – but all other activities were chores into which he had to be dragooned. Swimming was too wet. Walking was an exercise which inevitably returned to its starting point. Talking only proved that no one had anything new or interesting to say. And badminton, as he now seemed hell-bent on demonstrating, was the most mind-numbingly pointless game ever delivered up by humanity's quest for social distraction. In order to make this clear, James was grimly intent on not missing a shot while playing with one hand in his pocket and affecting an expression of irked boredom. Rachel, meanwhile, having worked hard to get James to pick up a racquet in the first place, was embroiled in the joyless impulsion of the shuttlecock and deeply regretting it.

'Hey, you two! Come and look at this!' someone shouted. The others were gathered around the patio table, chuckling at Jessie's snapshots. Seeing her opportunity, Rachel lashed wildly at the shuttlecock and let her racquet slide to the ground.

James looked suitably appalled, as if, after making this enormous concession to Rachel, he'd been betrayed. 'Just as I was winning!' He tossed his racquet aside and wearily followed Rachel over to the patio, where the others had stopped giggling and were puzzling over one of the snaps.

'Daddy's wearing an insect,' said Beth.

'It's a bug,' said Matt. 'It must have crawled inside the camera.'

The snapshot showed Chrissie, Sabine and James sitting near the pool, faces rather sweaty and red from too much sun. The shot was slightly underexposed, but what attracted so much interest was the presence of a large insect settled on James's forehead. The creature had obviously been magnified by the camera lens and obscured one half of his brow. The superimposed image offered the illusion of the insect feeding nastily at James's right temple.

'Sucking your brains out,' said Matt.

Sabine made a remark about the thing going hungry, and everyone laughed at James's expense. Jessie, unlike her sister Beth, was not laughing. She gazed at the bug picture with horrified eyes.

The bug was present in the next picture, taken in sequence, a close-up of James smiling sleepily into the camera. The insect was enlarged but fuzzy and out of focus. Again it seemed to fasten itself to the side of James's head.

'Ugh!' Chrissie said unnecessarily.

When the next photograph was turned, the bug had gone. This was a shot of Beth and Chrissie splashing each other in the pool. The thing must have crawled out of the camera, someone observed;

perhaps it got wound into the film spool, someone suggested; lucky it didn't spoil all the shots, someone else remarked.

When the full set of snaps had been pored over and captioned and commented upon, Matt went indoors and uncapped a beer for himself and one for James. 'Game of backgammon?' he suggested, and James assented sniffily. As they counted the blots on to the backgammon board, Rachel and Beth drifted across the grass to play badminton. Jessie took her photos upstairs as Chrissie and Sabine slumped into deckchairs on the patio.

The sun shifted in the sky. The afternoon heat rose in a haze from the ground, and the cooked earth smelled proved and warm. Amid the sounds of the two women murmuring idly, and the backgammon blots being counted across the table, and the gentle thwack of the shuttlecock at the end of the garden, no one noticed Jessie re-emerge from the house.

Adjacent to the house was a stable, converted into a garage. James had secured it for his Mercedes, while Matt's lustrous new Ka was left to incandesce under the sun. The old stable doors were weathered grey, the grain in the wood split and fissured by sun and rain and colonized by spores and grey-green lichen. They were held in place by a single beam of wood, similarly weathered. Jessie's attention was focused on the heavy beam. She'd been staring at it for a full ten minutes before her mother, on a sudden impulse, looked up at her.

'Jessie,' Sabine said softly. Then, more alarmed, 'Jessie?'

Jessie only blinked, her breathing stilled, her features set.

Sabine recognized an intent. She scrambled out of her deck-chair but was too late. 'No, Jessie!'

Jessie lowered her head, braced herself and ran at full speed towards the stable doors. There was a sickening crack as, head down, she launched herself against the doors, her forehead impacting with the wooden beam. She toppled backwards. Unconscious, she sprawled in the dust.

6

The troposphere is the lowest layer of the earth's atmosphere and is the theatre of all weather processes. It extends to an altitude of roughly eleven kilometres above the polar regions, and to about sixteen kilometres above the equatorial region. It contains 99 per cent of all the water vapour in the earth's atmosphere.

Indeed, it is an ocean of gases and water vapours, and we live on the bed of this ocean, subject to all the disturbances of the prevailing tides, buffeted by its streams, subject to its vast, swirling currents.

7

While all of the other adults and Beth too had gathered around Jessie, lifting her to her feet, examining her wounds and clucking in alarm, it was Matt who hung back. Not that he lacked concern. On the contrary, he tapped the table with his backgammon blot in consternation. He was as fond of Jessie as any of them. Indeed, having no nephews or nieces of his own, he had adopted the role of uncle to Beth and Jessie. And being avuncular was not enough for Matt; he had to be *favourite* uncle.

Being favourite uncle came easily to Matt. All you had to do was give lots of presents, make jokes over the telephone, speak in funny voices and send unusual objects through the mail. No, it was not that Matt was unconcerned; it was that he never knew what to do.

Other people always seemed to know whether to call the emergency services or merely to produce a glass of lemonade, whether to apply antiseptic or to send someone to bed without supper. So Matt hung back, preferring to do nothing rather than risk doing or saying the wrong thing, reflecting instead on his own inadequacies.

What a good thing it is, thought Matt, that little girls don't know the truth about their favourite uncles. He, by his own good-natured admission, was lazy, useless and lecherous. In all three departments, he would point out, he was at least a champion. In his working life he was a jack-of-no-trades. He had tried almost everything in his time. His impressively broad CV was depressingly consistent in the time it took him to quit a job. He'd trained and qualified, and worked and quit, as an accountant after leaving university. Too boring. He'd retrained as a teacher. Too limiting. He'd had a spell as a youth worker. Too table-tennis. For a while he'd knocked about in the USA. Then he knocked about in Thailand, and then in Paris, and for a time it seemed all he was going to do with his life was knock about. Later he'd sold life-assurance schemes. Too manipulative. That particular work he traded in for a period of number-crunching in market research. Too full of existential *Angst*.

'What?' Chrissie had cried, for he had met her by then. 'Too what?'

'Black moments,' he'd said. 'In the middle of calculating how many C2 industrial workers eat cereal for breakfast. Moments, Chrissie, of genuine dread.'

Matt had met Chrissie during his Paris period. Matt saw himself as a Left-bank artist, but when anyone asked he admitted he was a painter without brushes, a poet without words. He claimed to have invented something called anti-media, an art form which existed only in the mind of whoever thought it up. It was supposed to be a joke, but Matt heard himself speaking so frequently about it to people that he almost started to believe in it and wondered briefly if he could make money out of it. To be truly anti-media, however, you had to starve and suffer, and, of course, Matt didn't like that either. He made a few francs by acting as a runner for backpacker hostels, by washing dishes, by distributing leaflets for disco-nightclubs.

He saw a Goth coming towards him one day on the Boulevard de Sebastopol. She was sweating under her white make-up in the surprising afternoon sun of a day early in April. 'Have a leaflet. You look hot.'

'It's these black clothes,' she'd answered in English.

He didn't mean that sort of hot. He meant that her fanny was eating its way out of her black jeans. 'Give me a cigarette.'

She did.

'Buy me a coffee,' he said half an hour later.

She did.

'Get undressed,' he said that evening, back at her squalid room.

She did.

After Chrissie had showered and removed the greasepaint, Matt had been astonished at what emerged from the cracked shell. She was shiny like a moist new seed. She smelled like the kernel of a species of nut. Her mouth tasted of almond, her saliva of aniseed. He wanted to eat her, to sate himself on her. He was maddened by her odour. He breathed deep and made a deranged sacrament out of her body perfume. The inordinate scent of her sex inspired in him an almost religious delirium in which her cunt was the communion wafer. Her genital incense smoked the air; it was like spiced breath condensing on him. It drenched him. He emerged each time from her blinking into the light like someone rebirthed, reincarnated. The odour of her triggered a holy terror.

For three days, except for calls of nature or to make raids for food, they didn't get out of bed. From time to time he would cast a glance at the pile of black clothes in the corner, the spike heels and the lace gloves and the BMW bangles, and he would wonder if under it all was a white mask with crimson lips. It haunted him to think that a fleshy spirit had climbed out of the Goth regalia, a new animal, a succubus.

Chrissie ever afterwards spoke of the time when Matt rescued her from Paris. But Matt knew she had rescued him. 'What are you doing in Paris anyway?' she'd said.

'I don't know.'

'Neither do I.'

'In that case, let's go home.'

So together they went home. They left Chrissie's hovel owing rent. Chrissie dressed in some of Matt's clothes. She abandoned her Goth gear where it had fallen: the gloves, the silver bangles, the black T-shirt and the mask hidden beneath. It was as if some creature within her had been banished or exorcised. They travelled to Calais and took an overnight ferry to England, sleeping in each other's arms on the floor of the bar as the vessel made rough crossing.

The fact was that when Matt met Chrissie his rationale for remaining in Paris evaporated. He was in Paris, he used to tell himself cheerfully, because it was a splendid city in which to indulge a lecherous disposition. Matt was inspirational and architectural in the quality of his sexual fantasies. He would collect women in the street and assemble them into Busby Berkeley spectaculars of lavish and obscene proportions. The athletic and pyrotechnic quality of his imagination suited his lazy character. He had never done very much to begin to enact any of these fantasies until he met Chrissie.

Her life fell on his like a carelessly discarded cigarette on tinder-dry landscape. She consumed and scorched him. It was three years before the blaze began to die down.

Indeed, when the smoke did begin to drift away Matt found himself living with a woman he still felt he hardly knew but having to put on a suit every day to drive up and down motorways taking orders for bars of chocolate at service stations and at various outlets between them. He was doing it, he understood, because he loved Chrissie, and their love was so aeriel a power that it needed the anchor of ordinariness. But when he could no longer make algebra out of the equation, he quit that job, just as he had quit many before. He had married Chrissie, and during that time various jobs had come and gone, not because he wanted them but because he thought that that was what married people did: they worked. It never occurred to him that one or two unmarried people might hold down a job because he couldn't see the point. He'd had so many jobs over the years he thought they might make impressive author's notes on the jacket of a novel, if he could write one. Not so long ago he'd even worked for James, enjoying a brief spell as a copywriter at Hamilton & Poot, which appealed to his sense of creativity. But after six months James had to 'let him go'.

'Let me go? You mean, you're firing me?'

'Firing you? Hell, Matt. I've been in there fighting to keep you! You know how I protect my people. I've used every trick I know. But we've lost three major contracts this year, the figures just don't add up and it's last in-first out. You're a friend. It's hard, it's tough, but that's how it's written.'

Matt said nothing, though he was deeply hurt. He'd worked

incredibly hard in the short time he was with Hamilton & Poot. But he blamed himself, having made a couple of small errors. Matt had thought himself almost immune, since James, who'd achieved the barrel chest and the hip-swivel that came with the status of creative director in advertising, did indeed throw a protective cloak over his own unit. Once James had bawled Matt out after he'd been indiscreet to a female colleague over things he knew about James. Then he'd had a run-in with an account executive who'd failed to present his ideas to a particular client; the account was lost, and no one was interested in recriminations.

'If I kept you on at the expense of another colleague, how would that look?' James had said. 'Work and friendship have to be kept in separate boxes. You can see that, can't you, Matt?'

Matt said he could see it. Eventually he found another job, his current one. Another friend had found him a position. He'd invoked some of his old youth-work contacts and was selling playground equipment to local education authorities for a Scandinavian manufacturer.

But then Matt cared very little. Work was a leech, plumping itself on your blood as you waded through the swamp of life; it was a tropical worm, entering the bloodstream through the soles of one's feet and swimming up to the head to feed behind the eyes until they closed for ever. A less career-ambitious man it would be difficult to find.

But Matt was not in all things apathetic. He was, for example, prepared to work hard to preserve his relationship with Chrissie.

Those few days in Paris, and the voyage home to England, and the ensuing months had become fixed for Matt in acid light. Something had walked into their lives and had enfolded about them golden wings. They had been chosen, set apart. They had taken their place among the elect. Work never mattered; they could do anything. Love made them bullet-proof. Love made them invulnerable.

Matt never knew when or why it happened, but one day he woke and saw Chrissie readying herself for work. She was applying make-up in the mirror, smacking her lips at her reflection. His vision misted by a hangover from the wine they had shared the night before, he blinked around at the damp, one-bedroom flat they had occupied since coming back from Paris. Then, day by day, the golden light cracked and began to peel back like foil. The photochemical light faded.

Matt panicked, and in his panic he asked Chrissie to marry him. She agreed instantly; he had, after all, rescued her from Paris. Matt was astonished at how easy it was to become a married person. He telephoned the registrar and found that all you had to do before the wedding was to turn up with a cheque and make a promise to a man in shirt sleeves and braces that you were not a bigamist. He had been prepared for what? Ordeal by fire and ice; quests for a black rose in the mountains at the rim of the world; public examination at the hands of perfectly ascended spiritual masters.

'You don't live in the real world.' Chrissie laughed at him when he came home with the documentation. 'You don't.'

Their wedding at the register office was attended by a couple of trumped-up witnesses. They couldn't afford a honeymoon but spent their wedding night in a hotel, dining lavishly and succeeding in pulling the huge velvet drapes from the window in their love-making. The golden light returned and suffused their world and their bodies. For a week or two.

Matt couldn't understand it. There were no conflicts, no differences, no sticking-points. Neither got mad if the other forgot to replace the top of the toothpaste tube or left a grimy ring around the bath. But he couldn't bring himself to talk about it with Chrissie. He didn't know if the acid light was still there for her; and if he had to ask, then it would surely be turned off. Moreover he blamed himself. He felt he had been given a rare and precious gift, and he had not been worthy. The gift had faded in his hands. He who was once one of the elect was now one of the preterite, the passed-over.

It made no sense to have been so elevated, only to be dropped.

Matt devoted his time to trying to restore the fabled condition to his life. He took jobs and tried to build a home. He quit jobs and persuaded Chrissie they should travel together through Indonesia. They returned and he took a job again. Then he wanted to quit again and return to Paris. Perhaps it was there, in the city of lovers, that the golden light could be restored. Chrissie refused. She wanted nothing more to do with Paris. The only good memory of Paris was of escaping it, she told him.

And here he was, several years later, moment by moment still trying to lay the ghost of the acid light, while a delinquent child lay sprawled in the dust after headbutting a stable door. Matt got up and surprised everyone with his authority.

'Stop fussing! Here, let's get her to her feet. Jessie.' He held his hand in front of her, three fingers splayed. 'How many fingers do you see?'

'Three.'

'That's it, you're not concussed. Sabine, you bathe that cut and put antiseptic on it. Then we'll all have a swim, right, Jess?'

'Right,' said Jess, her eyelashes fluttering.

Everyone looked open-mouthed at Matt. 'So what?' he said. 'So she headbutted the door. I feel like doing it all the time.'

Then Matt tore off his shirt, stormed down to the swimming pool and threw himself into the deep end.

8

The following day the housekeeper visited, arriving on a bicycle so old it might have served the Resistance. Her name was Dominique, and because she spoke almost no English she seemed greatly relieved to find Sabine in the house, with whom she could chat happily. She was delighted too that Jessie and Beth had been raised to speak French. She quizzed them about their ages and their school life, and she promised next time to drop by with chocolate croissants. How had the girl hurt her head? she asked Sabine. Jessie's mother lied and said that Jessie had dived into the shallow end of the pool.

Why did she lie? thought Jessie. *Why not just say my daughter is disturbed?* This was a word she'd heard about herself on more than one occasion. The French word for disturb was *déranger.* Deranged. *Am I disturbed or deranged?* Jessie thought. *And does it depend what country I am in?*

Dominique squinted at the bruise. 'You must take greater care,' she told Jessie in French, mock-scolding. 'Especially around here.'

'What's your name?' Jessie asked, involuntarily and for the third time.

'Dominique,' the woman stated again.

'Yes, I know,' said Jessie, and wanted for Dominique's sake to add, 'I'm deranged.'

Eventually Sabine and Dominique were left alone to drink coffee on the patio. Rachel, who could speak French reasonably well, wanted to join them, but she could see how happy Sabine was to slip back into her mother tongue. Sabine spoke rapidly and with elation. She seemed girlishly happy with the opportunity, so Rachel left them to it.

Dominique established that the holidaymakers had everything they needed and had negotiated their way around some of the eccentricities of the house. It was old, she said, and inclined to malfunction in every department. Sabine denied this and said she found it all perfectly charming, even when the electricity went off and reappeared for no apparent reason. Sabine mentioned the scuffling in the roof and Dominique confirmed that it was an owl nesting in the rafters, and not rats as everyone suspected, though she did warn that any scraps of food left out overnight would attract unwelcome visitors.

Though the *gîte* was owned by English people, Dominique and her husband maintained and cleaned the place, never seeing its owners from one year to the next. Sabine so enjoyed the visit from the housekeeper that she invited Dominique to come to dinner one evening and to bring her husband. Dominique left on her bicycle, shouted goodbye to the children and peddled towards the dipping yellow sun.

'Oh, you *didn't*,' James whined when Sabine told him about the invitation. 'We're supposed to be here to relax.'

'So you can't relax with French people any more?'

Rachel saw much in the question but said, 'It will be lovely to have some local company.'

'That's right,' said Chrissie. Ganging up against James had become the house sport. 'Ambience and colour. Good idea, Sabine.'

Sabine clamped her lips tight together. She got up and cleared away the coffee cups, making the china clink with aggressive duty. She didn't want the group's support.

'Do you miss your family in France?' Rachel asked her afterwards.

'I feel cut off,' she said briefly. Rachel decided to leave the issue until Sabine added, 'My family were not pleased about me marrying an Englishman. James was able to charm my mother eventually, but I think my father saw through him from the beginning.'

'Saw through him?'

Sabine didn't get a chance to respond.

'When did this appear?' James wanted to know. He was standing on the patio, gazing at the stone lintel over the old farmhouse door. Matt, roused from his paperback, got up to look over James's shoulder. 'Anybody notice it before?'

Wedged into a crevice between the rough-hewn stones over the lintel was a small wooden cross. The precise angles of the cross were cut from oak, grained, mellowed and blackened with generations of dull varnish. James lifted it down, pulling a black fleece of spider's web along with it.

'I've never clocked it before,' said Matt, losing interest and returning to his book.

Sabine and Rachel came to take a look. Neither of them had noticed it either. 'Perhaps it's normal in this region,' suggested Rachel, 'to leave a cross over the door.'

'Maybe a horseshoe,' said Sabine, 'but not a cross.'

The cross was engraved with a Latin inscription, almost lost under the layers of wax: *Absit omen.*

'May there be no ill omen,' said Rachel.

Everyone looked at her. 'You're making it up,' said James.

'No. That's what it means. It's one of the things I learned in my . . .' Rachel tailed off. Her cheeks flamed. No one else in the group ever felt the need to explain a point of education; they took it for granted.

'It's weird,' Matt said without looking up from his book. 'Throw it away.'

'You can't do that!' said James.

'Burn it,' said Matt.

'Do you suppose your washerwoman put it there, Sabine?'

'If you mean Dominique, she sat with me almost the whole time. I don't know why you're making a fuss over nothing.'

'Throw it on the fire,' said Matt, turning a page, 'or you'll be sorry.'

James ignored Matt and carefully replaced the cross above the stone lintel.

'God,' said Sabine, 'but it's so *hot* today.'

*

'Do you know why you sweat, Jessie? Or should I say perspire? Do you know why we perspire?'

'No.'

'It's to keep you cool. You lose heat in the evaporation of sweat from your body. The body wants to even out its temperature, like the weather.'

'Can you sweat when it's cold?'

'Sure. You can get yourself into a nervous state. That will make you sweat. And people sweat when they make love. That's got more to do with the mental condition they're in than with the exercise of fucking.'

Jessie thought about this but said nothing. Sometimes she was alarmed by her instructor's candour. Her instructor was inclined to talk at length about things that made most adults clam up in front of children. The adult world comprised a beach full of open secrets, half-hidden like shells among the shingle, but when you lifted them to your ears the secrets roared like the sea. Adults whispered or lowered their voices in the presence of children, or tried to speak in a ridiculously transparent code. Jessie had already found several such shells on the Beach of Growing Up. In her collection she had Sex, a bright-pink, sea-scoured subject which often raised a dirty laugh; Drugs, a weird conch of an issue and something which Matt put in his long, dog-legged cigarettes and tried to hide under the table every time she or Beth approached; Money, a brittle razor-quill of puzzling interest, her father's favourite; and Illness and Death, black lustrous shells still containing the rotting remains of some unpleasant marine life. There were many others, lesser shells, but these were chief in her collection.

Her instructor, however, was different. On any of these subjects her mentor was likely to say more than was comfortable or could even be taken in. When she was alone with her instructor, the beach grew vast and though the shells winked and became luminous, the waves crashed and roared and dashed at the shingle in a most frightening way.

47

'Is fucking the same thing as making love?' Jessie asked at last. There seemed to be a vast grey area here.

'The act is the same. The state of mind is sometimes different. You are certainly the product of your mother and father fucking, as are we all; and they may have been making love. The trouble is, Jess, it's just words. You can fuck without making love. And you can make love without fucking. Having the two things in place at the same time is best. Now then, the air pressure dropped, even as we were talking. Did you feel it? Storms are coming. Won't be many days now.'

Jessie smiled. She very much wanted to be able to say that she had felt the air pressure drop, but in all truthfulness she couldn't. Her instructor had explained how air pressure was different from temperature; that a lowering of air pressure was a reduction in the weight of the atmosphere. Her instructor had also explained how Jessie was more prone to fits or outbursts of temperament when the air pressure was high.

'You don't kill a bug on your head by running at a door, Jess.'

Jessie was astonished at the ability of her mentor to see right though her. 'How did you know . . . ?'

'I understand you, Jessie, in ways that the others don't. Only I know that you are a sensitive, as I was when I was your age, and as I still am. It's no good trying to explain about the weather to the others. They just don't get it, which is why I ask you not to talk about these things to them.'

'I don't tell them.'

'I know. You're a good girl. A great kid. But I'm trying to prepare you because you're going to start bleeding any day now, and then in addition to the weather we'll have hormones to worry about. And this thing with you, well, it could go either way. You understand that, don't you?'

Jessie nodded. 'This thing' referred to Jessie's problems. Her waywardness. The spirit that got inside her from time to time. The thing that made her ask a person's name over and over, though, curiously enough, she had never had to ask her instructor a second time.

The subject of impending menstruation had been graphically, even garishly, covered by her instructor. Jessie's mother's efforts to deal with the subject had been inadequate, focusing on the paraphernalia of keeping clean, of hygiene, of pads and towels and tampons and leaks. Jessie felt, after Sabine's ministrations, that she would be able to get through menstruation in great style without knowing much about why it was happening. Her instructor, on the other hand, had been arcane, gross at times, a dark pool of mysterious allusion, while leaving little of the physical to be guessed at.

'Something turned up at the house today,' Jessie's instructor said. 'Did you notice?'

'You mean the cross?'

'Yes. I hope it's not a threat. To us, I mean. To you and me.'

'Why would it be a threat?'

'Perhaps it isn't. Perhaps it was there all the time, and none of us noticed it. We'll see. Come on, let's get back to the house before we're missed.'

Beth's grace that evening ended with the usual murmured amen. James offered his amen by raising a glass of deep burgundy-coloured wine to his lips. The course of his hand followed a precise arch, the glass deviating not one millimetre on its journey up to lip or back down to table. It was the practised, machine-driven track of the accomplished alcoholic. Savouring the kiss of wine on his tongue, he looked up and almost shouted, 'Hey! Who moved that thing?'

'What thing?'

'That chunk of wood. Cross thing. From over the door.'

The table fell silent. Then everyone protested and shook their heads. Eyes turned to Jessie.

'It wasn't me!'

'Are you certain?' James said.

'Yes!' Jessie was almost tearful.

49

'Beth?'

'I didn't touch it.'

'Right,' James said, 'who's playing silly buggers?'

No one, it seemed, had moved the cross.

Jessie looked from one face to another. She certainly hadn't moved the cross, and she knew her sister couldn't reach it even standing on a chair. That meant one of the adults in the company had moved it; and unless it was someone not resident at the house, that in turn meant that one of the adults at the table was a liar. Jessie felt none too comfortable about breaking bread with a grown-up who was a liar.

'Please,' Sabine said, and her voice was slightly shrill, 'please, everybody,' reaching a serving spoon into the *boeuf bourguignon*. 'This meal is going to be so *cold*.'

'Wake up! Wake up, Jessie!'

Jessie blinked. It was Beth, standing over her in her striped pyjamas. 'What time is it? Go back to sleep.'

'Wake up! There's someone in the garden!'

The excitement and anxiety in Beth's voice made Jessie sit up. Beth beckoned her over to the shutters, which were open just a crack. The grey light of a false dawn gave everything poor definition as Jessie blinked sleep from her eyes. She went to the window. Outside, the garden was shrouded in nacreous mist. There was not a breath of wind, and the mist gathered here and there in cotton-bud clusters: it was like an attempt at Creation by an inexpert and childish hand.

'I can't see anything,' Jessie said.

'By the pool,' Beth whispered.

Then Jessie saw that there was indeed someone sitting on the edge of the pool, perhaps with their feet in the water. The form was adult, though in the heavy grey mist she couldn't make out who it was, or even if it was male or female, though she suspected the figure was naked. She couldn't even tell if it was one of the occupants of the house.

All the rules have changed, Jessie thought as she peered through the mist at the still poolside figure. At home it was different. At home everything had a precise order and a place until she, no matter how hard she tried, was responsible for disrupting things and in ways she never understood. That was how she saw herself, as Jessie out of order, while her mother and father and Beth were all in order. But here things were different. Other people were out of order, and that was strangely comforting to her, as if they were allies or fellow travellers.

'They woke me up,' said Beth. 'I heard them moving about.'

Then Jessie saw another figure emerge from the mist, carrying a blanket, which was draped around the shoulders of the first figure. Jessie closed the window shutters. 'Go back to bed,' she told Beth. 'It's all perfectly normal.'

9

Jessie's instructor, in the peace of the darkened room, doing her own share of mirror-staring. Naked. Leaning forward. Touching her reflection with the tip of her tongue, trying to taste the past summoned there. Breath condensing on the mirror. *Don't mist the mirror!* Who said that? Oh, yes, that pornography thing. Remembering now. That pornography thing. How had she got there? What path?

Yes, it was the angel. She could see it all now, in the mirror, in the dissolving light. That was it.

It was after the angel gave her an instructive crack on the head that she'd decided it was time to get out of London. The big city had not been good to her, never had been since she'd left home a decade ago. As if she needed proof, here she was, nursing a hangover and a slight head wound in a city where the streets were paved not with gold but with a creeping amber slime generated by pre-dawn halogen street lights and the light drizzle that had already soaked her coat.

She probes that wound. It hurts. Her hair is wet from the rain, alarming at first. But the blood, such as it is, has dried, comes off on her fingers in tiny, iodine-black flakes. She looks up at the angel that has laid her out cold. It looms over her, wings spread in celestial glory and triumph, hands outstretched in what is meant to be a gesture of beneficence but which at this moment seems like an aggressively offered challenge.

'I've had enough,' struggling to her feet. 'You win.'

The angel stands impassively over her. She licks her fingers, massages her wound. Her hair is plastered to her face, coat spattered with mud. Huge, golden parchment leaves are stuck to her boots.

Looking around, trying to figure a way out between the angels and the urns and the undreaming white spires.

Highgate Cemetery. Remembers the party, vaguely, and recalls coming here, indistinctly, with four or five other party drunks, strangers who'd either abandoned or forgotten her after her fall. Negotiating her way between the gravestones and on to the main path, the scene in the Half Moon Inn comes back to her. Black Russians at a steady trot; raucous conversation with a quarrelsome posse of young men; yes to a party invitation and bundled into a car with same young men, one of whom in the crush put his hand down the back of her pants, and she'd let him; a dark, heaving household, lighted-coal end of spliffs passed back and forth; a toilet bowl full of vomit; French-kissing a man who waited to use the toilet after her; music pumping up and changing gear; dancing; some filthy kind of rum punch; a window pushed in – out – from the inside and the party threatening to break up; reviving again, and some banana-flavoured liqueur; then, from somewhere, an idea to raid Highgate Cemetery – what for?

Jessie, you wouldn't want to know all this. Good thing you're not here to see this.

Lots of shouting and dancing on gravestones. Stepping from one grave to another, overbalancing, leaping clear and then looking up just in time to see the stone wingtip of an angel flapping at her head.

Then morning.

She leaves the cemetery feeling like a wraith, insubstantial.

The journey back to the squat in Seven Sisters is hell. She's shivering badly when the tube train arrives in Highgate. At Euston, changing for the Victoria line, can actually feel her blood pressure rising and falling with the advent and departure of the trains. Tears squeeze from the corner of her eyes: for one appalling moment she thinks it is blood. The rumour of an approaching train whispers like demons alive in the track. The hollow roar into the vacuum of the tunnel reaches a lonely and terrifying note. At Seven Sisters her hands tremble so badly she finds it difficult to insert her ticket at the barrier.

Worse, her vision distorts. The crack on the head leaves her journeying through a snowstorm like poor reception on an old TV set. Moving through a mild flurry of tiny sparks of light, brilliant but minute flickers, worms, flashes at the blue end of the spectrum. Like walking in violet rain. Violet rain.

Back at the squat, walls sweat. Embossed-rose wallpaper peels at its damp corners, ready to roll itself away from the plaster. She tells herself to get out of the squat. London is killing her. Have to get out. But where? Maybe to her sister, who seems so far away in the Dordogne. Maybe her sister. Wherever. Whoever.

Stripping off her damp clothes and climbing into bed, she falls into a forty-eight-hour sleep. She wakes, bruised and sticky. Feeling herself, she wonders if it is possible someone has fucked her while she was unconscious. Thirteen others live in the squat. Someone has stolen one or two of her things. Returning from Highgate, concussed and shivering, she'd been too sick to remember the standard survival procedure of barricading herself inside her tiny room. Not much to lose, but the sound-blaster, now gone, was something she'd always thought she might one day convert into ready cash. And today is that one day.

Cut losses. In the squat things are getting worse. Violence increases day by day; one of the girls downstairs hacked off her own hair after being raped by a freak from off the street; toilets all backing up; the one bath full of used hypodermic needles.

Sitting naked on bare floorboards, she composes herself before a slab of cracked mirror propped against chipped skirting board. The violet rain hasn't gone away but has subsided slightly. Pulling a cosmetics pouch from her leather bag, she reconstructs her face, heavy on eyebrow pencil, generous with burgundy lipstick. She has good features, knows how to enhance them; what's more, she understands the mileage of a painted face. Knows that in order to reach her sister she is going to have to find a little more cash.

Stroking eyelashes with a pencil brush, she squints through the violet rain. 'I'm not a prostitute,' she argues with her reflection, searching her own eyes, the way someone might in order to detect whether another person is lying. 'I'm not selling my arse.'

She finds a phone box and telephones Malcolm. A recorded message hisses on. Someone snatches up the receiver. 'Hullo.' Rich, fruity timbre, Oxbridge modulated to Estuary English.

'Malcolm, is that offer still open?'

'What offer? Who is this?'

'The offer you made before.'

An exhalation of breath. Malcolm has obviously forgotten. 'Come down any time. Any time.'

'Like today?'

'Today? Where's the fire? Hang on a minute. All right, come down after one.'

Underground to Shepherd's Bush, finding her bizarre new sensitivity to the onrushing trains heightened. Her heart still squeezes and contracts with the rise and fall of her blood pressure as trains approach. She finds her way to Malcolm's studio without recalling the address, having been once before.

Her finger trembles slightly as she presses the buzzer, and a voice crackles over the intercom. The door hums. She shoves it open. Malcolm greets her without enthusiasm on the third floor, looking as though he's just remembered who she is.

'Sweetheart, you look fucking awful.'

'Thanks.'

'I mean, last time I saw you you had a bit more meat on you.'

'Disappointed?'

'A bit. Come in.'

Through to a lounge with oversized white leather sofa and giant fern. Half the leaves on the fern are browned. Malcolm, six four with tiny, sun-tanned choirboy's face and rugby player's physique, plumps down on the sofa, gestures for her to do the same. 'How long you been a blonde?'

'Ages.'

'Your roots are showing.' Squinting at her head, 'How did you do that?'

'Dashed my head on a stone angel.' Finds herself refining her accent, talking herself up as Malcolm trades her down. Are we classless? Like could call to like, she knows it.

'Strange thing to do.'

'Inadvisable, Malcolm.'

Malcolm's tiny nostrils twitching. Rubbing the end of his nose vigorously, flicking a disparaging finger at her hair. 'I don't know. I really don't know.'

'I need it, Malcolm. I've got to get to France to see my sister. It's vitally important and I have a liquidity problem.'

'You mean, you're skint. And you let me down last time. I gave you a chance and you let me down.'

Eyes are moist on demand. 'I need the cash.'

Malcolm in barrow-boy mode. 'Cash? I'm a businessman. I don't fuck about wiv cash.' Even as he says this, produces his wallet, digs out a roll of notes, tosses them at her. 'Get your arse in there. Pots of shit to cover up those dark roots. You hide those bruises. And I don't like the way you're made up.'

10

'It's coming,' Jessie's instructor said later that day. 'Can you feel it? Surely you can. It's coming.'

'But every day seems just as hot as the last one. Sometimes I think it's getting hotter.'

'It is getting hotter, and so it will continue. But that will only bring it along more quickly.' Jessie's instructor lovingly stroked the girl's hair from behind. 'Shall we go and swim?'

Sabine watched Matt and Rachel and Chrissie and Beth leaping in and out of the pool. Matt picked up Jessie, swung her in his arms and then flung her into the deep end. Jessie screamed as she hit the water. Chrissie balanced on the lip of the pool, clinging on only by her toes, pretending to be distracted so that Beth could sneak up behind her and push her in. Jessie climbed out, ran at Matt so that he would pick her up and fling her into the water again, shrieking and screaming. And again. And again.

Sabine blinked, lizard-like, at Rachel before speaking to James. Rachel still seemed to be asleep. She spoke in a low murmur, hardly making her lips move. 'Jessie is spending a lot of time with Matt, don't you think?'

'So?' James grunted, himself near to sleep on the sunbed.

'She gets cow-eyed every time he says anything. And don't you think it was odd how protective he became when she bashed her head on the door?'

'Hmm.'

Sabine put on her Raybans to study the cavorting without being noticed. Matt swept up Jessie and tossed her over his shoulder. She kicked and screamed and grabbed the waistband of his swimming trunks in mock panic as he jogged round the pool. He dived in, still with Jessie over his shoulder. Then he swam a length with her clinging to his back.

'Don't you think they're just a little too intimate sometimes?'

'What exactly are you saying?'

'Nothing,' said Sabine, collapsing back into her chair. 'Go back to sleep.'

Rachel, lying on her stomach a few yards away, frowned thoughtfully.

The sun rolled in the sky like a dry miller's stone, pummelling them, pressing them flat until they lay stretched, proving like dough on the griddle of the earth. Matt woke from a deep sleep and gazed blearily at a vision of Rachel poised on the edge of the pool. The sun was dipping behind her, and the temperature had dropped a couple of degrees. She was wearing a microscopic black bikini. She stood unselfconsciously on the edge of the pool, flexing before the moment of making a dive. The sun pulsing behind cast her almost in silhouette, painting her lithe figure with sticky, caramel light.

Matt recognized a perfect moment. It was as if the day had been a shell baked and cracked open by the sun, from the inside of which a new life was about to stir.

Raising her arms in the air, Rachel suddenly became aware of Matt's eyes on her. She paused only to smile at him, cocking her head slightly to one side, before flexing again and executing a perfect dive. Matt passed a hand across the involuntary erection inside his swim shorts. He glanced across at James, realizing that the other man had been studying him watching Rachel. James arched his eyebrows cryptically before taking a swig of beer.

Sometimes James found it difficult to keep his eyes off Matt. And when he did look, it was not with admiration or affection, nor was it with envy or malice. It was with misgiving. Matt wasn't a competitor, yet the man had a way of inciting deep suspicion.

Take the irksome matter of his car. When Matt had worked for James, he'd played a part in securing a lucrative contract, earning for himself a generous bonus. Inordinate back-slapping and cork-popping followed before James suggested that now he was earning serious and steady money Matt might want to go in for a 'decent' motor. James was profligate with advice. He walked Matt around the coveted spaces of the executive carpark, where inaccessible automobiles languished like aloof, fat courtesans in haremic seques-tration: lipstick-red BMW coupés trying to out-pout silver S-class Mercs, seemingly carved from a single piece of ice, abreast of Audi A8s sighing Teutonic confidence from every vent. James cooed about solid-chrome gearstick knobs, made ecstatic orations over genuine walnut dash-panels. He seemed to want nothing less than for Matt to invest in the space race.

After several days of instruction James was perplexed when Matt drove directly from the showroom in a new but modest Ford Ka. After all James's generous tutelage and Zen-like insight, Matt had turned up in this . . . this . . . *sculptured teardrop* and asked him what he thought.

'I'm speechless,' said James.

'I know. Takes your breath away, doesn't it? A hymn to sim-plicity, this. The apotheosis of design.'

James didn't know whether he should laugh. 'God love us. And what clinched it for this, dare I ask?'

Matt thought very hard for a minute. 'I think it was the name.'

'Huh?'

'The Ka. Ancient Egyptian. Transmigration of the soul from one life to another. Oh, yes.'

'You can't buy a car because of the poxy name!'

'Isn't that we're in this business for? Selling concepts? Names?'

This time James did laugh. 'You're not supposed to believe all that crap just because you make your living out of it!'

'But I do believe it,' said Matt earnestly. 'I'm committed. One hundred per cent.'

Exasperated out of all proportion, James started shouting. 'And what about this colour? It's *purple*, for crying out loud!'

'Belladonna, actually,' said Matt.

It was that choice of car that first made James deeply suspicious of Matt. Though he could afford something more ostentatious, he had declined. James nursed the notion that Matt had deliberately done this to vex him, to spurn his advice, to berate his values. He was playing at not playing the game. In buying a Ka the little shit was being deliberately subversive. From that moment on James decided that he would have to keep a close watch on Matt.

'Where do you keep disappearing to?' Beth said to Jessie. They were in adjoining beds, having been woken up by the wine-jolly adults stumbling to their rooms, as they were every night. Now they couldn't get back to sleep.

'What do you mean?'

'You keep disappearing. Why don't you take me with you? Where do you go?'

'Nowhere.' Jessie turned over, showing Beth her back, knowing it would be unwise to say anything about her instructor. Jessie's perennial problem was shaking off the attentions of a sister who would cheerfully follow her to the jaws of hell in the hope of a nod or wink of approval.

'Why won't you tell me?'

'Tell you what?'

'Where you go. Who you go with.'

'Go to sleep,' said Jessie.

'I know,' said Beth. 'I know who you go with.'

Sabine cuddled up to James, wrapping her slender arms around his large frame. She interpreted his grunt as a signal of approval. After a few moments she sat up in bed. 'Too hot for this,' she said slipping off her satin nightdress. She snuggled down again, pressing her amber nipples against his leathery back. Her arm reached round between his thighs, her fingers closing round his flaccid cock. James sighed contentedly, but failed to respond.

Sabine kissed his neck. She raked her fingernails gently along his spine.

'Ow! Sunburn.'

Sabine let go and rolled away from him. 'Perhaps you'd prefer her.'

'Who?' said James, thinking Sabine was referring to Chrissie.

'Rachel. I saw you looking at her.'

'When?'

'Today. By the pool. You find her sexy, don't you?'

'If you say so.'

'I say so.'

'I've told you. I don't feel well. Helen of Troy in a leather bikini couldn't do anything for me at this moment.'

Sabine clamped her lips. She was not Helen of Troy and she had no bikini, leather or otherwise. She gazed up at the swimming darkness.

'I saw you,' said Chrissie.

'What?' Matt, laughing. 'What?'

'Looking. Lecherous. Lascivious. Lusting. Libidinous. Licentious.'

'Ow! Haha! Ow! Ow!'

'Admit! Admit it!'

'OUCH! Get off! Haha!'

'Admit!'

'Admit what, you little witch?'

'That you were lusting after her. By the pool. Today. I saw it.'

'After who? Sabine? It's true. OW!'

'Rachel! Lusting after Rachel. You'd like to fuck her, wouldn't you?'

'I'd rather fuck you. Then Sabine a close second. Then Rachel a close third.'

'Animal. You're an animal.'

'As you well know. As are you.'

'But, really,' Chrissie serious now, 'you'd go for Sabine rather than Rachel?'

'Yes. She's classy. Plus she's got the pheromones. Class plus pheromones is it.'

'You mean social class?'

'No, I don't mean that. Anyway – don't tell James – Sabine is from peasant stock. But she's got class. In the way she walks. In the way she holds her head.'

'So you would fuck her?'

'Given half a chance.'

'And Rachel?'

'Given half a chance, her too.'

'Right then,' Chrissie said, straddling him, pinning his chest with her knees, 'we'd better not give them even a quarter of a chance.'

'What's that noise?' Beth wanted to know. The ceiling overhead creaked ominously, and phantom gasps punctuated the rhythmic squeaking of ancient bedsprings and old timber floorboards from the room overhead.

Jessie, who knew that Chrissie and Matt occupied the room above, said, 'It's the owl in the roof. Go to sleep.'

'That's not an owl,' said Beth nervously.

'Yes, it is.'

'No, it's not!' After a pause the two girls began to laugh, giggling themselves to sleep.

Rachel, in the quiet of her own room, could hear James and Sabine beneath her arguing in low tones. She could also hear Matt and Chrissie making love, and for a while, the suppressed laughter of the two girls in the adjacent room.

She could also hear, busy in the rafters above her, the scrabbling and scratching of the barn owl, the real creature this time, the restless white ghost. The owl's nocturnal adventures and scuffling reports woke her every night and sometimes wouldn't allow her to sleep. She snuggled deeper into her pillow, her hand crooked between her legs, rocking herself into a slumber.

I I

Change in air pressure is one of the consequences of atmospheric motion. Air pressure simply means the weight of the atmosphere. If air is drawn up away from the surface, a region of low pressure is created beneath it.

A mercury barometer is used to measure changes in air pressure, even though the human body is itself an excellent barometer.

12

When at breakfast one morning Beth asked Rachel, 'Why is your accent funny?' Jessie sniggered.

'Don't be rude,' said Sabine, whose own almost flawless English was still lightly seasoned. 'Rachel is from Essex.'

'My accent isn't funny,' Rachel told Beth. 'It's your accent that's funny.'

Rachel wasn't especially aware of her social background until one of the others drew attention to it. Of these, Beth in her innocence was the only one who did it directly. It was not as if any of the others wanted to put her down; it was the inevitable consequence of working-class qualities and attributes butting up against middle-class mores and idiosyncrasies. Scissors cut paper; paper covers stone.

So that when Rachel laughed loudly at something, she might see Sabine's uneasy glance and instantly hear her own laughter echoing back at her. Or when Matt talked about his early life travelling with a father in the diplomatic service, she thought of her own father's travels as a train driver for British Rail. Or indeed when Chrissie exhibited an aggressively verbal and open sexuality, she felt her own experience to be comparatively limited and repressed. And then when James stuck his nose in a glass of plonk and told you whether there was too much lime in the grape-producing soil, Rachel openly conceded to an inferior nose.

She did nurse a suspicion, however, about James's wine nose: that it was made of moulded rubber and belonged in a box with greasepaint and an orange wig. But it was more than all of that. It was the confident note on which the others lived their lives. As if they knew by instinct how to move the pieces around life's chessboard while she was still counting the squares and avoiding the diagonals.

It amazed her, for example, that Matt could cheerfully talk insignificant nonsense in a flight of self-possession available only to someone who for the first eighteen years of his life has been told nothing but how truly wonderful he is. And that Sabine could place serviettes and sit to stiff, elegant attention knowing there is no other way in the world to place serviettes or to sit, even though it were possible her neck might snap under the pressure. And that Chrissie could, with posh vowels, chatter incessantly about sex and cross and uncross her legs and stroke her own thighs until it seemed that her cunt might at any moment leap from beneath the table and bite a passing waiter's leg. And that James's enjoyment of his fine wines was spoiled by his determination to find, in every second and third bottle, wormwood and poison and gall.

This at any rate was how it seemed to Rachel. She wished that one of them would openly call her an Essex Girl, since that was how they thought of her, and then she could make light of it. Despite all of this, at first Rachel genuinely liked the other four. She lamented the gaps in her own education, her lack of social graces, her capacity to become loud and raucous at moments of enthusiasm, the moments when candour deserted her. But she was earnestly grateful that she was not, unlike her holiday companions, so obviously fucked up.

'Why have you got tattoos?' was the next thing Beth wanted to know.

'Beth!' said her mother.

Beth was disgusted. 'Why can't we ask anyone about anything?'

'It's not polite,' said Jessie, peering closely at the lustrous Celtic knot patterning Rachel's right arm.

'It's all right, you can ask. I got it on my travels. When I was living in the Welsh mountains, in a tepee.'

'Really?' Jessie's eyes were ablaze.

'Really?' Sabine said sceptically.

'You were a New Age traveller?' put in Chrissie.

'I was a traveller. There is no New Age as far as I'm concerned.'

'What is there then?' said James, passing by the table, suddenly interested.

Rachel's brief affair with James had been a mistake, and perhaps it had been a mistake to accept this invitation to holiday with James's family and the others. But the affair was two years in the past, and though she wondered about James's motives in inviting her along, she was certain that neither of them had any interest in rekindling old torches.

When the bone-chilling damp, the cold, the streaming noses and the indomitable grime of living in a tepee had finally driven Rachel down from the Welsh mountains and into the city, she'd taken on secretarial work with an agency. She arrived at Hamilton & Poot as a temporary PA/secretary to James when his usual PA had some kind of nervous breakdown. Rachel didn't get to meet James until her third day, but on arriving on her first morning she was shocked to find many of the staff dressed as if for an evening at the theatre. Even the so-called Jumpers – the moody creatives – observed the style-magazine orthodoxy. She was required to liaise between the Jumpers and the Suits, the accounts bagmen. Rachel shrugged and next morning dug the little black number out of the wardrobe, unrolled the sheer, fine-dernier nylons, slipped on a pair of fuck-me heels, and layered her face with pre-stressed creams and quick-dry cosmetics. Then she let her hair fall free.

'This is a working day.' she told herself in the mirror. By eleven thirty on that second morning she had had three offers of lunch dates, passing on all of them. An experienced temp, Rachel had been down this road before. By the time James returned from business in the north of England, she had a handle on things in the office. When all of her letters were perfectly spelled and neatly presented he was pleased. When she alerted him to a double-booking, he was surprised. When she took a call from a client in Paris and dealt with it in passable French he was impressed.

'What are you doing for lunch?' James asked.

'There's an interesting lecture at the British Museum.'

It was meant to be a joke. It missed James. 'Oh. Perhaps another day.'

Rachel became a mystery in the office. Efficient, cheerful and detached, resisting all invitations to join colleagues for lunch or for drinks after work. And with hidden tattoos, she mocked the posturing Jumpers and stood up to the pushy Suits.

'Would you like to make this job permanent?' James asked her one day.

'No. I hate it. It's schizoid. The Jumpers sulk and slop about like wannabee rock stars; the Suits bustle round like Eighties stockbrokers.'

'Really? Is it so bad?'

'Not bad, but dull. Tedious and repetitive. You get all the fun.'

'Fun? You think my job is fun? Look at that bloke out there.' Rachel followed his gaze through the glass partitions to a man she knew was called Matt. 'Friend of mine. Known him for years. Going to have to make him redundant.'

'Why?'

'All part of my job. Which you think is fun.'

'I only work to save for my next trip,' said Rachel, feeling the need to fill the air with words. 'Me and my boyfriend are planning a journey across Africa.'

'Africa?' said James, and left it at that.

But within a week of that conversation there was no boyfriend and consequently no prospect of Africa. Rachel made high demands on boyfriends, and if they didn't match up, she didn't always grieve when they left. On the Friday that James dispensed with the services of the man called Matt, whom Rachel had met briefly and liked, James claimed to be depressed and upset.

I've known him for years. Years.'

'It must be hard.'

'Come and have a drink with me.'

Rachel shrugged. 'Sure.'

Drink turned to dinner. James was witty, generous, expansive, experienced. They drank a lot of costly wine. When the wine waiter poured for tasting James's histrionic assessment of the grape made Rachel laugh. She thought his theatrical and faintly disgusting sloshing was all done for comic effect. It was the first in a series of occasions when Rachel mistook James for a master humorist.

James, getting progressively drunk, told Rachel that he found her beautiful, electric and terrifying and that he wanted to go to bed with her.

'You're married, aren't you? I can tell, even though you've never mentioned a wife. Even though no wife has ever telephoned you at work. Even though you keep nothing in your office to suggest you have a wife or a family.'

James coloured.

'Don't worry,' said Rachel. 'I've decided to fuck you anyway.'

But not that night. And not there in London either. Rachel dictated that if he wanted her, James would have to take her to Rome. She was tired, she'd decided, of being used and upset by men, and if she was going to give herself, then she was going to extract some mercenary pleasure out of it. James had looked perplexed, dismayed and anguished before he capitulated.

'Book it,' he said to her. 'You're my secretary. You book it. Invent a client in Rome.'

So the affair started, and somewhere in the Sistine chapel, post-coital by a couple of hours and gazing up at the ceiling, Rachel was already lamenting its shortcomings. Where fingertips strained to touch there was no cosmic spark – just the unmodified earth, neither smoking nor transformed, a place for cooling heels to stand. But it went on, tepid adultery. They managed to keep it a secret from the rest of the staff at the agency.

One day James asked Rachel to arrange for flowers to be sent to his wife Sabine that afternoon. It was their anniversary, he said, and he had forgotten. Rachel was furious.

'I'll go to the florist's personally,' she said.

'No need,' James had said, missing it all again. 'Just pick up the phone.'

'No, I'll go in my lunch break.'

At the florist's, Rachel picked out a miniature, unimpressive, phallus-shaped cactus in a pot. She had it wrapped in a yellow bow and delivered, with a 'Happy Anniversary' note, to James's address.

The following day James was icy but never spoke about the incident. Rachel too said nothing. The affair was showing every sign of fading without even a protest before Rachel had a strange conversation in the ladies' toilets with another agency employee.

Paula Wolf was an account director in charge of all below-the-line contracts. A glamorous, tough cookie with lopsided lipstick and – it was said – a collection of a hundred and fifty pairs of shoes. 'How do you like working for James Clegg?'

'Not bad.' Rachel was combing her hair in the mirror.

'Not bad, eh? Fucking slime bag, more like.'

The trick was to avoid glancing at the other's reflection when being quizzed about James. 'Why?'

'Did you know Matt?'

'Matt? The one who got the bullet recently? Not really.'

'James had been trying to get in my pants for two years. Then Matt came along. Nice guy. Him and me got on really well, used to lunch together regularly. Then a story went round that we were having an affair. James was furious, so he put the boot in. Goodbye, Matt.'

Rachel forgot the brief and turned to stare at Wolf.

The other woman pouted a kiss at herself in the mirror. 'Must dash. Contracts meeting.'

Rachel was shocked. Distrustful of Wolf, she asked around the department about Matt's work. Then she asked James why Matt had been released.

'To be honest, his work was crap. He couldn't hack it.'

'I was talking to a few people. They said his work was first rate. "Superb" and "brilliant" were also words used.'

James turned nasty. 'What is this? Why are you making yourself busy? Interfering in how I run the place, is it? Get back to your desk. Who we hire and fire is no concern of yours.'

James's regular PA/secretary had made a recovery and was ready to return. Rachel didn't want there to be any issue of obligations. She went out to lunch with James and concluded the affair over coconut crème-caramel desserts. James appeared to accept the situation calmly.

On the way back, however, depressed and subdued, James stopped and pointed out something across the street. 'Look at that poor old sod. The poor old girl.' It was a London baglady. She wore a filthy coat and a woollen hat. Curiously, she had an apron tied over her coat. She was busy at a Pelican crossing. In her hand was a rag with which she was lovingly polishing the electronic button box, like any old-fashioned housewife trying to make the brass letterflap gleam on the front door of her house. As they watched, she breathed on her bit of rag and started rubbing the glass of the WAIT–CROSS window.

James marched across the road, already feeling for his wallet. Rachel scampered after him. 'Stop doing that, mum,' James said, pushing a wad of notes into the old lady's hand. 'Here you are. Go and get yourself a cup of tea.' He retraced his steps, hardly looking back to see if Rachel was following.

It would be a good cup of tea, thought Rachel. There must have been two hundred pounds in that wad of banknotes. They walked the rest of the way in dismal silence. It began to rain. On Charlotte Street, outside the doors of Hamilton & Poot, Rachel stopped him. 'There's a good man inside you, James.'

James looked at her with loathing. 'It takes more than that, sweetie. A lot more than that.'

'I just meant –'

James wouldn't let her finish. The expression of loathing had changed to despair. 'Promise me something. When people split up, they say pitiful things about remaining friends, without meaning it. But the thing is I only wanted a friend. I didn't want a lover. So promise me you won't be my fucking friend.'

James hadn't waited for an answer. He'd ducked inside, leaving Rachel defeated. The rain came harder, stinging her cheeks.

'So what is there, if there isn't a New Age?' James asked again.

'Recapitulation,' said Rachel. 'Endless repetition of the same successes and mistakes as everyone else's, for all time.'

James, Chrissie and Jessie looked on at Rachel, fascinated. Beth looked bored.

'Yes,' said Sabine, getting up from the table. 'And I'd better get on with the endless repetition of making lunch.'

13

Rising early one morning, they breakfasted in relays and prepared to take both cars to see the famous cave paintings at Lascaux. Then James, who hadn't emerged from his room, announced he wouldn't be going.

'If you're sick, for God's sake tell me what's wrong with you!' Sabine was heard to screech at him from behind a closed bedroom door.

Feet shuffled and glances were exchanged as they awaited the outcome. Jessie felt sick too. She sensed her father's illness and her mother's anger swelling and cross-stitching inside her stomach. She stood on the patio, staring across the valley. Chrissie moved to put a friendly arm around her, but Jessie didn't thaw.

'Daddy always spoils it,' said Beth.

'No, he doesn't!' Jessie shouted. Suddenly her face was puce with rage and she heard herself roaring at her sister. 'NO, HE DOESN'T, HE DOESN'T, HE DOESN'T!'

James stepped out from the kitchen on to the patio. 'Good gracious! What's all the screaming about?' He picked up Beth, who was cowering under her sister's onslaught. 'Are we going to this cave or aren't we?'

Jessie was hyperventilating. Everyone's attention was now fixed on her. Turning, she sprinted across the grass, leaped the rickety palisade and ran down the steep hill of the open meadow. The booming of her heart and the singing of blood in her ears almost drowned out the calls she heard behind her. When she reached the road, the world tilted, and she ran until it began to come level again.

There was a field with a white horse. The grazing animal calmed her. She sat down by the gate.

After a while, Chrissie and Matt came along. They said nothing to her, simply climbed on to the gate and sat, patiently waiting. Matt lit a cigarette. After twenty minutes, Jessie said, 'I'll come back, but I'm not going to a stupid cave.'

Back at the house, Jessie sat at the kitchen table with her head in her hands, staring down at the grained oak of the table. Sabine tried to talk to her but elicited no response. James had a go but got nowhere. Rachel too made an effort, but everyone entirely failed to engage her. Sabine said she was going to make some coffee.

'If the trip to the cave is off,' James said, 'I'm going back to bed.'

Jessie rose from her seat like an automaton, grabbed her coat and went and sat in the Mercedes.

'Save the coffee,' said Matt. 'I think the trip is on again.'

The sisters seemed happier to be separated so Beth travelled in the Ka with Rachel, while up front Matt navigated as Chrissie drove. In her rear-view mirror Chrissie noticed Sabine was driving the Mercedes behind them. It was unusual for James to allow her to take the wheel.

'What exactly is the matter with James?' Chrissie wanted to know. Before anyone answered she said, 'I mean, beyond the obvious. Medically.'

'Some sort of virus,' Matt said absently, looking through the window at the passing landscape.

'But Sabine said he's been like it for months. Almost a year. And he looks pale. Don't you think he looks pale?'

Beth piped up, 'Jessie said Daddy's got AIDS.'

For the next five minutes they proceeded in silence. The car, with windows open, swished by the tree-high corn; then the road dipped suddenly and flipped the stomach, and the sun broke through the morning mist with highly defined yellow rays, like the rotary arms of a vast propeller.

Chrissie made a fuss of getting Matt to find her sunglasses to protect her from the glare reflecting off the road. 'Are you sure that's what Jessie said?'

'Someone told her.'

'Who told her?' said Matt, pretending to read a road map.

'Are you sure that's what she said?' Rachel put in.

Beth, sensing that her casual remark had tripped some unfathomable switch, shrank back into her seat.

'Maybe,' Chrissie said after they'd driven a further few kilometres, 'it's just a word she's picked up.'

At the Lascaux cave they were denied entry. All tours of the cave were full. At the kiosk beneath the frowning limestone outcrop a slab of torn hardboard was chalked in four languages. 'Bookings Adviced', it warned. James sniffed round the surly attendants as if this was all some Gallic trick. He looked from Sabine to Rachel, and from Rachel to Chrissie and Matt, hunting for someone to blame. Matt sniggered, and the children stood by the Ka playing a hand-patting game.

'"Bookings adviced",' James said at last to Matt. 'Why didn't you *advice* us?'

'You're more likely to be the one going around *advicing* people,' Matt snorted. 'I mean, you're the boss.'

James squinted, as if to see to the bottom of Matt's remark. Then Sabine suggested that there were other caves to which they could go, and they did. Only to find the same problem at all of the major sites in the region. At every cave of the hunter-gatherers queues of British tourists stood in line, whining over the strength of the franc. They seemed drawn from a narrow band of regionless middle-class society, loitering at the cave mouths like prospective diners in a canteen queue or emerging into the light at the other end with a burp of mental satisfaction. Matt called them visitor-gatherers.

'I've gone off the idea of seeing a cave,' Rachel said.

'Me too,' said Chrissie.

But a cave they had come to see and see a cave they must, James decided for everyone, even if it contained only the humbler spectacle of stalactites. An expensive but desultory tour of an illuminated limestone grotto was conducted by a melancholic guide in French, so that only Sabine and the children properly understood what was said. Nevertheless, the mission, for such it had become, was accomplished. They emerged from the dripping grotto in single file.

'Can we go home now?' said Beth.

On returning from the unsatisfactory trip to the famous cave they found Dominique at the house. She was accompanied by the man who once a fortnight came to clean the swimming pool. He was complaining about the state in which he'd found it. No one understood exactly the nature of his complaint; Sabine established only that something unpleasant had turned up in the filter.

Dominique asked Sabine about their day. When Sabine told her about the queues of bloody English, Dominique cocked her head to one side. 'But it wasn't necessary to go so far to see cave paintings!' She pointed to the craggy limestone outcrop across the valley. 'There is a cave up there. Of course, there are no lights, or guides, or tickets. But if you have a torch, we can take you there.'

'But do the authorities know about this cave?' Sabine exclaimed.

Dominique shrugged. 'Maybe. We don't shout about it, because if you do, then some fool from the Ministry comes to take away your land.'

So they would have their excursion to see cave paintings after all. Sunday – they would all go together on Sunday, taking a picnic and torches, and Dominique's husband Patrice would show them some cave paintings.

Later that evening, with dusk settling like a light fall of soot around the house, Matt, Rachel and Chrissie sat on the patio. Chrissie had made Earl Grey tea. The others had gone for a stroll up by the old church. 'You've been very quiet today,' Chrissie said to Rachel.

'Yes.'

'I've been thinking,' Chrissie continued, 'about what Beth said in the car.'

'Yes?' Rachel squinted at her. There was an outside chance that Matt knew about her affair with James, and even though it had ended almost two years ago he might have told Chrissie.

'I mean, I've been looking at him all day. He does look tired.'

Matt, without lifting his nose from his paperback, said, 'I'm sure Beth and Jessie haven't the faintest idea what they're talking about.'

'You should ask him,' said Chrissie.

'I can't just ask him,' Matt said.

'Yes, you can. You're an old friend. You should ask him when he's on his own.'

'Why? To satisfy your curiosity?'

Chrissie was stung. 'Not at all. It's more important than that. We need to know. What do you say, Rachel?'

Rachel offered only a minute shrug. Matt looked up and saw something in her eye that for a fraction of a second made his own heart stop. He looked back at his book. 'Maybe I will,' he said, rapidly turning a page. 'Maybe I will ask him.'

So Matt asked him before dinner.

James was sprawled on his bed, 'exhausted' after chasing caves around the Périgord. He was sipping claret from a wine glass. Matt picked up an almost empty bottle from the cabinet and studied the label.

'A wasted day,' said James.

'Wasted? I don't think so. The big cave was a fake anyway.'

'What?'

'A concrete gallery built into the cliff. Replica paintings. You don't think they'd let you into the real one, do you? Not at Lascaux anyway.'

'Well, why didn't you say so? We could have stayed at home.'

'I thought you knew,' said Matt. 'I thought you could tell when something was authentic. Is that a good wine? Beth told us you have AIDS.'

James drained his glass, set it on the cabinet and folded his hands before him. 'Fabulous.'

'We could do with knowing. One way or the other.'

'What do you suggest? A formal announcement over dinner? Or a quiet press release?'

'I can think of at least two women in the company who would appreciate a less satirical approach.'

James filled his glass with the last of the wine. 'What do you know about that? You were gone from our place before all that.'

'I continued to lunch with former colleagues for a while. I did pick up the occasional breath of gossip.'

'No, Matt, thank you for your kind but robust inquiry. I don't have AIDS or HIV for that matter.'

'Good. Someone should tell Rachel. Someone should also tell Beth and Jessie, who are busy announcing your demise. And you might also tell me what exactly *is* wrong with you.'

'I'm just sick, Matt.'

'What kind of sick?'

'I get giddy. Faint. Short-of-breath kind of sick. The doctors say the symptoms are like an infection. A parasite. A tropical parasite.'

'You've never been near the tropics!'

'They say the symptoms are *like* that of a tropical parasitic infection. Only they can't find it. Can't identify it, I mean. Can't detect it.'

'You mean, they can't find anything wrong with you,' said Matt. 'I see.'

'I don't want you saying anything, right? Anything at all. Promise?'

Matt didn't get time to promise, as Beth appeared in the doorway, silent as a ray of light. 'Hello, Mrs Rabbit,' said James.

'I'm the dinner gong,' said Beth.

'Really? I didn't hear the gong, did you, Matt?'

'Bong,' said Beth. 'Bong. Bong. Bong.'

14

What to tell? And what to leave out? To a precocious girl who asked her parents shocking questions about necrophilia and Golden Rain, how much should an instructor – a truly conscientious instructor – reveal? Honesty had to be the watchword. If it was possible to be honest about one's history. Yet you couldn't be expected to tell everything, not the highs and lows. Lord forgive me the sins and offences of my youth.

Jessie's instructor peered at herself in the mirror, searching for a candid reflection. Memory, after all, was a distorting mirror. What was it that animal said? *Don't mist the glass.*

Touching her reflection in the mirror with the tip of her tongue. Without misting the glass. At the same time hoisting her right inner thigh parallel to the dressing-table itself, extending her leg outwards and pressing the foot into the air. Holding this position is uncomfortable in the extreme and quite painful on the strained tissue of knee cartilage.

'Nah, nah, nah, you dull tart, you've breathed all over the glass!' Malcolm, coming up behind her with cloth and spray, dragging her away from the mirror. 'Get down while I clean the glass.'

Climbing off the dressing-table as Malcolm goes to work on the mirror. Folding her arms across her breasts and crossing her legs at the ankles, a concession to modesty. The cloth in Malcolm's hand squeaks in protest at the vigorous buffing.

'There. Now don't breathe on it.'

'I'll try not to breathe at all.'

He, twanging her suspender strap, elastic snapping sharply against her buttock, 'Get back up on there, and keep the mirror *clean.*'

Seriously considering giving Malcolm his money back. Then thinking of France and the Dordogne again. Finally protesting, 'It's cold in here.'

'Tell your fucking union.'

White stockings, suspenders, white spike-heel shoes. Nylons snagging slightly on the mahogany furniture as she hoicks her leg up, shifting her buttocks. Not until she touches her mirror reflection with the tip of her tongue does she hear the rapid auto-wind of Malcolm's motorized camera. A sharp spasm in her ligament forces her to bring her knee back round.

Malcolm nosing from behind his camera again. 'No, you untutored little tart, you have to stay *open*! Do you get it? Do you get the concept? Do you appreciate the concept?'

Climbing down again, turning to face him, she lets her hands drop to her sides. 'Yes, I think I appreciate the *concept*. I don't expect I need a degree in philosophy from Cambridge University to grasp, more or less, the fucking concept of showing you my snatch.'

Malcolm is more accustomed to abusing his models for their perceived ignorance or stupidity. Some of them even answer back, but not many counter by suggesting that any limitation of intellect is wholly on his side of the camera. Holding up his hands, he drops the phoney barrow-boy accent, now all oleaginous Charterhouse charm. 'You're just not relaxed, darling. Let me see if I can find you something.'

Fumbles with a desk drawer on the other side of the studio, producing from a small plastic sachet a mirror-compact and a couple of lines of cocaine. He abandons the sachet open on the table. She's promised herself she will avoid this, but as Malcolm rolls a ten-pound note into a tube and snorts the white dust from the mirror, she knows it will get her through the next half-hour. Malcolm's eyelashes fluttering wildly as he offers the compact. Taking it from him. Steadying the rolled banknote over the powder, seeing her own eye inflamed in the compact mirror. The violet rain still not gone from her vision. Blinks, snorts the coke. Violet flickering lights flurry like a shaken snowstorm-paperweight. Now, in the harsh studio light, her eye seems jaundiced and red-ringed, an eye that has seen too much, an owl's eye.

Deep breaths. Climb back up on the dressing-table.

As the tip of her tongue lightly brushes its reflection, she thinks of France, of the Dordogne, and in the mirror, misting slightly even though she struggles to still her breath, behind the flickering violet rain she sees herself as a girl of eleven. There the garden, and there the plum tree heavy with fruit, and there the lively dovecote. As doves flutter and settle and resettle, a white, cocaine-like dust shakes from their feathers. The garden is bathed in a strange golden light, light which penetrates only when the sun has burned off the mist and yet exudes from the people around her, as if everyone is lit from behind for a camera-shoot. Mother. Father. Melanie. All at play in the biblical light.

Then Melanie stands on her head, the plum tree behind her, a pulsating yellow sun tangled in its branches. Cousin Melanie, two years older than she, clever Melanie, her legs spread in a wide V, juggling the plum tree and the golden sun-disc between her ankles, balancing them there like a circus performer; her blue cotton skirt rucking and falling over her belly, exposing her knickers. Daddy looking. Mummy looking at Daddy looking.

The plum tree! Fresh fruit falling every day. Daddy says we can have them, some so swollen and plumped and heavy they're sucked to the bone-hard earth by their own weight, skins splitting on impact, spattering the earth with red juice and bruised flesh. Like a daily ritual of bloodletting, tanging the air, fermenting in the heat.

'Breathing.' Malcolm's voice, from a long way off. 'Don't breathe all over it.'

White pigeons break from the dovecote, go winging up into the sun and are consumed. Melanie topples from her headstand. She tries to imitate Melanie but can't. The baked earth makes for a hard fall. The days are long, the evenings full of stars. Daddy standing behind them, her and Melanie, one hand on her shoulder, the other pointing up at for ever. 'Look at Gemini. Your sign. You're looking into the past. What you are seeing is light from a long time ago. What's your star sign, Melanie?'

Sighing at the past. Mirror misting. In it, distorted, predatory behind her, Malcolm advancing slowly. She feels a nudge at her bottom.

'Don't try it!' Snarling, climbing off the dressing-table. 'Don't even think about it.'

'Just friendly,' Malcolm trying to joke, adjusting his clothes. If it is a joke, it misses by a long mark. She is spitting-mad. 'Calm your nerves, girl!' Barrow-boy again. 'I was only going to give you a squeeze. We're all done and dusted.'

'Just back off!'

Malcolm curling his lip. 'Go on. Get dressed. Get out of here. You've had your money.' Disappearing into his office, still mouthing abuse, but his instructions are redundant. She has already stripped off stockings and suspenders, is climbing into clothes she came in. Before leaving, she uses the small toilet adjacent to the studio. Her eyes fall on a tin of powdered bleach.

Back in the studio – he is still out of the room – she tips a handful of bleach into Malcolm's plastic sachet of cocaine. Put that in your sinuses. Moments later Malcolm appears again. 'You want your head looking at, that's what you want.'

'When I want psychological counselling from a half-wit pornographer I'll turn in my card.'

'What card?'

'Owl's eye to you, Malcolm. Owl's eye.'

'What? You're rickety, you are. Touched. Cracked. Get out of here.' But she's already out and halfway down the flight of steps. 'And don't' – over her shoulder she can still hear Malcolm bellowing – 'ever come back.'

She waits until she's on the street before counting her money.

15

High in the blue, fifteen kilometres high, preside the jet streams. A concentration of winds into narrow belts accelerating at the limits of the troposphere, drawing the air from the earth in an updraught and leaving a region of low pressure beneath.

A region of low pressure is known as a depression. The depression will attract towards it cold, polar air (in our case from the north) and warm, tropical air from the south. As these air masses are sucked into the depression, they are deflected by the rotation of the earth. Thus the winds in a depression move in an anticlockwise spiral, as do their vapour trails (but clockwise in the southern hemisphere).

As the depression matures, the boundaries between these warm and cold air masses become distinct and form clear 'fronts'. These are zones of highly active weather change. It is by their coming together that these fronts become the source of almost everything we call 'bad weather'.

16

'I have some news for you, Jessie. It seems your father does not have AIDS after all. He has something else.'

'Is that better or worse?' said Jessie.

'Well, it's a relief because if he had AIDS, then he might not be with us for very much longer. But what I wanted to talk to you about is Beth. You know, she's a lot younger than you are. You shouldn't tell her everything I tell you. And, anyway, I only offered my suspicions of what afflicts your father. Suspicions, that was all, and I was wrong. Beth has a habit of blurting out everything you tell her, and at the most inappropriate times. So remember: the things I tell you are not only a secret from the adults, they're not for Beth's ears either.'

Jessie, understanding she was on the end of a ticking-off, let her concentration drift. Her eyes crossed slightly, and her gaze sailed to the middle distance.

'*Come back*. Don't you do that to me,' her instructor said sharply. Jessie's attention returned immediately. 'You can play that game with your parents and even with your teachers at school, but I don't want you to do that with me. If you don't want to be with me, just say so and that's an end to it. Understand?'

'OK,' said Jessie. She really didn't want to lose her friendship with her instructor.

'Good. Then we're still friends.' It was early morning. The others were all back at the house, still sleeping. Jessie's instructor had woken her with a hand over her mouth, told her to get dressed and to come outside. The valley was wreathed in mist, strange terraces of vapour, cloth of grey with a yellow lining where the dawn had broken through. They were going to look for mushrooms of a certain species, Jessie was told, as a special surprise for the others.

So far they hadn't found any. Jessie pointed to a field mushroom with grey cap and pink gills. Her instructor shook her head. 'Poisonous, that one. Keep looking, and tell me what is happening with your mirror-watching.'

'I did it yesterday for a long time. Well, half an hour before Beth came into the room. It was a bit frightening.' It had been more than a *bit* frightening, but it was important to Jessie that she didn't sound like a wet little girl.

'I did tell you about that. You'll have to put up with it for a while. Were there sparks?'

'Yes. A blue spark jumped across the mirror, and then two smaller white ones. Then, after the sparks, I waited for a while and nothing happened. Then a shadow came across my face, and that's when I started to get scared.' Really scared.

'But you persisted?'

'Only because you told me to. The shadow came out of the mirror and settled on my face. I didn't like it. I couldn't see anything else in the mirror because all the room had disappeared. Then my cheek began to twitch and move. It was as if someone had grabbed my cheek with their fingers, and they were pulling it. Next thing that happened was that my eyebrows changed. They kept changing. Like one of those Identikit toys, as if someone was looking for the right eyebrows but couldn't make them match. I felt scared. I wanted to stop but I didn't. Then Beth came in and asked me what I was doing.'

'What did you tell her?'

'Checking for spots.' Jessie hated spots. She would spend long periods engaged in another kind of mirror-gazing, searching for skin blemishes.

'Good. You're making sound progress, Jessie. Keep it up. Soon you'll find your angel. Here. This is what we're looking for. This is the only time of the year you will find this mushroom. It loves the warm weather and the damp mornings.'

They collected the speckled blue-grey fungi in brown-paper bags. Jessie's instructor checked her wristwatch and shot a nervous glance back across the fields to the house. 'Now, before we go, tell me what you can feel from this morning's weather. But we mustn't be long. I think your mother is beginning to suspect.'

'Why are you so different?' Jessie asked suddenly, impulsively taking her instructor's hand.

'Different?'

'From all the other grown-ups.' It was true. Her instructor treated her as an adult, and that had earned her loyalty and respect.

'It's just a question of honesty, Jessie. Adults, almost all adults, think that young people should be protected from honesty. So they lie about things, usually the things they are frightened of themselves: sex, drugs, religion, love, hate, language, the weather, what comes out of the mirror. They think you are better off with lies.'

'Why?'

'Because they think if they are honest, they will steal some of your childhood away from you. They think the truth will spoil your days as a child.'

'But in some ways it's better not to know things, isn't it? I can see that, and I'm only eleven.' Although she wanted to know everything, she recognized that there was a dark and angry place inside her, a place she sensed sometimes when she began to drift.

'How can you grow, Jessie, if you are deceived or kept in ignorance? By lying to you they force you to remain a little girl for as long as possible. But you mustn't repeat these things, or it could mean trouble for me.'

Contradiction. In the teaching. Something not quite right. 'I don't understand. How can telling the truth get you in trouble? A moment ago you said it was all a question of honesty.'

'Remember what I told you about your mother and father making love, having sex? Well, if everyone grew up seeing it happening naturally, often and in the same room, then you would never feel that it was anything bad or unnatural. But if people heard me suggest this, they would shoot me or have me burned

86

alive. Because they desperately want to believe that children grow up in a state of innocence. Even though it isn't true, and no child is innocent. The purpose of lying is not to secure the child's welfare. It's to preserve the sanity of adults that they have to believe in this golden age of innocence.'

Jessie gazed into the thinning mists across the valley, as if to determine whether her own golden age was being sullied by knowing all of this. Yet everything she was being told seemed a storehouse of riches.

'Bring the mushrooms,' said her instructor. 'Let's get back before the household stirs.'

Late that morning everyone tucked into a breakfast of fried gourmet sausage selected by James, tomatoes and mushrooms, with bread still warm and aromatic from the baker's oven.

'Delicious!' said James as Chrissie set a plate before him. The sausage had a deep, gamy smell.

'You should try it first,' someone said.

'It smells funny,' said Beth, who knew Jessie had brought the mushrooms from the field.

'Surely not,' said her father. 'Do we know these mushrooms are all right?'

'Clever Jessie found a book about wild mushrooms,' said Matt.

'In the house,' said Jessie. 'On the bookshelf.'

'I checked it.' Rachel broke a baguette and handed it on. 'It's the sausage I'm not sure about.'

'We all checked it. Very thoroughly,' said Chrissie, pouring coffee.

'Wild mushrooms! My daughter is a genius!' Jessie glowed in her father's praise.

'*Bon appétit!*' said Sabine.

'Toadstools,' said Beth.

Two hours later James went to bed claiming he was feeling unwell. Then Beth was sick in the yard. Alarm bells started to ring when Chrissie locked herself in the toilet with stomach pains, and

Sabine went to find the book Jessie had used to identify the mushrooms, which she herself had judiciously not eaten. No one knew where the book was. 'There definitely *was* a book, was there?' Sabine sniffed suspiciously.

'Of course,' Rachel said quickly. 'I checked it out myself.'

'I'm not lying,' Jessie said, her voice keening. She wasn't. She just couldn't remember what she'd done with it.

Then James came out of his bedroom. Finding the upstairs toilet occupied by Chrissie, he lurched heavily past everyone and into the downstairs lavatory. His groans and the sound of retching were audible throughout the house.

'Oh, dear,' said Sabine. 'Oh, dear.'

Jessie backed into the corner like an animal at bay, her hands clasped under her chin. No one had pointed the finger; but they didn't need to.

'I'm all right,' Rachel protested, 'and I ate the mushrooms. So is Jessie. And Matt.'

Matt, with perfect timing, stepped out of the kitchen and on to the patio, where he vomited violently on to a geranium in an earthenware pot. After a few minutes, ashen-faced, he came back inside and crouched down to speak to Beth, who sat on a kitchen chair holding a hot-water bottle to her tummy. 'Beth, answer me honestly. I just saw a pile of mushrooms scraped into a flower pot. Did you put them there?'

Beth nodded. 'Toadstools. I didn't want them.'

'Did you try one?'

'No.'

'Right,' said Matt, sweating profusely. 'Sabine and Rachel didn't eat the mushrooms and they're OK. Beth didn't either, but she's not OK. Who ate the sausage?'

Only those who had eaten the sausage were ill. A doctor was summoned. He arrived, put his hand on each tummy in turn and diagnosed a mild case of food poisoning. Then he left. Despite being exonerated, Jessie's frozen posture didn't alter during the entire visit of the doctor or for some time afterwards.

'Come on, Jessie,' Matt said softly. 'Your mushrooms are in the clear.'

But Jessie appeared to be in a state of paralysis. Sabine, who had seen this behaviour before, ignored her. Chrissie suggested Matt leave her alone. Sabine checked on her after a while and found she had gone up to her bedroom. The victims of James's sausage spent the rest of the afternoon recovering in the cool shadows of their bedrooms, with shutters firmly closed.

17

Sabine had her suspicions. Packing the picnic for the excursion to the local cave, she paused to brush a stray curl from her eye and gave vent to a deep and long-suffering sigh. Beth, counting hard-boiled eggs into a basket, looked up, and Sabine forced a smile for her. It was important to her that Beth should not guess that her mother was struggling against a rising panic.

It was the sense of leakage. Everywhere around her she sensed life leaking, draining, diminishing, sucked away by some unseen force.

Someone was filling Jessie with ideas. This she knew not so much from what Jessie said but from what Jessie had ceased to say. If it was possible to grow accustomed to being shocked, then Sabine had done so; at least, she was no longer surprised by some of the precocious things Jessie had to say. But since arriving in France for this holiday, Jessie had become secretive, inclined to disappear across the fields or into her room for long periods, and when she did have anything to say, she hardly seemed to speak in her own words.

Sabine knew, as only a mother can, that someone was usurping her influence over her daughter. Someone in the company was stealing her away.

She thought it might be Matt. Though she liked Matt, and welcomed his cheerful and relaxed attitude, she understood that his laid-back posture disguised a brooding undercurrent in his nature. She suspected him of deep seriousness. There was another matter. Sabine intuited in Matt a simmering resentment towards James. Matt kept the lid closed, so that resentment never manifested as hostility, at least to people with no antennae. Sabine had no idea what it was about, and ascribed it to some jealousy over James's success. But her own antennae made her afraid that Matt, by winning Jessie's affection, had found a way to punish James.

She also felt uncomfortable about the way Matt played with Jessie, and picked her up, and touched her in the swimming pool. But in this she had been ashamed of her own suspicions.

Then there was Rachel. Against her instincts she liked Rachel, yet always felt prickly around her. The problem was difficult to pinpoint. Rachel was charming and natural, and always very pleasant and positive towards Sabine – perhaps too pleasant and too positive. She was assiduous in doing her share of the work, in cooking and in helping with the children, but fractionally over-helpful and microscopically deferential. There seemed to Sabine something odd in all of this. It was as if behind this deference and desperate need to get along, Rachel was playing with a different deck of cards. Rachel seemed to pretend to be inferior in order to hide some secret knowledge which made her superior.

'You know what your problem is?' James said to her when she voiced her thoughts to him. 'You've got too much imagination.'

Too much imagination. That may be the case, Sabine thought. But she felt uneasy whenever Rachel took her daughter for a walk. It was true that Rachel always invited Beth along too, and although Beth went with them occasionally, she would usually decline. Sabine felt unhappy about the opportunities this gave Rachel to get closer to Jessie: not because she was possessive in the usual sense but because she feared Rachel might in some way want to use Jessie to get at her, Sabine.

'Why do you think people are out to get you?' James had said. 'You always think people are plotting to take something from you.'

James had a way of making her feel mentally unstable.

Dominique and her husband Patrice arrived for the short expedition to the cave. With Patrice guiding the way, they decided to walk the two kilometres across country. After shaking everyone's hand warmly, Patrice injected a mood of high spirits into the group, smiling broadly from beneath a vast, twitching, iron-grey moustache. They locked the house, and the cheerful group of nine set off with the sun at their backs. The babbling of the company trailed behind them in the dry air like a banner on a pole.

They passed a field of tall, ripening corn, and Patrice, laughing, told the girls in French that they shouldn't risk going inside the corn because there were spirits living there who waited to prey on little girls.

'*Imbécile!*' Dominique shouted gaily.

Beth looked up at Chrissie, who held her hand as they walked. 'Is it true?'

'I'm sure it must be,' Chrissie said, 'if Patrice says so.'

'Really?' said Jessie. Chrissie only smiled enigmatically.

Sabine allowed herself to fall behind a few metres, so that she could watch the group. Jessie was nothing if not sophisticated for her age. Sabine wasn't at all surprised by Beth asking if such a thing were true, but here was Jessie, checking it out with Chrissie.

Oh, yes, Chrissie. Now there was someone she could really dislike, and with enthusiasm. Sabine disliked Chrissie because of the way she treated other women; and the way Chrissie treated other women was defined by the way she treated men. Even now, as she marched at the head of the group with Jessie and Beth, Sabine despised the overt swing of her hips, the unconscious flicking of her long, dark hair, the perpetual moistening of her lips. Even now, in her skimpy cotton frock, she exposed sand-coloured thighs and wind-burned shoulders to the hot tongue of the sun. It was plain that she'd enjoyed the glitter in Patrice's eye when they'd made their introductions – how self-possessed of Dominique to seem not to notice. And there was Matt, sweet Matt, caught and led in chains across deserts of sex in the eternal caravanserai of this woman's vanity.

In a civilized and coded world it was crucial to maintain social balance and to check destructive impulses, and to do this it was necessary to live beyond the obvious. In this, Chrissie broke the rules. It wasn't Chrissie's sexuality that offended Sabine. She herself liked nothing better than to turn a man's head in the street or in a restaurant. Chrissie's offence lay in the fact that she signalled only the question 'Are you interested?' when it was a woman's job to signal the challenge 'Are you worthy?' Sabine despised Chrissie because she reduced the sexual game.

She was also convinced that Chrissie was having, or perhaps had had in the past, an affair with James. She was the kind of woman who couldn't help herself, just as James was the kind of man who couldn't help himself. Sabine had felt her suspicions confirmed by the manner in which Chrissie had spent most of the holiday carefully avoiding her. So far they had never actually been alone together in one place. There was definitely something sinister and covert in Chrissie's behaviour. Some guilty secret.

Sabine felt more jealously disposed over the business with Jessie than she did over James. If James wanted a woman like that, he was welcome. Chrissie represented the bedrock of biological function rather than a serious threat, and Sabine could let the matter go. God knows, James had his affairs but always came back. In Jessie's case, however, it rankled deeply to see her so impressed by Chrissie. Being wild, being reckless, being irresponsible was easy, and yet everyone – particularly an eleven-year-old – seemed to think it made one more interesting. She made a mental note to talk to Jessie about that.

Was Chrissie the one? She had walked into the girls' room on one occasion and had found Chrissie and Jessie sitting on the bed, their heads together, talking intently about some matter. She had hovered at the door, trying to catch what it was they were talking about so intimately. But then they had looked up, and Sabine realized that Chrissie was simply helping Jessie to load her camera and was demonstrating how to loop the film in the sprockets of the winding mechanism.

Sabine was an intelligent woman. She knew her animosity towards Chrissie could lead her into making the wrong guess about whoever was whispering in her daughter's ear.

'Don't lag behind, Sabine! Here, let me carry that!' Matt jogged back a few paces and relieved her of the wicker trug.

'You are always so thoughtful, Matt.'

'No, I looked back and I saw you thinking thoughts. I often see you thinking thoughts. It's like hearing a taxi-meter clocking up the fare. What goes on, I wonder, in that mind of yours?'

'Oh, you know me. Sweetness and light.'

They arrived at an outcrop of limestone at the edge of a field. Further to the east climbed higher ridges of stone, cliff-like in their formation, where Patrice said there were even more caves. The exposed rock was bleached like the bones of some mammoth creature, smoothed and polished by the sun. They had to push their way between angry, scratching brambles bearing blackberries powdered with white dust. Behind the brambles was a narrow, cervix-like slit in the rock.

'Are we going in there?' said Beth, expressing the doubt everyone else was only sensing.

Patrice switched on his torch and stuck his head through the hole. Withdrawing, he turned round and said, 'Boo!' Then Sabine translated as he spoke rapidly.

'He says it gets wider inside. He knows this place from when he was a boy. He suggests we all link hands because he doesn't want anyone falling down a hole.'

James looked the most doubtful. He wasn't even sure he would be able to squeeze in. Dominique beckoned him to follow her.

'What's the matter?' said Matt. 'Too many lunches?'

They formed a daisy-chain and passed, with some effort, through the cave's aperture. The children each carried a dim torch to supplement the light offered by Patrice at the head of the chain and by Rachel bringing up the rear. They had to pass through a damp section of cave and ascend slightly before stumbling into a wider gallery. The cave was indeed shaped like a womb, and the interior wall, when caught by flashlight, was veined with red ochre and some yellow pigment seeping from minerals in the rock.

Patrice put his fingers in his mouth and produced an ear-splitting

94

whistle. The sound ricocheted back and forth across the cramped gallery, reproducing itself and attacking the wall like a flock of disturbed bats frantic to find a way out. Then the sound cut off instantly.

'He wants to show you his sound-and-light show,' Sabine translated for Patrice, who kept up a barrage of cheerful talk. 'Everyone must crouch down and train the lights on the far wall.'

Dominique signalled encouragement, all smiles. Everyone did as instructed.

'I want to get out,' Chrissie whispered to Matt.

Matt ignored her. Then they were told to switch off their torches and wait for a signal.

'I want to get out,' Chrissie said again.

'It's all right,' Jessie tried to reassure her.

'*Shhh!*' said Patrice. '*Ecoutez!*'

They listened hard. After a few moments all they could hear was the sound of each other breathing in the dark. One of the children shifted slightly. Then even the breathing was stilled.

Jessie strained to listen, reaching deep into the pool of silence to pick up a single sound. In the quietest places of the countryside one could hear the drone of insects. She supposed that even in the desert there was the wind. But here it wasn't possible to detect the sound of one's own blood singing in the veins. It was like being deprived of the most basic vibration of existence itself. Jessie liked the idea, but at the same time it unnerved her. The thing beyond silence began to seem predatory, fattening in the dark, spreading like a contagion, eating away at the wall between the inner and the outer, threatening to show itself as –

The silence was fractured by Chrissie. 'I have to get out!' She leaped upright and scrambled back towards the cave entrance.

'Take the torch!' said Rachel, but Chrissie had already gone.

The other torches flickered on. 'She'll be all right,' said Matt.

Chrissie had upstaged Patrice's idea that on a given signal they should flash their lights upon the cave drawings. Instead he directed their attention to the near wall, where there were etchings of a very primitive, possibly pre-historic species. The drawings tended to follow fault lines or contours and shadows in the rock itself. Grouped around a central figure were several small, sooty renditions of horned animals, perhaps a herd of reindeer. The central figure, however, was much more dramatic, though it was difficult to determine its exact character.

As they pressed forward James relieved a disgruntled Beth of her torch to pore over the charcoal-coloured extremities of the drawing. He was deeply impressed, as were they all except for Beth, who was gamely trying to win back her torch. Jessie stared into the shadowy folds of the figure as if mesmerized.

Patrice kept up a running commentary in French, and Sabine gave a partial translation. 'He doesn't know exactly what it is supposed to be. As you can see, it has far too many limbs and a set of horns. Maybe it's a bison with a man chasing it.'

'Yes!' James shouted. 'There's his spear! That would add up to the right number of limbs and –'

'No,' Matt broke in, 'it's a man in a costume of some kind. Look, a head-dress. Perhaps a shaman or something?'

'I don't see that,' Rachel protested. 'It's a chimera, a mythological figure, half-bird and half-man. Here, these are wings.'

'Wings?' James wasn't having any of it.

'Yes, wings.'

They all stared thoughtfully at the wall, as if somewhere in the shadows a Cro-Magnon artist waited, having said, 'Give me your honest opinion.' They were still looking when Jessie broke the spell. 'It's two people fucking.'

Her words reeled back from the wall like Patrice's whistle. In a moment of renewed silence, James and Sabine stared hard at their daughter. Beth giggled nervously as Chrissie and Rachel looked away.

'*Qu'est-ce que la petite fille a dit?*' said Patrice. 'What did the little girl say?'

'Either that or it's an angel,' said Jessie.

18

'I'm cold,' said Chrissie.

After returning from the cave, she had gone directly to bed, having developed a temperature. Matt made her a cup of herbal tea from a sachet produced by Rachel. 'Drink this. Tell me what happened at the cave.'

Following Jessie's surprising interpretation of the cave drawing, they had all come out of the grotto, squinting into the light, to find Chrissie sitting on a rotting molar of a rock and hugging herself. Everyone made a fuss of her. Dominique stroked her hair. Patrice gave her a little squeeze. Sabine looked at the sky. She was all right, Chrissie told them; she didn't know what had come over her.

She was quiet on the way back. 'I just didn't like it,' she said to Matt.

'What was there not to like?'

'I don't know. First there was the smell of the place.'

'I think it was bat-shit. Like ammonia.'

'No. Something other than that.'

Matt nodded. He'd seen Chrissie like this before. 'Did it remind you? Of that time?'

There was a pleading rinse to her eyes that begged him not to talk any more about that.

'Drink your tea,' he said. 'Sleep if you can. I'll look in on you in an hour.'

Later Matt stood over her bed as she slept. Her dark-brown hair fanned across the white pillow, and she slept with her small fist clenched near her mouth. He loved her, and he was afraid for her in ways he found himself unable to define. They had taken each other from guilt to innocence, and he hoped it hadn't been too late. He wished they had met each other when they were both fourteen years old and that they had known nothing and no one but each other, and he knew it was like wishing on a dead star. He left her to sleep and went down to dinner.

'Daddy, it's gone again!' Beth reported at dinner that evening.

'Yes,' said James, 'but if we pretend not to notice, then that stops someone playing games, doesn't it?'

Jessie's ears pricked up.

'So who keeps moving it?' Beth wanted to know.

'Someone with nothing better to do. Probably Matt.'

'I can think of other ways of spending my time, thanks,' Matt said evenly.

'That still doesn't answer the question,' Jessie said. 'Why would someone keep moving the cross?'

'I think we can guess,' James sighed. 'Eat up, Beth.'

'Well, I can't,' said Rachel.

'Oh, I think we can.'

Jessie searched the faces of everyone at the table. It astonished her that they could go on eating with the matter unresolved. Towards the end of the meal, Rachel asked if they should take some food up to Chrissie. Sabine for some reason immediately interpreted this as a suggestion that the job should fall to her. She stood and picked up a plate.

'I didn't mean you,' said Rachel.

'I'll do it,' said Matt.

'No,' Sabine insisted. 'I've finished my meal. I'll take it.'

Chrissie was out of bed and sitting at the dressing-table, brushing her hair in the mirror, when Sabine knocked and walked in with a tray. 'That's kind. You needn't have. I was just about to come down. It's so hot in this room.'

Sabine shrugged and set the tray down on the table across the room. 'I'll leave you to it.'

Chrissie turned from the mirror. 'Stay a minute.'

Sabine stopped at the door. 'Why?'

'I want to ask you something.'

Sabine considered a moment. She bumped the door shut with her bottom and, folding her arms, leaned her back against the door.

'You don't like me, do you?' said Chrissie.

Sabine shrugged.

Chrissie put her brush down. 'Goodness. It must be hard to have so much integrity that you can't soften a direct question with a white lie.'

'There's too much lying around here.'

'Really?'

'Yes, really. Now let me ask you a question. Do you know why he is ill?'

Chrissie glanced back at the mirror for a second. 'He's not the one who is ill. Not any more. And anyway, right now he's just depressed. He has mood swings. You would, in his situation.'

'Would I? Really? But then I know so little about his *situation*. You would know so much more than me.'

'Of course I would.'

'I don't know why I should be surprised at this.'

'Neither do I. Look, can we please begin this conversation again? We are talking about Matt, aren't we?' Chrissie saw Sabine's eyes widen. She gasped. 'My God, we're not, are we? We're not talking about Matt. Is this conversation about James by any chance?'

Sabine had realized her mistake, but it was too late.

'You're asking me what I know about James? Why should I know anything? Do you think we're having an affair? Is that it? Whatever gave you that idea?'

'I've made a fool of myself. I'm sorry.'

'No, don't run off. You've made something very clear to me. Now I understand why, ever since we arrived here, you've sniffed and sneered and practically dislocated your nose to get it high in the air every time you see me, and why you wince every time I talk to Beth or Jessie, and why you squint at me every time I try to make a joke. I should thank you. You've solved quite a mystery. Now I know you weren't motivated by a sense of superiority. Well, listen to this, lady. Not even sealed in a Vulcanized latex suit would I be tempted to go anywhere near James. And to think I started this conversation to ask if we might be friends.'

Sabine slipped out of the door, her cheeks flaming.

'I'm too hot,' said Jessie.

'That's the English half of you,' said Beth. 'Patrice said that the English spend all day talking about the weather.'

Jessie knew something about this. 'That's because when we talk about the weather, we're really talking about something else.' Beth looked puzzled, so Jessie adopted the same posture as her instructor might when imparting a new and important piece of information. Jessie was so impressed by her instructor that she had decided she wanted to be an instructor herself. Even though she'd been told to be careful not to pass information on to her sister, she needed a subject to practise on, and so she'd chosen to be Beth's instructor.

'What?' Beth wrinkled her nose.

'When people talk about the weather they're really talking about how they feel. But they don't always know it. When they say, "It's nice now," they mean, "I'm happy now." When they say, "It's freezing outside," they mean, "I'm glad I'm inside." And when they say, "Looks like change on the horizon," they mean, "I'm worried I might not be happy in a while."'

'Who says, "Looks like change on the horizon"?' Beth wanted to know. 'I've never heard anyone say that.'

'That's not the point.'

'Who says?'

Jessie almost blurted out the name of her instructor. It wasn't always straightforward being an instructor of someone as dumb as Beth. Instead she said, 'You'll learn as you grow older.'

But Beth wasn't satisfied. 'Why do they say these things? Why not just say, "I'm sad, even if the sun is shining"?'

'No, you can be happy even if it's snowing. It's the *way* it's said.' At least Jessie thought this was what her instructor had told her. It wasn't coming out quite right now that she was trying to pass the idea on to Beth. She thought about it for a moment. It seemed to her there was a kind of language that you had to learn: saying the same things but in other words. Jessie had learned French from the first day she was breast-fed by her mother, and it came naturally. Other children at school, however, found it a daily grind. Weather-language, she decided, was learned at mother's knee, and that's why Beth couldn't see it in terms of another language.

'It's stupid,' Beth concluded.

If there was another pupil in the house with the potential to benefit from Jessie's teaching, she would have dropped Beth from her class immediately.

'Feeling better?' Matt asked Chrissie when she emerged from the house.

'Much.' The heat of the day had died down and a slight breeze had picked up from the valley, dispersing the torpor of the afternoon.

'Chrissie!' shouted Beth, running to her, tugging her arm. 'Come and play with us! We're going to play in the corn!' Beth was hugely excited. Her eyes glittered at the prospect; she jumped up and down on the spot. Chrissie looked across the grass to the edge of the cornfield where James, Rachel and Jessie, though lacking enthusiasm, had been recruited for Beth's game. 'We mustn't let the farmer catch us,' whispered Beth, leading Chrissie and Matt over to the others. Matt looked a trifle unsure.

But Sabine was the only one who had resisted. 'Don't go too deep into the corn,' she called after them, giving voice to some irrational, barely formed unease.

'We're playing Fox and Hounds,' Rachel explained. 'Everyone is a fox hiding in the corn. One person is a hound –'

'Me, me, me!' said Beth.

'– and when caught, each fox becomes a hound until the last fox remains.'

'Right, let's go,' said James, disappearing into the corn. Jessie, Matt and Chrissie followed.

'All right, Beth,' said Rachel, 'count to a hundred and then come looking. Shout if you get lost.'

'I won't get lost,' Beth said, indignant.

Rachel crept deep into the corn, squatting behind a thick, wizened stalk. In the struggle for growth little could compete with the voracious corn, and the earth at the crop base was hard-baked, cracked and dry. Only dim, lime-coloured light penetrated beneath the nodding corn-cobs, and hardly any sound carried inside other than an eerie rustling as faint cross-breezes stirred and parted the wide, parchment-like leaves. Rachel listened. The sound of Beth counting, loudly at first, diminished. There was a sudden swish as someone else nearby changed position. Then all fell silent again.

Rachel's own breathing began to still. The light filtering from above was a green-and-mustard haze. It was a foreboding place inside the corn: the breezes conspired with intimate whisperings, and at times it seemed a mouthing spirit world in which unseen wraiths rippled an uneasy passage between the stalks. More than once she thought someone was coming up behind her, or in front of her, only to see the stalks part briefly without consequence.

She was relieved when she heard the cry of someone caught by Beth at a short distance. Crouched in the shadowy light and nursing a growing unease, she hoped to be caught soon. There was a swish of leaves behind her, and she felt a breath fall on her neck as two arms enclosed her from behind. Two male hands rested themselves on her breasts. She recognized the hands.

'Don't you know,' – her voice came out in a cracked whisper – 'Don't you know not to creep up on women?' James merely nuzzled her neck. She unclasped his hands and twisted away from him. 'Don't do this.' A swishing in the corn mocked her hoarse whispers. He seemed unafraid that he might be caught. 'Your daughters . . .'

'Why are you avoiding me?' James hissed.

'Avoiding you? What are you talking about? Don't try to start it up again, James. I don't want it.'

More swishing, and a stiff breeze flushed the corn. But someone else was coming. James looked angry. He turned and slipped away, going deep into the crop.

'You should be careful,' said a voice behind her. Rachel turned quickly. It was Chrissie. She had a haunted look and was smiling oddly. 'The corn knows everything.'

'What?'

'You can't keep a secret in the corn. Listen. You hear that whispering? That's the corn spilling everyone's secrets. Yours and mine.'

Rachel didn't know what Chrissie had heard or, indeed, how much Chrissie knew. She didn't get an opportunity to ask. Chrissie reached out a hand and touched her lightly on the shoulder. 'Now you're a hound,' said Chrissie, before disappearing into the corn after James.

The following afternoon, when James, Sabine and the girls went to visit an aquarium, Matt found an old hammock in the outbuildings. He rigged it up between two trees and was so pleased with himself he fell asleep in it immediately. Rachel and Chrissie stretched out down by the pool.

The yellow sun throbbed in the sky. The baked white earth, the grey roof-tiles and the honey-coloured housebricks exuded a warm and peppery tranquillizing gas. It numbed the limbs. It slurred the speech.

'Something strange is going on here,' Rachel murmured, without lifting her head.

'Ha!' Chrissie agreed.

'You've noticed?'

'Ha.'

'I'm glad. I was starting to think it was me.'

'Maybe it is.'

'Maybe. But I know that Sabine and James are quietly going off their heads. No wonder Jessie is disturbed.'

Chrissie raised her head and shielded her eyes from the sun. 'Sabine is on to you. She came for me. She thought it was me.'

Rachel looked hard at her. 'It's in the past.'

'You don't have to explain anything at all to me. I'm just warning you. She's figured it out, though her first guess was wrong.'

'I shouldn't have come here. It was a mistake. I thought I could keep my friendship with James and draw a line under the past. Did she confront you directly?'

'She tried to, oddly enough. If you're worried about it, then there is a solution. You should make up to Matt.'

'What?'

'Nothing obvious. And, anyway, I'd have my eye on you, wouldn't I? That way Sabine would be confused. I'll let Matt in on it. He knows all about you and James.'

'Oh?'

'Yes, he knows a lot about James. He knows James cost him his job, for example.'

Now it was Rachel's turn to sit up, but Chrissie rolled on her back and looked at the sky. A lone, straggling cloud, high in the blue, drifted in from the west. Chrissie pointed up at it. 'First one I've seen since we got here.'

19

What happened next, after the Malcolm episode? How much could be recalled in the mirror's dissolving light?

On her way to her sister, that was it. Hitching a ride in an articulated lorry to the port at Ramsgate, yes. Rain, lots of it. Wiper blades, steady, hypnotic. At the docks, letting herself down out of the cab. Waving at the driver, a cheerful and burly Midlander who looks at her oddly and says, 'Bye-bye, Blondie.' Sprinting through the downpour to get a ticket. A three-hour wait.

Then holding a discarded newspaper over her head and walking a quarter of a mile in the rain until she finds a hotel. Knowing enough about hotels from her brief, tough experience as an escort. Shaking water and pulped newsprint from her hair, she steps through revolving doors, marches boldly across the brightly lit reception to the concourse lavatory. From her bag she pulls a number of bottles stolen from Malcolm's studio, setting them on the washbasin. Fills the sink with hot water, strips off her wet jacket and blouse, uncaps the bottles, snaps on a pair of latex gloves.

Checks herself in the mirror. 'Bye-bye, Blondie.'

'Bye-bye,' says her reflection. A tiny white spark forks from her iris. She searches her own eyes for more sparks before shaking the bottle of black dye, mixing it with activator solution. Squirting mix on to her head, massaging it thoroughly into her hair roots. One or two women come in as she works away, their nostrils twitching at the whiff of ammonia and peroxide, but they choose not to comment. Some black dye splashes on to the carpet. The porcelain is discoloured, but she largely manages to keep it off her skin. Her wrists, however, are manacled with rings of dye. Half an hour, job done, hair black as a raven. Discarding the gloves, she proceeds to apply Cleopatra lines to her eyes. Girl *noire*.

On the ferry she finds a seat in the observation lounge, pulling her coat over her, hoping for sleep. Uncomfortable crossing. Same one: Ramsgate to Dunkirk. Years before that, when she was a schoolgirl; Mother, Father, Melanie, her, all out on deck, gazing back at the receding coastline, each blink offering a different snapshot in a series of photographs. Holding Daddy's leathery hand. His other hand resting on Melanie's shoulder. Then driving south to the Dordogne, to the sun, to the plum tree and the dovecote and the biblical, golden light.

'French coffee,' Father had said, 'Fresh croissants. French bread. Steak *au poivre*. Red wine.'

'Can we have wine?' Melanie had said.

'Can we?'

'Melanie is almost fourteen, so Melanie can have wine,' Father said, and he kissed Melanie on the lips; but when he broke the kiss Melanie's lips were bleeding.

'Can I have wine?' said Mother.

'And I?' she shouted. 'Can I have wine?'

'In Paris,' said her father, 'in Paris you can have wine.'

Dreaming. She's been dreaming. Feeling slightly feverish, she's still not right since that crack on the head. The dull headache is unrelenting along with the migraine vision. The flickering persists even with closed eyes.

Then someone is shaking her gently awake. The ferry has docked, people are disembarking. She blinks. Wine in Paris. *Guidance*, she thinks. *I'm being guided by angels*.

At the thought of guidance, and at the memory of wine in Paris, Jessie's instructor blinks into the mirror, into a past momentarily arrested in its unfolding. Here was something a young girl should know. She herself had no difficulty in believing in the existence of angels. The problem lay in distinguishing them when they appeared. People encountered angels on a regular basis but without recognizing them. This was because they appeared in the guise of ordinary people. Correction: they were ordinary people, or at least they were ordinary people whose bodies were inhabited for a brief few moments by the angelic spirit. Angels were messengers, or even messages. That's what the word meant; 'angel' was a Greek word meaning 'messenger'. They didn't arrive beating wings of fire or bearing long-stemmed trumpets. No, they were messengers, impromptu teachers and instructors, moments of inspiration. Sometimes they carried notes from the higher to the lower self, as when they came in dreams. Or they made external appearances, evident in the clouds or appearing in mirrors. Performing walk-on parts in the never-ending movie of life, there to be recognized only by those whose eyes were not scaled over with weariness.

Indeed, when they came as people angels chose an appropriate host, descended, entered at a tangent, intervened, and left their host none the wiser. Because of this it was sometimes difficult to distinguish an act of simple kindness from an angelic intervention. But in her case she discerned the glittering residue that always betokened guidance and instruction.

At the moment when she'd arrived in Paris she'd known it was entirely probable that someone would help her, steer her, guide her. Even there, at the Gare du Nord train station, it was likely that there were angels at large, and, given how critically important it was for her to get to the Dordogne, those angels must necessarily make intercession.

But it hadn't happened like that. Her eyes return to the mirror, where the past is rolling again.

Three days later, still in Paris and waiting for guidance, she is living in a cheap hostel near the Porte du Montreuil on the east side of the city, running out of money and afflicted with a strange malaise that prevents her from moving on. It seems the closer she gets to her destination, the more vague her purpose. Sister, sister. One morning she wakes unable to remember even the name of the place she's supposed to be heading for. Then it comes back. Dordogne. Dordogne. Tolling like a cracked bell.

Visiting Notre Dame, wandering in Montmartre, loitering near the République, she eats almost nothing. She is like an amnesiac whenever her quest to return to the Dordogne comes to mind. As if remembering to forget. And yet so close now. Made it this far. What is stopping her? What is blocking?

On the fourth evening, about half an hour before dusk, she wanders into the cemetery of Père Lachaise and is astonished. It is less a cemetery than a necropolis, and less a necropolis than a settlement of and for the living. Marble edifices are more like small houses than headstones. Paths between the graves are all tidy, well-maintained streets. The scale of the cemetery resembles that of a small town. Water is laid on in drinking fountains and standpipes, avenues are kept in impeccable repair, litter is minimal, damage to the monuments only incidental. It occurs to her that some strange administration is overseeing the necropolis.

Surely some hidden authority is at work, a workforce beyond the municipal, a secret alliance that does not count its numbers among the living. Hugging herself, she steps between Gothic monuments, threading her way between miniature classical temples and ivy-strangled angels, between spires and fluted columns and marble porticoes, while shadows of twilight deepen behind the razor-sharp angles of the sepulchres. With the descent of darkness the number of cracked vaults seems to increase; broken plinths double, cleft slabs multiply, hairline fractures in the stone feed on dusk, expanding. And something comes out of the tombs: not the dead, not dancing corpses, but something else. An exhalation, a soft radiance, a gentle, comforting violet light.

And then the cats appear.

The next day is spent indoors at the hostel, waiting until dusk, waiting to visit Père Lachaise again. Ostensibly to feed the cats, taking stale bread. The feral cats, perhaps chased away by the cemetery attendants, come out at twilight to scavenge for scraps left behind by visitors. Extraordinary in number, they move silently between the tombstones. She feels at one with them, though it isn't food she is after; it is fragments of something else, a thing flickering at the periphery of her vision, twitching at the edge of consciousness.

Flitting that evening between the monuments, herself like a shade, she sees ahead of her a man in a leather trenchcoat, the wings of his collar turned skyward, his pallid profile offered to her. She stops. He turns, their eyes lock, and something very strange happens. The visual storm, the migraine-intense sparking of light before her eyes, changes. It is subdued, and though it doesn't disappear entirely, it resolves, softening into an eerie backlight, illuminating the man with ultraviolet radiance as if from behind. Meanwhile the man lifts a kid-leather glove to his cheek and caresses his face gently. He passes between two stones and is gone.

Intrigued, almost dizzy with relief after the abatement of the visual storm that has dogged her for days, she moves to the spot where he was standing. Three red roses lie across a cracked tomb. The broken slab covers the grave of a woman who died over a century ago. The roses are already wilting, turned the colour of dried blood in the crepuscular light. She looks up from the inscription on the stone, sees the man pass along an avenue of headstones to disappear again from sight.

She follows, careful to stay a respectful distance. The figure appears briefly, passing behind a carved Valkyrie trailing marble robes. Each time she loses sight of him, she turns to see his fleeting form passing between another avenue of densely packed gravestones. Almost as if he is leading her through a maze. Finally she steps out from between the stones on to a main thoroughfare of the necropolis. The man is nowhere in sight. There are only cats.

The following night, faint with hunger, she returns to Père Lachaise. She has enough francs in her pocket to buy a good meal, but something else prevents her from eating. That day she's had only three cups of coffee and a small piece of bread.

She finds the stranger in the same place as the previous night. As before, the violet light intensifies and gathers around him. She turns, pretending to be interested in some other tomb as he takes a step towards her.

'Why are you following me?' English. His voice has a slight rasp.

'I'm not,' she protests. 'You're following me.'

'That's absurd. Do you think your first words to a stranger should be a lie?'

Guidance, she thinks, her breathing shallow. 'No,' she says defiantly, but she is transfixed.

Very slowly he peels off a kid-leather glove. Gently reaching out, he slips his hand inside her coat, laying it lightly across her belly. She has no interest in resisting him. His fingers press lightly just under her navel. Then he withdraws his hand and puts his glove back on.

Her eyes are turned up towards his. The next move is entirely his. He asks her, 'Would you like to come with me?'

20

At the warm front, the air mass climbs, producing clouds whose structures change with altitude. Seen from the ground, an approaching depression is signalled by high, thin wisps of cloud, fine brushstrokes. First cirrus, meaning 'lock of hair', 'curl'.

Then, after cirrus, the layer of cirrocumulus, 'heaped or massed curls', and then altocumulus, 'high heap or high mass', otherwise known as a mackerel sky. Thickening, the cloud descends as altostratus, as stratus and finally as the heavy blanket nimbostratus, the aureole depositing the light and widespread rain typical of a warm front.

At the cold front a different hierarchy. Cold air noses in under a warmer block. Warm air ascends rapidly, cooling as it rises, and water vapour condenses. Cumulonimbus is formed, sometimes towering fifteen kilometres high, spreading out on top in the shape of an anvil.

And the anvil of cumulonimbus awaits the hammer of the storm.

21

'Things were coming out of the mirror.'

'What kinds of things?'

'I couldn't see properly. They were hidden. Hidden behind a dark cloud. First this fuzzy cloud came out of the mirror, like smoke. Then the smoke settled on my shoulders.'

'Then what happened?'

'I didn't like it. I got scared, so I sent it back.'

'Back into the mirror? You shouldn't be afraid, Jessie. You shouldn't be afraid of angels. If you don't let them out of the mirror, they can't help you, can they?' Jessie's instructor lay back in the grass, gazing up at the fine wisps of cloud in the sky. 'Clouds, Jessie, look. Clouds comprise an alphabet for those who can read them. A language, laden with meaning. A litany, evoked by air masses, themselves like a hierarchy of angels. You know, even the names of clouds are angelic, Latinate, beyond the reach of us the profane, us the vulgar, us who have lost the tongue of clouds. Do you know what altocumulus means? It means "high mass". No accident, that. Oh, yes, the angelic language of the clouds is complex and difficult.'

Jessie wasn't at all interested in the clouds. She pulled at the grass as she spoke, agitated. 'But you said there are good angels and there are bad angels. How do I know it isn't a bad angel in the mirror?'

'I've told you before. There's no difference between good angels and bad angels. That is, it's you who decides whether it's going to be a bad or good angel. It takes its shape from the things that are in your mind at the time it forms. That's why it's important for you to keep an honest disposition. Bad angels feed on lies and

112

mean thoughts. That's why I told you that when you meet someone for the first time, you should never lie to them, in case they are an angel.'

Jessie snatched at a tuft of grass. She was growing red in the face. 'I don't get it! I just don't get it!'

Jessie's instructor sat up. 'Be calm. Take a breath, Jess. You do yourself no good when you get worked up like this. If you get into a state, you'll have one of your fits. Take a deep breath.'

'Well, explain it to me.'

'Not everything can be explained. Remember what I told you about sex? When you have sex you open yourself to good and bad angels, depending on the purity of your thoughts. You let them in accordingly, and they can be passed on to your children that way.'

'You mean this thing . . . these things that are supposed to be wrong with me. Do I get them from my mother or my father? I want to know.'

'I can't answer that. It depends on what either of them was thinking when they were having sex. Pure thoughts or corrupt thoughts.'

'But I don't know about sex.' Jessie jumped to her feet and hurried away towards the house. 'Sometimes I think you forget I'm only eleven.'

'Come back, Jessie!' It was the first time that Jessie had turned her back on her instructor. 'Come back!'

Dominique arrived on her bicycle with gifts of home-bottled jam and plums and tomatoes. She found folk idling on the patio. They'd been living in the villa for a few days now and everyone said, '*Bonjour!*' quite comfortably, with no trace of selfconsciousness. Such was the speed of English people in acquiring foreign languages. Then Dominique said something in French, and Sabine looked startled.

'What did she say?' someone wanted to know.

Sabine's eyes widened. 'She asked if we knew that our little girl was on the roof.'

Chrissie, Matt and Rachel all got out of their chairs. James didn't. 'Oh, Christ,' he said softly. Sabine stepped off the patio and saw Beth squatting in the barn doorway, playing with her dolls. Like choreographed dancers everyone else stepped on to the grass and turned their gaze to the roof of the house. Jessie stood on the ridge of tiles next to the dovecote, holding on to the weather-vane. She was naked.

'Don't shout at her,' said James. 'Don't anyone get excited. Don't let her hear any panic or anxiety in your voices. It will only makes things worse.'

'*Merde!*' Sabine said.

Matt cupped his hands around his mouth to make a megaphone. 'What are you doing up there, Jess?' he asked evenly.

Jessie ignored him. She continued to gaze over their heads at the horizon, as if watching for something. Her face was red, from exertion or anger.

'For God's sake!' Sabine shouted. 'Why are you doing this?'

'Sabine!' James hissed.

'Doesn't look too safe up there, Jessie,' Rachel tried.

Jessie pivoted her head to look at Rachel. 'Inside every beautiful woman,' she snarled in a voice that was almost not her own, 'is an intestine full of a good kilo of steaming shit.'

They all stared at her. Beth had come too to see what was going on. 'Get inside,' Sabine told her.

'Why is Jessie on the roof?' Beth asked.

'*Get inside! Get inside! Get inside!*' Sabine screamed. Her face was contorted, almost demonic. Beth went inside.

Dominique entered the barn, saying something about fetching a ladder.

'Can I talk to you, darling?' James called up. 'Can I talk to you?'

'We're all dying anyway,' Jessie shouted. 'You start dying from the minute you are born. All flesh is decay. Rotten. Putrefying. All stinking corpses.' She dislodged a tile and it skated down the roof. They had to dive out of the way as it shattered on the ground.

'Everything you eat. Everything you touch. If you have sex, you're having sex with a dying person.'

'I'd like to know,' Sabine said in a low growl, 'who has been filling her head with these things.' She was trying hard to remain calm. She knew James was perfectly correct. They'd been through this kind of thing enough times before. Anger and excitement merely raised the temperature; and when the temperature was raised, Jessie internalized the chaotic emotion; and when that happened she was prone to blackouts. If she had a blackout here, she was in danger of toppling from the roof.

'All the soil,' Jessie said, 'is manure. That means shit and dead things. So everything that grows does so in a dead thing or in the shit of a dying thing –'

'Stop this,' Rachel said. 'Stop this now.'

'You can't stop it,' Jessie said. 'And inside every man –' Suddenly the weather-vane swung fractionally. Jessie looked at the vane as if it had been a sign from God. 'It's changing,' she said. 'The direction of the wind is changing. That means the weather is changing.'

Dominique returned with the ladder. Chrissie helped her to set it against the roof. Matt offered to go up, but Chrissie stopped him. 'Can I come up, Jessie? Can I come up and talk?'

'No.'

'Just us girls. Me and you. Girls' talk. Girls have to talk in private sometimes, you know.'

Jessie thought about it. 'You can come up. And Rachel. But no one else. And one condition.'

'What's that?'

'You have to take off your clothes.'

Dominique, Sabine, James and Matt sat in the kitchen drinking coffee. Beth also sat at the table, exhibiting a sense of privilege that she was allowed to join the adults during a crisis. James was brooding, staring hard into his cup. Sabine spent some time explaining to Dominique in French the vexed nature of Jessie's condition, her volatility, her temperament, her tendency towards startling behaviour. Dominique nodded sympathetically, sipped her coffee. The others sat in silence.

Dominique concluded that if Jessie had behaved like this before, then it was not really a crisis. '*Alors, c'est normal.*'

Sabine agreed. '*Oui, c'est normal.*'

'Yes,' Matt sniggered. 'We've got three naked females perched on the roof of our *gîte*. What could be any more normal than that?'

'You think that's funny?' James said sharply.

'Yes, I do as a matter of fact. Very funny. Very funny indeed.'

'Perhaps you could explain the hilarity of the situation to those of us not blessed with your superior comic insight.'

'I'll try.' Matt was warming to it. 'Sabine, translate, please. I'd hate Dominique to think this was an aggressive exchange rather than a discussion. I think it's funny because you, James, run around striving for perfection. Nothing wrong with that, lots of people do it.' Sabine obliged with a simultaneous translation. 'Only you have this daughter. Bless her, I love her. She's gorgeous. A really terrific kid. I wish she was my own daughter. But she's imperfect. And that causes far more problems for you than for anyone else. You'd like this holiday to be fine wines, gourmet meals and sophisticated conversation. The *bon viveur*. But instead we've got three nude girls sitting on the roof discussing corpses, as far as I could understand it.'

'Good,' James replied. 'Sabine and I are uplifted to hear that our family misfortune gives you a belly-laugh.'

Sabine didn't translate for her husband, and Matt said, 'Don't drag Sabine into it. I'm talking about you.'

'So I manage to make you happy all by myself? Fine. Don't feel obliged to stop laughing at me. I wouldn't want your fun to be spoiled in any way.'

'It's not me that laughs at you, James. It's life. Life laughs at you.'

James glared hard at Matt. It was a poison, dry-eyed stare.

Dominique broke the gaze by saying, in thickly accented English, 'I agree. The life is imperfect. It must be.'

Dominique's clever intervention had the effect of making a feud seem like a debate. Now James looked as if he wanted to evict her from his kitchen. 'Did I say wrong?' she asked quickly.

'No, you are right,' Sabine reassured her. Then she turned to the men. 'But it's more complicated than that. One of those women on the roof is poisoning my daughter's mind.'

Having got these women up on the roof with her, Jessie didn't exactly know what to do with them.

'It's nice up here,' said Rachel. 'Only I think I've burned my bum on the tiles. You never warned me that the tiles were hot, Jessie.'

'We should get them to send some drinks up,' said Chrissie. 'Maybe we could lower a bucket on a string. Do you think they would send supper up?'

'I'm not staying here all night,' Jessie said indignantly.

'Why not?' Rachel said. 'The view is terrific.'

Jessie couldn't but agree. The afternoon sun sank low in the west, dispatching warm gules of light, like the rotor-blades of a huge turbine above the distant limestone hills. Heat ripples streamed from the baked earth. The tall corn, stiff and erect, stretched away from the house for acres. Tiny movements amid the corn suggested the presence of restless spirits, and the blue vault of the skies was boundless.

All three were seated on the tile-ridge, toes pressed flat against the roof slope. They sat in silence for a while, enjoying the sensation of the late sun on their skins. Jessie, leaning against the dovecote, was pink and slightly burned. Chrissie, in the middle, was a deep caramel colour, her bikini outline strikingly visible, white, like a photographic negative. Rachel's skin was peach-yellow, tanning slowly.

'Hold hands,' Jessie said. 'Let's hold hands.'

They had to shuffle closer to do so. After a while Chrissie said, 'Arcadia.'

'Why did you say that?' Rachel wanted to know.

'I don't know. It just popped into my head. I was feeling very happy and it popped into my head. I don't even know what it means.'

'You're mad.' Jessie giggled.

'Why?'

'Because you're up on a roof with no clothes on, and you say you're happy. You must be mad.'

Rachel started sniggering, and the tremors passed from her bottom to Chrissie's. The sniggering skipped to Jessie like a wave, and in a moment they were cackling from the rooftop like witches. James came out to look at them. He gazed up in puzzlement and disgust. The expression on his face only made them laugh more loudly. He went back inside.

'Let's get Sabine and Dominique up here,' said Chrissie. 'Then we can all laugh at Matt and James.'

'Dominique might come up. Sabine wouldn't,' said Rachel, and Jessie agreed.

'Only,' said Chrissie, 'because James might disapprove.'

'Just remind me,' Rachel said to Jessie, 'why we're up here.' Jessie focused on the middle distance. Her attention, compelled by the question, was elsewhere. '*Don't do that!*' Rachel said sharply. 'That's a bad habit, Jess.'

'What?'

'That game of switching off when people are talking to you. If you don't stop, it will set for life.'

'Sorry,' Jessie sang, and Chrissie looked on with interest.

'Now then,' Rachel tried again. 'Remind me of why we are here. On this roof, I mean.'

'I've forgotten.'

'Not that easy,' Chrissie said to Rachel.

'Look.' Jessie was pointing. 'Clouds.'

'What sort?'

'Cirrus. Wisps of cloud, far off.' She pointed east. On the horizon thin curls feathered the sky, slightly mauve, barely discernible. 'That's why we're here: because the weather is changing.'

'Ah.'

'Of course.'

'Jessie's right,' Chrissie said to Rachel, speaking out of the corner of her mouth, though Jessie could hear her perfectly well. 'The weather is changing. Remember what I said: she's on to you.' Rachel looked deep into her eyes. 'I mean, the one who wouldn't come up here. She thought it was me. But she's on to you.'

'I'm ready to go down now,' Jessie said quickly.

'Good. You first,' said Chrissie.

Jessie went ahead, using the ladder Dominique had leaned against the roof. Rachel came down last. Their clothes were still at the foot of the ladder. They got dressed, and when they went indoors they received a round of applause. But not from James.

22

New things were also coming out of the mirror for Jessie's instructor. A procession of events once in train, difficult to stop now.

She is taken back by the man called Gregory to the decaying grandeur of an apartment off the Boulevard Voltaire. All that remains of its former glory, however, is its scale. The apartment occupies the third floor of an elaborate eighteenth-century residence. A sweet, cloying but not unpleasant odour clings to the stairs. The place is hardly renovated: plaster cornices and architraves are broken, and original floorboards are exposed and damaged in places by clumsily installed central heating. Faded damask wallpaper bubbles on the walls of the entrance hallway.

Shown into the main sitting-room, she pauses in the doorway. 'Goodness! Do you like looking at yourself?'

He says nothing, slinging his coat across the back of a sofa. The comment is prompted by the vast array of mirrors hanging on the walls, a disconcerting collection of disparate styles, classical to kitsch. There are a number of huge eighteenth-century mirrors with ornate gilt frames, glass mottled or distorted or both; mirrors framed in heavy mahogany and in metal filigree; Art Nouveau and Deco frames; mirrors with artless plastic frames and others set inside gaudy coloured glass. No section of wall space left unhung. Her eyes are drawn to the ceiling, searching for some relief, only to find it entirely covered with large mirror-tiles.

'You can't escape that easily. Would you like to sit down? I make very good coffee.'

'Escape from what?'

'From yourself.' He goes out. She sits down, her nostrils twitching, still trying to identify the sweet, florid odour. The furniture also comprises a wild assembly of ill-matched designs. The springs in the sofa are broken and uncomfortable. She tries not to look into the infinite fan of images powered by one mirror reflecting another.

He comes back, still wearing his kid gloves, carrying a silver tray and an elegant coffee service. Suddenly remembering the gloves, he mutters an apology before removing them. 'I'm not used to people. I'm an incompetent host.'

His blond hair is unfashionably long and bleached. He is a photographic negative or positive, she thinks, of herself. His eyelashes flutter nervously when he looks at her. His skin tone is pallid and his fingers, now removed from their gloves, are remarkably long and elegant. Is he a messenger? An angel? A clumsy, incompetent and dithering angel, unable to be at ease with people, unaccustomed to them?

'What do you do?'

'You mean for a living?' He thinks for a second. 'I'm a musician.' A swift glance around the room reveals no instrument. 'So I'm lying. You saw it instantly. Good. I'd prefer it if you know when I'm lying. Do you think we might be allowed to go on lying?'

'Pardon?'

'Then we would avoid any betrayal. When people first meet, they begin perhaps to speak frankly. Then inevitably, quite soon in the case of most people and immediately in the case of many, one or the other will lie. Seems impossible to avoid this, in my experience. But if we could agree to lie to each other from the beginning, with integrity, as friends, then we could never betray each other.'

A laugh. 'You're joking!'

He sips his coffee, looking earnestly at her across his cup, 'No, I'm not. I'd really prefer it that way. You think I'm eccentric.'

'Not at all, I –' The first lie. A palpable hit, pure reflex.

He smiles. 'Good. You can lie easily, and that's what I prefer. Now, tell me what you do.'

Say anything. 'I'm a meteorologist.'

'Fascinating. You know what's coming, then.'

'In certain cases.'

'Our behaviour is more influenced by the weather than we like to admit, don't you think? Consider the characteristics of different races. Or the behaviour of birds and animals before rain. Now I'm pretty fed up with discussing the weather. I propose instead that we go and get your things, so that you can be more comfortable here.'

'What?'

'I know you're not going to be banal. I know you're not going to tell me I'm moving too fast. There's a spare room. It's quite comfortable, and it bolts from the inside – not that I'm the prowling type.'

'You're not serious?'

'Alternatively, you can continue to pay rent for your squalid room in that dirty hostel.'

'How did you know?'

'I followed you, of course.'

She catches her own reflection gazing back at her, wide-eyed, off guard, off balance. Behind the reflection a staggered image of herself retreats into endless mirror-space on a virtual curve. A hundred snapshots of her own surprise.

'Why? Why did you follow me?'

'Do you believe in the divine spark?'

'I believe in guidance. Is that the same thing?'

Putting down his coffee cup, he says with an air of finality, 'I knew it. What do you say? Do we get your things?'

The Parisian evening is wet. They walk slowly through the rain, through streets the consistency of wet charcoal and under lamps the colour of sulphur. They take the Métro in silence. Having checked out of the hostel, Gregory carries her single bag back to his apartment, frequently switching it from one gloved hand to the other. The spare room, unlike the sitting-room, has a single mirror. Heavy, faded velvet curtains hang at the windows. The furniture amounts to no more than a bed, a dressing-table, a single bentwood chair and an oak wardrobe. He shows her a round the apartment – but not his own room – and gives her a key to the front door. He is tired, he explains. He is going to bed.

She is left in the sitting-room to examine the puzzled expression of her own face in a large, ancient mirror. Her reflection speaks sharply to her. 'Have you forgotten something? Weren't you trying to get somewhere?'

'No, I haven't forgotten anything.'

After six days she begins to suspect Gregory who, with ample opportunity, has failed to make a single advance or anything that could even be interpreted as a move. Evenings are spent either strolling in central Paris or eating, conversing and reading at the apartment. Gregory insists that they perpetuate the lying game and encourages her to fabricate exotic stories about herself.

Occasionally he suspects her of straying near the truth. 'I don't believe you did that,' he says, observing the untruth formula himself.

'Really? That means you think I did.'

'Don't complicate things. Just lie *exclusively*.'

But it is complicated, to lie persistently. It requires concentration, needs focus. One frequently drifts back to the truth. To lie consistently is like trying to fold your arms left across right, against form, before discovering that truthfulness is a habit rather than a virtue.

'Have you ever been in love?' Gregory asks one evening when the game is working particularly well.

'Never.'

'Ah! But I have. Many, many times, and with many lovers.'

With this remark she gets her first and unexpected whiff of his profound loneliness. Hard, while playing this game, ever to approach. With how many other people has he played like this?

'Has any man seen you naked?'

'No. None.'

He nods. 'So you're a virgin.'

'Of course. Would you like to? See me naked?' It is a bold step, but her extreme curiosity is awake and stalking. Because she knows men. Knows that in all cases and in every relationship, in her experience, from the moment of chance encounter or formal introduction, men are in a state of countdown. Their individual clocks are set differently, it has to be conceded. Some come at you head on, some pounce from behind and some come sideways, struggling for words and with eyes averted. But they all tick towards the same smoking and critical value.

It never occurs to her that not all women move through life in this condition, causing this much atmospheric disturbance. She does not guess that the proportion of women who will be delighted to find themselves in this position is matched by the numbers who will detest it. But because she's experienced this *frisson* for as long as she can remember she assumes it is the norm and for this reason dismisses the notion of unconsummated friendship between a man and a woman as luxurious and inherently idiotic. The only men in whom she's felt the absence of the ticking clock have been gay or asexually impotent. She concludes then, after the sixth day, that Gregory is one of these.

Strolling the Père Lachaise on a damp evening, he points out the tombs of Chopin, Oscar Wilde, Proust. She asks him to show her the burial place of Jim Morrison. There are a couple of French punks, a boy and girl, almost comatose, sprawled over the graffiti-strewn, vomit-spattered, condom-littered tomb like wraiths from a bad horror movie. By Morrison's tomb, the Greek inscription *Kata ton daimona eytoy*. 'Against one's own demons,' Gregory translates, inaccurately. 'So be it.'

The door of her room by now is left unlocked and unbolted because she wants to know whether he is in fact prowling at night waiting for this sanction. She needs to know. So she asks him. The question hangs in the air, waiting for the dissembled answer, pulled this way and that by mirrors. 'Would you? Would you like to see me naked?'

Gregory smiles. 'Yes. Very much. I have an overwhelming desire to see you naked.'

She is confused. It's not the expected answer; on the other hand, it confirms her suspicions. But if he is homosexual, if he is uninterested in her sexually, then what does he want? And on his first approach in the graveyard, when he pressed his hand on her belly – why did he do that if he wasn't drawn to her physically?

She badly wants to ask these questions directly, but the convolutions of the lying game require a long and tedious strategy. In any event, Gregory drains his wine glass, offers a sigh and a rather brief goodnight, as if somehow disappointed with her. But, as usual, he plants a cool, chaste kiss on her cheek before retiring to bed.

Leaving her to wait up for a further hour, sipping wine alone, exasperated by the nonplussed expression on the face of the woman in the mirror. A face which finally drives her out of the room and to her cold bed.

23

'A what?'

'An owl watch I promised the kids an owl watch. So we'll give 'em an owl watch.'

Sabine loaded baguettes into the shopping trolley as Matt wheeled it along the aisles of the supermarket. The others had gone to visit a château where Cathars had been butchered in the thirteenth century. Matt had generously offered to relieve James of shopping duty, and James had finally relinquished his self-appointed role as culinary overseer. Sabine became lighter when not in James's presence. A girlish spring returned to her step. She flushed easily at Matt's jokes, and he in turn took a strange pleasure in strolling through the market with her, knowing other folk would think them a couple. He sensed she reciprocated.

'We sit up all night until we see the owl.'

'All night?' Sabine said. 'I'm not letting my children sit up all night!'

'It won't be all night; just until we see the creature. It's a great sight, and then Beth and Jessie will know.'

'Will know what?'

'That life goes on in the dark. That there's another world active while we are all sleeping. That things are happening that you don't know about.' Sabine blocked Matt's trolley. He pretended to be fascinated by a jar of mayonnaise. 'And while everyone is watching for the owl,' said Matt, replacing the jar on the shelf, 'we can watch for something else.'

'Such as?'

'You were the one who said someone is filling your daughter's head. A bit of careful observation might reveal exactly who it is without anyone knowing they'd given themselves away.'

Sabine stroked a clump of celery and squinted at Matt. 'Let's pay for this and go for coffee.'

They found an aromatic café near the medieval covered market-place of the *bastide*. Sabine bought a packet of Gitanes and luxuri-ated in smoking along with her coffee. She popped her lips. She blew rings. She exhaled thin jets of blue smoke down her nostrils. She held her cigarette exactly perpendicular to the ceiling. In order to prevail on James to smoke less, she explained to Matt, she'd had to quit smoking herself.

'He came to France. He told me he'd fallen in love with France and with the smell of Gitanes. So for some reason I had to stop him smoking them.'

'That's partners for you,' Matt said. 'They're too bloody good for your own good. Me, I love the blue, blue packets.'

'What if it turns out to be Chrissie?'

'Huh?'

'On your owl watch. I'm sure it's either Rachel or Chrissie. What if it turns out to be Chrissie?'

'You never know. She's a strange character. I wouldn't swear to knowing her entirely.'

'But she's your wife!'

'Would you say you know everything about James? I'm sure he has his secrets, small or large. Don't you have your secrets from him?'

Sabine blew smoke.

'Anyway, there are other people to consider. You shouldn't narrow it down to just Rachel or Chrissie. There are others.'

'I know. I haven't entirely excluded Dominique. She likes to take Jessie for long walks. And then there's you.'

'Quite right. But you're forgetting one other person.'

'Who? James? No, I know the things Jessie is saying are not coming from James.'

'I'm not talking about James. I'm talking about you.'

'*Fou!* You're mad.'

'I'm serious. People can do things without even knowing it themselves.'

Sabine drained her coffee and stubbed out her cigarette. Pink lipstick ringed the butt. 'Let's go. You're in danger of cheering me up.'

Jessie was amazed and delighted to see her mother come properly awake that evening for the first time during the holiday. With Rachel and Jessie helping, Sabine bustled and joked her way through her turn to prepare the evening meal. She drank claret as she chopped and mixed. She sang songs in French. Jessie complained that she even *hummed* in French. James came in briefly to sniff at the kitchen activity. Something made him frown, and scratch his chin, and eye his wife speculatively. Sabine had told him she and Matt had coffee together in the town, and he had asked her if the coffee had been laced with bong-weed.

Sabine even found time to go upstairs and change into a glamorous red satin dress before dinner was served. Jessie was thrilled. Extra candles were placed around the table and lit.

'What's the special occasion?' James wanted to know.

'The owl watch, of course,' Jessie said, blowing out a match.

'Of course. The owl watch.' James wrinkled his brow and poured himself another glass of wine.

Jessie and Beth were in a state of excitement because they'd been told they were to be allowed to stay up late, sitting in the garden with the adults. Rachel encouraged their excitement, stoking their expectations. Chrissie shrugged and suggested chilling a few extra bottles of wine, while James, against his better judgement, refused to be the only one to drag his heels and happily joined in the spirit of the thing.

When dinner was over and the dishes were cleared away, Matt instructed everyone to go and find something warm to wear and to bring whatever they might want to drink for the duration of the owl watch. Then everyone was instructed to drag a chair on to the grass and to form a tight circle. He had a piece of paper and a pen for everyone.

'What are these for?'

'For the owl watch.'

It seemed to take an age before everyone was settled. Chrissie wanted to change her chair; Rachel felt inclined to fetch another pullover; the ink in Beth's pen had dried, so she insisted on finding another; Jessie needed something firm to lean her piece of paper on; and by the time all of this had taken place Matt had consumed another glass of wine and was ready to uncork a further bottle. Only Sabine, it seemed, was installed and eager to go, with pen poised.

'Everyone ready?' Matt wanted to know. 'What is it, Beth?'

'She wants to go to the toilet,' Jessie said helpfully.

'Then you must go. We'll wait.'

And they did wait, in a curiously nervous silence, for Beth to return and take her place. When she did so, Matt put a finger to his lips to ask for silence. He asked each in turn if they were prepared to commence the owl watch. They were.

'Right,' said Matt, 'wait for the signal. Ready. Steady. *Go!*'

There was silence. They sat in the darkness, everyone regarding Matt steadily, Beth and Jessie with bulging eyes, Chrissie quizzically, Rachel with the same wide-eyed expectation as the girls, James with one eyebrow cocked emphatically. It was Sabine who broke the silence with a high-pitched shriek of laughter. Her wine glass fell from her hand on to the grass. She crossed her legs and tried unsuccessfully to stifle her mirth with her hands, wheezing and shrieking.

Now everyone was looking at her. She glanced up at them, and then another wild cackle of laughter went shrieking across the night sky like a firework rocket. 'Your faces!' she cried. '*Your faces!*'

Is it you? Jessie thought, looking at her mother. *Do I get it from you?*

'I think Mummy's had a little more to drink than usual,' James said.

'Is there a points system?' Rachel asked.

'There's always a points system,' said Matt.

'May we be permitted to know what it is?' James inquired.

'Tell 'em, Beth.'

'One point for a hoot,' said Beth. 'Three for a screech. Five points if you see the owl perched. Ten if you see it in flight.'

'Who told you?' Sabine wanted to know, now recovered.

Beth looked at Matt, who mouthed something to her. 'Secret,' she said. 'And if it turns to look you straight in the eye, you get *fifty* points.'

'Are we allowed to talk?'

'Of course,' said Matt. 'This is meant to be fun, James. Pretend you're having fun. But be careful that while you're talking you're not missing anything.'

'I didn't know owls both hooted and screeched,' said Chrissie. 'I thought they did one or the other.'

'But we don't know what sort of owl it is, since no one has seen it. It might be a barn owl or it might be a little owl.'

'I'm not sure which one hoots and which one screeches,' James admitted.

'Lose five points for being an ignoramus!' Matt shouted, making the girls laugh.

'Daddy's stupid.' Beth giggled.

'Daddy's an ignoramus,' echoed Jessie.

Already James didn't like the way the game was going.

They listened. They looked at the stars. The constellation of the Plough was so huge and low in the sable night sky it seemed ready to till the soil. The Milky Way was as clear as an *autoroute* through space. Jessie noticed that every face was turned upwards towards the night sky, reflecting the limited grace of starlight. Gravity stopped working for a moment as a cosmic switch was thrown, and they tumbled together, in a single group-mind, into the outermost reaches of space. It was an instant during which Jessie would never be able to say with confidence that they were not transported for five seconds or five minutes or fifty minutes. Who would bring them back?

It was Beth, the youngest and therefore the least star-bound. 'Why doesn't the sky look like this at home?'

'It does, but you have to go away from the cities,' said Matt.

'There's so much light,' Chrissie murmured, 'that in our cities we can't see anything.'

'That,' said James, 'sounds almost profound for you, Chrissie.'

Chrissie slowly rotated her head away from the stars and locked eyes with James. For a moment the heat in her gaze went supernova with hatred, then cooled, then whited over with catch-light. She smiled. 'I have my moments.'

'I'm cold!' said Beth.

'Come here,' said Chrissie. Beth skipped over to Chrissie and jumped on her lap. Chrissie draped her blanket around both herself and Beth.

'It's freezing!' said Jessie.

'You've no staying-power, Jess!'

'Come here,' said Rachel. 'Let me give you a cuddle too.' Jessie, exaggerating the chattering of her teeth, went over to sit with Rachel.

'Was that a hoot?' said Matt.

No one else had heard anything, but Sabine said, 'I think it was.'

'I didn't hear anything,' Chrissie said.

'Perhaps it wasn't,' Matt conceded.

'Oh, I think it was,' Sabine insisted.

'You have to be careful,' said Matt. 'Sometimes you can trick yourself. You can hear a hoot only because you're *listening* for a hoot.'

Jessie noticed that her father seemed lost in his own thoughts. It reminded her of the times people called her back from her own moments 'apart'. Adults were obviously allowed to get away with it. James stood up. 'I'm sorry, folks, I can't keep my eyes open. I'm going to have to turn in.'

'You're already minus five points,' Matt shouted after him. 'You'll end up bottom of the heap.'

'I'm already there,' he quipped over his shoulder, before disappearing indoors.

Pretty soon Beth fell asleep in Chrissie's arms. Chrissie whispered that she would carry Beth to bed. Sabine watched her jealously, but Chrissie returned after a few minutes, kissed Matt on the forehead and said she too was going to bed. Jessie remained silent as the others stayed and talked. Comments were made about the weather. It was changing, they felt. The temperature had certainly dropped a couple of degrees and the evening was really quite chilly. Jessie yawned and grew bored, and got up and said goodnight. The owl had been forgotten. Finally Rachel peeled away. She started to clear up wine glasses, but Sabine told her to leave them, that she would tidy up.

Matt and Sabine were left to talk. They chatted about What is Important, and stayed for another hour or more.

And the owl never came.

24

Wind is air in motion. Winds are generated by differences in atmospheric pressure, which are in turn attributable mainly to variations in air temperature.

Temperature is not the same as heat. Heat is a form of energy, whereas the principle of temperature is the transfer of heat between bodies. In the case of two bodies at different temperatures, heat will always flow from the hotter to the colder body until the temperatures are identical and thermal equilibrium is reached.

25

Rachel was in the lounge giving Jessie her first piano lesson of the holiday, and so it was against a background of an inaccurate rendition of *Für Elise* that James announced he was going for a stroll. Sabine looked pleased and asked him to wait while she put on her hiking boots and called the children. No, said James, he wanted to go for a walk alone – yes, alone – and was there any need to make that kind of face, couldn't a grown man simply go for a walk on his own now and again, Christ, it wasn't much to ask, was it, well, was it?

The piano fell silent. No, Sabine was forced to agree quietly, it wasn't much to ask. James slammed his feet into his walking boots, dodged Matt and Chrissie in the kitchen, ignored Rachel and Jessie in the lounge and brushed aside Beth on the lawn. He soon put the corn behind him. His boots clacked on the sweating, gunmetal-coloured tarmac of the country lane.

The air smelled of limestone and of the vast corn crops and of horse-chestnut. He passed a fig tree in the tangled hedgerow. White dust mottled the leaves and the plumping fruit with an impression of corrosion. He saw that the dust was everywhere like an insidious poison, suffocating the hedgerow. The land needed rain, a downpour to wash away the corrupting white dust.

James was almost three kilometres away from the house before he reached a crossroad sign leaning at a prodigious angle. There he stopped, venting a deep sigh.

Something was killing him. Eating at him, a morsel at a time. It was as if someone in the group was poisoning him. That morning he'd been sick again, had actually vomited for the third time since their arrival, though he'd been able to prevent Sabine or anyone else from knowing about it. But it couldn't be a case of poisoning because he'd been affected by the same symptoms for several months now.

The doctors, after a battery of tests, had been unable to find anything seriously wrong with him. Once again James rejected the infuriatingly facile diagnosis of the NHS (slightly high blood pressure) and paid handsomely to have someone tell him something that made more sense – any kind of sense. At last a brass-plate Harley Street specialist had (under pressure from James and for a fee so spectacularly high it transformed hazarded guess into inspirational diagnosis) suggested to him that he might have been infected by a rare parasite of tropical origin. Having made this diagnosis, the doctor was unable to suggest any treatment. He prescribed Temazepan to help James with his sleeping and advised against drinking.

Yet the condition sapped his energy, fed from his blood, weakened his will and destroyed his temper. Plus his own breath smelled awful. Occasionally he caught the whiff of decay, and it flipped his stomach. Even so he found himself cupping his hand to his mouth or breathing against a mirror to try to catch the corrosive stench, scientifically, as it were, to measure the progress of the rot.

More significantly, he suspected that someone near to him had deliberately infected him. He knew the idea was paranoid, yet there was no other explanation. He'd never been near the tropics. He even avoided Asiatic restaurants of all descriptions because of a declared prejudice, he said, against bad food. Where would he have ingested a tropical parasite?

He knew he had many enemies. In the Eighties he hadn't simply trampled on people in the climb up the greasy pole; he'd decapitated them bloodily and extracted teeth for trophies; he'd banqueted, gloating, on hearts and livers. But it wasn't the executive corpses who haunted him; it was those around him whom he counted as friends.

James didn't trust Matt because he knew he'd hurt him; he didn't trust Rachel, who he knew saw through him; and he didn't trust his wife, who knew him better than he knew himself. It was outrageous, he admitted, to think that one of these had done this thing, that one of them had deliberately infected him so that he would suffer like this.

But somebody had done it. He didn't know how; he didn't know when. He only knew that someone had found an ingenious way to infect him with a tropical parasite. He knew also that he felt measurably worse around the people who were closest to him. He'd felt worse for the duration of this holiday: the symptoms of his sickness had become more manifest, and his condition had deteriorated. He felt some relief only when he was able to put a distance between him and them.

Behind him, to the north-west, clouds were beginning to form. To the south all looked clear. He proceeded south.

After walking for another three or four kilometres he looked back. The landscape had changed slightly. He could see nothing of the house or the surrounding corn crops, or the exposed lime-stone hill. He could easily pretend they were not there at all, that he had no family, no wife and children, no dangerous friends or embittered lovers, no large house in Surrey to maintain, no bullshit advertising empire to oversee, no executive parking space to scrap for, no Merc or Citroën for the wife, no school fees or dog's dinner, no power tools no cast-iron saucepan-set no solid silver cruet no doctor's fees no bloody Temazepan no no no . . . It was easy. As he walked, so he could shed these things. He sensed them spinning away behind him, clattering as they hit the road. He felt lighter, stronger.

James's eyes remained fixed on the southern horizon. There was the French Riviera, easily walkable; and Italy, easily reachable; and beyond that Greece, a mere step; and Asia Minor, almost visible, beckoning like a jewelled finger. He could go anywhere.

New life. Health. Youth. Vigour. He would walk towards these things simply by following the wonderful winding road.

*

'These clouds you see, Jessie, these are not good clouds.'

'Some clouds are good and some clouds are bad?'

'Exactly that. Some bring refreshing rain. The land needs rain. But these are of a certain kind. Look at them. They are a messy brown colour.'

'They look more like purple to me.'

'No. They are the colour of a dirty bruise. Look. You know why? They're made up from unclean air and from polluted water. They are contaminated clouds. You know why they're contaminated?'

'No.' Jessie was afraid of her instructor in this mood. Her instructor's eyes were fixed, almost immovably, on the cloud formations swelling in the distance. There was a certain lost quality about those eyes. Though they shone, they did so with a strange kind of absence, one that Jessie had seen before. When Jessie was waiting to see the Harley Street specialist, a woman had come out of the doctor's surgery and stared at her and laid a finger across her cheek. 'Is it because of chemicals?'

'Chemicals? No. That's another kind of pollution. I'm talking about the contamination of clouds that is brought about by people's thoughts.'

Jessie laughed, then wished she hadn't. Sometimes she suspected her instructor was quite mad.

'You think I'm joking?' her instructor said. 'It's something very few understand. If people are feeling unwell, unhappy, angry, hurt, confused or upset, they give off a special kind of heat. This heat draws perfectly ordinary cloud like a slow-acting magnet. Then it contaminates the cloud. What you see, Jessie, is the colour of dirty heat. The cloud is rolling towards us out of all the people across this valley. It's coming our way. Something is going to happen.'

Jessie looked again at the distant cloud. It was beginning to take on a brooding quality. She wasn't sure what to make of her instructor's words. She suspected that her instructor couldn't entirely be trusted.

*

137

By nine o'clock that evening James still hadn't returned. Having held off dinner until this time, they proceeded to eat. Sabine picked at her food in silence.

'Where the hell is he?' Rachel said, almost on her behalf.

'It's too soon to jump to conclusions,' said Matt.

'Which conclusions do you suggest we don't jump to?' said Sabine.

The meal was finished quickly. Sabine went upstairs to see to the girls. The others sat outside while Matt opened a bottle of wine and enumerated the possibilities: James could have got lost; he could be lying hurt somewhere; or he could have simply decided to stay out late. They all agreed it was too early to do anything about it.

'You know him best, Rachel,' Chrissie blurted. 'What's he up to?'

Rachel shrugged and squinted angrily at the stars.

By one o'clock in the morning James still hadn't returned. Speculation was avid now, though it was all unspoken. It was almost possible to hear cog-tooth minds turning on the obvious fears. Sabine came back down to say goodnight. Rachel wondered whether they should contact the police.

'Would you in England?' Sabine said, a little too sharply. 'If a man stayed out all night?'

'No.'

'So. It's the same in France. I'm going to bed.'

'Don't worry. I'll wait up,' said Matt.

'I won't worry. And there's no need for you to wait up.'

'Why not?'

'Because the bastard has taken his passport and his credit cards.'

Sabine's profound sobbing resounded throughout the house. Her unhappiness pulsed through the cavernous dark, and her crying kept the others awake. She had given up pretending. Whatever stoicism and phoney reserve she'd picked up from her years of living the Anglo-Saxon life of self-restraint – and James normally insisted on composure in the same way that he insisted on a good wine – she had suddenly surrendered. The old house, with its creaking floorboards, precarious shutters and rickety furniture, seemed itself to ache and sigh in the shadows, dismayed and troubled by her anguish.

Rachel also lay in the dark, in a spillage of guilt and regret over her affair with James. Matt and Chrissie too lay wide awake, listening attentively without wanting to listen. 'One of us should go and talk to her,' said Matt.

'No,' said Chrissie, 'it wouldn't be welcome.'

So they lay there as the sobbing diminished and then grew louder again. It was interminable. Just when they thought she had cried herself to sleep, she would break out again like someone in pain, real physical pain, as if a new set of tormentors, hag-toothed and leather-winged, had turned on her.

The door to Chrissie and Matt's room swung open with a whisper of the hinges. Startled, they both looked up but could see no one. Then an apparition in a white nightdress floated before them. 'Jessie!' said Matt.

'Mummy's crying,' said Jessie.

Beth, diminutive in striped pyjamas, stood behind her sister with her hands in her mouth. Jessie too was crying. She looked at Matt and Chrissie as if they were empowered to intervene, to make everything right. Her eyes said, 'You are adults. You control the world. Why don't you do something?'

'One of us should go to her,' said Matt.

'You go,' said Chrissie. 'I'll sit with the girls a while.'

Matt put on a dressing-gown and slipped out of the room. Chrissie beckoned the girls to climb into bed beside her. 'Mummy's crying,' Beth said, echoing her sister.

'That's right,' Chrissie said collecting the girls to her, 'mummies do that sometimes.'

26

'Mummy's crying.'

It gets complicated, looking into a mirror only to see yourself in the past looking into a mirror. Two mirrors coming together should make a cataclysmic explosion, or trigger a storm, but instead the energy unleashed by the communion of mirrors is transported into the infinite. And the past is clearly reflected in the mirror that afternoon as she waits in the Paris flat for him to return from goodness knows where. Late-afternoon sunlight drenches the past in an amber glow. She looks in the mirror and suddenly remembers her deflected journey to the Dordogne.

'Mummy's crying.'

'Yes,' said her father. 'Mummies sometimes do.'

'Why? Why is Mummy crying?'

'Because, because, because,' he said, tight-lipped, distracted, 'because the Wizard of Oz.'

The Wizard of Oz? What sort of an answer was that? Mummy was crying because something was wrong. Everything was wrong. It was all wrong. This was the place of the plum tree, of sunshine, of the dovecote and never-ending summer. This was the carefree land of laughs, where you could perform headstands and cartwheels all day long if you wanted, where they came every year, each summer for as long as she could remember. A place touched by amber light, not a place of tears and anger.

'*Not a place of tears!*' she tells the mirror, and her words echo down the chain of mirrored images, a diminishing voice for each reflection, following the same scary virtual curve into madness.

What went wrong that year? What changed? That is why she has to get to the Dordogne, to find out what happened all those years ago. The answer lies in the pastel shades of remembering, in the green-and-golden light of the past; in that fan-shaped light streaming and flickering at the periphery of her vision. A scallop of time. Blades of green and gold, tigering the memory.

The answer lies somewhere in that biblical light.

'I love you,' says Gregory, startling her, coming up behind her unexpectedly. She sees him first in the mirror, a whole regiment of Gregorys standing to stiff attention.

'What did you say?'

'I said I love you.'

A lie. A lie which is expected to be received as a lie: does it become something else? Was Gregory saying, therefore, *I don't love you*, so that the opposite was true? That was another mirror game. Now it is no longer possible to check out the lie, to ask if the other is playing the game, because the answer yes or no can still be couched in terms of the game. And now the game starts to feel dangerous because it has no bottom. A touch of vertigo here. Better to take a deep breath, and to play with commitment. 'And I love you, Gregory.'

'The sun is about to set outside. It looks beautiful. Let's go to Père Lachaise.'

'Sure.'

He produces a pair of shoes from behind his back, placing them on the coffee table. 'Will you wear these for me?' Edwardian-style boots lacing up to the lower calf, spike-heeled, the soft black leather polished to a remarkable shine.

She picks them up. 'A fetish?'

'Not at all.'

She takes the boots to her room. Anxious to please, she unrolls a pair of sheer nylons and puts on a long black skirt. Making up her face in the mirror, she whitens her cheeks, finishing them with a slight rose flush.

When she emerges, his hand flies to his chest. He is unable to disguise a tiny gasp of delight. 'It gives me no pleasure at all to look at you. You're an abomination.'

141

She smiles. 'Let's go.'

Gregory stops to buy three long-stemmed red roses. He has something to show her, he says. It's already dusk when they reach Père Lachaise. The cats are out, scavenging between monuments. Grey marble shines in the gloaming with dull, phosphorescent light. Another strolling couple pass by on their way out of the necropolis.

She follows Gregory, clasping his gloved hand, along a maze-like path between the headstones. They stop at a place vaguely familiar. The place where she first spotted him, exactly a week ago. The withered red roses she noticed on that occasion still lie on the first step of the monument. Gregory lays the fresh roses alongside the withered. Sarah reads the inscription. Beneath it, chiselled in the stone, the Latin–Greek mismatch: *Et in Arcadia ego.* 'Who was she?'

'Bernadette Duchamp. A writer at a time when it was not easy for a woman to be a writer. Died over a hundred years ago in poverty, aged thirty-three. She could no longer get her work published. She went mad, or she was already mad, or at any event she was committed to an asylum, where she died. Then her contemporaries decided she was a genius. A group of wealthy Parisian writers paid for this monument. Then they forgot about her again.'

'Have you "adopted?" her?'

'In a way. I'm trying to have her work republished. She was a sexual revolutionary. She also said that everyone has several lives going on at the same time, each unknown to the other. Do you think that's mad?'

'No.'

'You're wrong.' He is smiling thinly. 'Of course it's mad. She was a damaged person. That's why I love her so much. Damaged people are the most beautiful. They fly so far out. They fall further. They fall burning.'

Climbing the three steps of the marble monument, she passes between the Corinthian columns supporting an entablature of leaves. A wrought-iron gate has been broken open; it swings back. It is possible to walk into the marble vault and touch the sepulchre, to stroke the cold stone. A brown beetle disappears into a crack in the corner of the trough. She feels Gregory's presence at her back and wonders why he has brought her here. She turns to him. His breathing has become shallow.

'Is that why you like me?' she asks. 'Am I falling? Am I burning?'

In place of an answer Gregory bundles her against the back wall of the porch, kissing her roughly, biting her lips, mashing his mouth against hers. She peers into his eyes. He reaches down and hoists up the hem of her skirt, pinning it against her breasts with one hand, flaying at her underclothes with the other. Tearing at her, he drags her nylons and her underwear down her legs. The chill of the evening air condenses on her skin. Releasing her skirt, he stoops, tugging the tangle of underclothes down to her laced boots. He produces a knife; he hacks through the nylons and cotton. His mouth presses against the instep of her boot. She feels the progress of his hot tongue as it climbs the length of her calf, feels it pause and flicker at the back of her knee; from there it leaps like a flame across the smoothness of her inner thigh before probing her cunt.

Shivering under the frenzy of the assault, she is caught between shock and confusion, wanting to resist, yet overwhelmed. She grabs his hair, releases it, presses back against the stone wall. Lifting her skirt again, he forces her bottom against the cold marble, hooking an arm under her knee and hoisting her leg high in the air. There is some inept fumbling with trousers; she helps him, releasing his burning cock into her hand. He lifts her and pushes inside her.

She is dry, and it hurts. The frenzy doesn't abate for some time, but then exhaustion stops him before he ejaculates. They slouch against each other in the shadows. She says nothing, holding him, waiting for him to recover. The shocking odour of their sex commingles with the smells of damp earth, decaying leaf, mouldering stone. Without warning he withdraws, adjusts his clothes, storms away from her.

Hurrying after him, she calls his name softly in the dark of the cemetery.

'Gregory. Gregory, answer me. You must speak to me.' She raps hard on his door back at the apartment. He has locked himself in and is refusing to talk. She knows he is standing just the other side of the door. She can feel his back pressed to the wood panel, can hear his breathing, can smell his perspiration through the door.

Furious, she leaves him. She runs a bath and locks the bathroom door. In the hot, perfumed water, with her skin turning pink and the rising steam dampening her hair and misting the mirror, she thinks again of the green-and-golden light. The bars of light separate in a haze. Green and gold, the light splits into long thin columns, shivering, slender, waving slightly as if in a breeze. The light wavers, like green leaves spangled by bright sunshine, like golden ingots of corn. She is deep inside a dense, high field of corn. That's it. Deep in the corn, and gone.

27

Rachel was doing enough worrying for everyone. She'd spent the last few days watching events with wide eyes growing wider. She also carried an ulcerous weight in her stomach on behalf of everyone at the house, a boil that was inflating like a football with each passing day. Now that James had gone walkabout, she began to prick her forebodings with the lance of conscience.

She'd been as surprised as anyone at his disappearance, but when Sabine announced that he had taken his passport and his credit cards, she saw his actions as a logical sequence of events. During their affair he had frequently suggested his willingness to leave Sabine and the girls for her – too frequently for Rachel ever to take it seriously – and the fact that she'd never asked for, or encouraged, this dramatic course of action seemed to irritate him. Mistresses were supposed to badger their lovers to leave their wives for a higher form of love. The thing was that Rachel hadn't needed to gaze into the tealeaves or peer into a crystal ball to see that if James was going to abandon his family it would not be to get another wife, it would be to get another *life*. As for Rachel, she was not the kind of adulteress, she told herself, who wanted things she couldn't have. It was the experience of James she'd wanted, not a future with him. She admired him, liked him, enjoyed the scent of him, but it was only a flake of him she'd ever wanted for herself. Collecting the stamps of another country didn't automatically mean that you felt the need to go and live there.

This had bothered James only inasmuch as Rachel was refusing to conform to the old archetype of the mistress. She was supposed to wait for him to turn up at odd moments at her Pimlico flat; she was expected to maroon herself on the dismal island of self-sacrifice.

Well, Jack Bollocks was the name she'd given to life as a mistress. Rachel figured it wasn't that she'd denied him a life of tragic sacrifice that had bothered James. It was that she hadn't acted out some script in his head. Her attitude left the same expression on his face as he had when the wrong wine was opened at the table or when the cork broke in the bottle.

Now that James had laced up his boots and walked away, Rachel could see how it had happened. The holiday was not going according to plan. There were too many cross-tensions, and the ship's crew was shaky. Jessie was given to holing the boat below the waterline, Sabine was muttering dark things in the galley and Matt was prowling the deck hatching unguessable plans. Captain of a ship threatening mutiny, James's solution had been to throw himself overboard.

Except that he was the only one among them who saw him as captain.

And if Sabine was muttering darkly in the galley, then it was Rachel who needed to beware of her running amok with the carving knife. Sabine had taken, in these last few days, to watching her closely, making no attempt whatsoever to disguise her strange looks. Chrissie had warned that Sabine had rumbled the affair; though how Chrissie knew this Rachel would have liked to discover.

Rachel was ready for confrontation. Her days of communal living had left her with a shrewd understanding of the limited patterns of human behaviour, and she sensed it would be coming any day now. Sabine seemed to be waiting for her moment, but with James going missing and Jessie's behaviour becoming more unpredictable, she had enough to worry about. But Rachel was ready, and she'd decided that if Sabine asked her outright, then she might just admit what had happened. Despite James's injunction, *admit nothing*, she felt she owed Sabine, and herself, more honesty than that.

Then there was Matt, and unless Rachel was very much mistaken, something there might intervene to prevent Sabine from daring to confront her. She had watched a tiny spark between these two growing wider and brighter. Rachel wondered how aware of it they themselves were, so latent was it, so early in its course. She considered herself a student of these things. She had watched it happen to other people. Sometimes she had watched it happen to herself as if it were happening to another person.

So far, the evidence was slight. Sabine brightened visibly whenever Matt paid her attention, anyone could see that. And Matt, Rachel had decided, was one of those men who was hopelessly, innocently, romantically compelled to assist women in distress. His innate sympathy for women excited him. He was drawn to women strapped to railway tracks, to women trapped in burning buildings, to women lashed to sea-sprayed rocks. He was a victim of the Andromeda syndrome, and Sabine had only to lift her arms and tinkle her golden chains.

On its own that would have been dismissible, even faintly risible. But what worried Rachel was that it was linked to the darker human emotion of revenge. Matt wanted his pound of flesh. He knew what had happened at the agency. On the one occasion that Matt had shown signs of blossoming, of demonstrating to everyone that he could succeed after all, it was James who, preferring his friend to remain in the role of failure, had whipped out his pruning knife. And it had all happened over a matter of sexual jealousy.

Rachel saw, with unflinching certainty and a hot intuition, that Matt knew how he could savour his revenge. And she knew too that Sabine might slake her thirst for revenge in exactly the same way. Though it should not have concerned her, it troubled Rachel. She could forgive anyone an affair if it emerged from a bruising, skin-flaying passion, the toxic white heat of unmanageable desire, or even the biological imperative of procreation which drove some people, but this, this had all the dangerous signs of happening because it might conveniently hurt someone else, even if they deserved it, and that in Rachel's book was wrong. It was an abuse of natural force. Like retreating armies blackening the sky by putting oil-wells to the torch and discharging radioactive slime into the sea. Everyone around would suffer from the fallout.

Only Chrissie, Rachel suspected, might not even notice. Chrissie was enigmatic. On James's mutinous ship, Chrissie was up in the crow's nest and refusing to come down. She always seemed distracted from the events going on around her, as if her eyes were half-fixed on another world. In fact, Rachel had her doubts about Chrissie. If Matt's wife sometimes seemed like a little girl playing in the sun, she cast a long shadow. And she had that inward stare, as if there were layers or echoes to the woman not accessible to anyone else. Rachel was unable to sound her. Fact was that she had never felt at all comfortable around Chrissie.

There was a slightly unwholesome aura about her. Of course, that whiff of sexual venery in Chrissie was guaranteed to infuriate every woman coming within her compass; but it was beyond that. There was a draught, a dangerous draught that inflamed Rachel's concern whenever she saw Chrissie talking to Jessie. It was ridiculous, but she felt a thrill of possessiveness about Jessie as if she were her own daughter. Chrissie was so absorbed in her inner world that she failed to recognize certain obligations: she was thoughtless with the things she said; she was lax with her language; she was careless with the young girl.

And Jessie needed especially tender handling right now. Influence, at her age, could be either a crucial advantage or an impediment. She was fucked up. Why? Because her parents were fucked up. You didn't need to be a Harley Street psychiatrist to work that one out. Rachel wondered when it had started, whether to ascribe it to her control-freak father or to her unspeakably repressed mother.

Rachel had not met Sabine before sending her the anniversary cactus. If she had, she'd have undoubtedly sent her a bigger one, with instructions and a tube of KY jelly. Despite promising herself that she would make every effort to give Sabine a fair trial, she had ended up despising the woman on all counts. Everything about the French that Rachel admired was undone by her. That wonderful French thing called *style* was unpicked by the woman's self-consciousness; even in an open field she fashioned every step

148

along an imaginary catwalk. That delightful, lilting French accent was an ugly parody in her mouth, as if she calculated it had the power to weaken all English men, and women too, at the knees. And even that charming and slightly remote femininity common to French women was an effete affectation in this hard-boiled bitch. Worse than that, Sabine had somehow managed, by an extraordinary and exact science, to make Chrissie, Matt and herself feel like guests in the house rather than holiday companions. Only that morning Rachel had heard herself apologizing to Sabine for wanting to use the bathroom.

And –

Rachel had to stop herself. She was surprised at how easily her analysis had run rabid. Surprised herself that what she thought was mere dislike of the woman was crystalline hatred. It was so much easier to blame her for what was happening to Jessie than it was to blame James. She could almost forgive James for running away. Indeed, she began to recognize his affairs or, more important, their affair as an inept attempt to escape from this appalling woman.

But the person for whom Rachel was most anxious was not James; it was Jessie. Rachel was doing her best to help Jessie. She took particular care over the quality of their relationship. She worked hard, careful in how she explained things to the girl, turning negative situations into positive ones, responding honestly and thoughtfully to all of her questions. But in the labour of it she struggled against the steep gradient of everyone else's influence – namely, James's and Sabine's neurotic obsessions, Chrissie's delinquency and Matt's juvenile laxity.

This was a child after all, a young girl. A tender mind, still in the bud.

Rachel had never been with people so careless with words in the company of children. Words had a life of their own – didn't they know that? Words were like currents of air, streaming hither and thither, trying to find an aggregate form. They were like weather fronts. The wrong thing said coldly to a girl of Jessie's age might harden into an attitude, and that attitude might butt up against one incoming from another person. Clouds would form. Storms would follow. Tears and anger, in a child who was already damaged and who continued to be damaged. It was appalling. Considering the psychological condition of all those around her, Rachel felt she should have come on this holiday dressed in a white coat.

If she had her way, she would take Jessie away from these other people, away from their banal taboos and shitty middle-class preoccupations, their disgraceful self-deceptions and their vile bourgeois values. Jessie was, or could be, a free spirit. A child of the clouds. But she needed undivided attention. Rachel would have to renew her efforts as Jessie's special teacher.

28

Dominique drew up in a shiny red Renault the day after James disappeared, offering to take the children into the *bastide* town. Either Beth or Jessie must have said something to her because when they returned a few hours later, Dominique wanted to speak to Sabine.

'Yes,' said Sabine. 'It seems like he's gone.'

Dominique stroked Sabine lightly on the shoulder. 'Come to the churchyard with me. I want to put some flowers on my mother's grave.'

The sun was a blister in the sky and the heat had stunned the afternoon. The corn hung exhausted with the effort of a season's growing, every cob ready at a moment's notice to thump down on to the cracked, hard earth. It was the fifteenth anniversary of her mother's death, and Dominique had bought an exotic bunch of russet-and-white chrysanthemums, which she fetched from the car along with a plastic watering can. She linked arms with Sabine. They spoke French in a languid whisper, almost in deference to the dry heat of the afternoon.

'My father disappeared like that, three or four times when I was a child,' said Dominique. 'Each time I thought it was the end of the world. There were tears, recriminations, my mother blaming herself, blaming us, blaming the weather, blaming the sky for being blue and the grass for being green. And each time he came back after a day or two. Nothing was ever said. They just carried on as if it had never happened.'

'I don't know if James is coming back.'

'And then, after I got married, Patrice played the same trick. Twice.'

'Really? You look so happy, you and Patrice.'

They reached the entrance to the churchyard. The iron hinges squealed as Dominique swung open the gate. 'Well, maybe it has nothing to do with happiness or anything else. Maybe it's the weather that has an effect on them. It was always at this time of the year. Or maybe it's that house.'

'Why do you say that?'

'Because that's where we used to live. My family. And then Patrice and I.'

'That was your family home? You never said!'

'No, I never said.' Dominique led the way between the tall marble headstones until she found a blue-grey slab bearing a photograph of both her mother and her father. She emptied a jar of withered sticks, replacing them with the chrysanthemums and refilling the jar with fresh water from her watering can. 'I feel a bit sad about it. We couldn't afford to stay there. We had to sell it to the English family who bought it from us. The price was so good. But I regret it.'

'You must come as often as you like,' Sabine gushed, and then immediately felt foolish.

Dominique, tending the flowers, smiled up at her. 'We could never have made it beautiful. Repairing the roof, converting all those old rooms, putting in the pool. It's much better now. It was decaying around us.'

'Anyway,' Sabine said, 'I don't believe in haunted houses.'

'Neither do I. But I believe that people are haunted.' The other woman got to her feet, brushing soil from her hands. 'Your husband will come back. They always did. They always will. It's the same heat, coming and going. But it was not him I wanted to talk to you about. It was your daughter.'

'Jessie?'

'I'm a little worried. No, I'm really very worried. She has a shadow.' The manner in which Dominique used the French word *ombre* flushed Sabine with alarm.

'What do you mean exactly?'

Dominique stooped again to tug at some stringy growth of weed around her parents' grave. 'You are not a Parisian. Like me, you're from the country, so you understand a little of this. It's something my mother always used to talk about. I'm not so good. I turned my back on those things, you know. But with Jessie . . . I've seen it.'

'What have you seen?'

'As I say, a shadow. Jessie is being overlooked. By whom, I can't say. But someone is exerting a black influence over her, and you should take steps to protect your daughter.'

'I already have an idea who it is,' said Sabine.

'Before you jump to any conclusions,' Dominique warned, 'my mother used to say this about the person doing the harm.' Here she kissed her fingertips and touched her mother's photograph. 'She would say of that person that they didn't always know they were doing it.'

Matt had to visit the bank and Beth asked if she could go along for the ride. In the town Matt bought her a huge ice-cream and a doll in a gingham dress. Whenever he was uncertain about the girls, he bought them something. If they looked slightly bored, even for a second, he would drag them into a shop and lavish money on them. Sabine had more than once accused him of spoiling them.

'That's right,' he answered each time. 'Spoil 'em to death.'

It was an honest enough policy and the only way he could show unconditional affection for the girls. Having no children of his own, he envied James the hugs with which his daughters frequently rewarded him. Matt too wanted to squeeze them but, in the shadow of taboo, every time he felt this innocent impulse he put his hand in his pocket instead and spent money on them, usually on tourist tat. And Beth, of course, loved dolls and would play with them all day.

'Is Daddy coming back?' Beth asked him during the drive back.

'Of course he's coming back, Beth. Why do you ask that?'

'Jessie said that Chrissie said ... No, Rachel said ... No, Chrissie ...'

'Beth!'

'One of them said to Jessie that Daddy had a storm in his head and had to go away to get rid of it. And he might not come back. Is it true?'

Matt stopped the car. 'Listen, Beth. Your daddy just went away for a couple of days. Like he's done before when he's gone somewhere on business. To sort out some things. That's all. OK?' But Beth seemed to have stopped listening. She was playing with her doll. 'Want to see a castle? A château? Let's go a different way home.'

Matt went several kilometres out of his way to show her an impressive, dour château, its towers festooned with rampant growths of ivy. Then as they drove back along the country lanes they passed more cornfields fringed with huge red- and yellow-headed poppies. Beth wanted to stop and pick some.

Matt parked the Ka on the side of the road. Beth grabbed at a poppy and held it to her nose. 'You should never go to sleep with your head among poppies,' he said.

'Why not?'

'Because you'll never wake up.'

'Is that true?' Beth wanted to know.

'Hey! I don't tell lies!'

Matt sat under the shade of the soaring corn, smoking a cigarette, as Beth gathered handfuls of the poppies. The corn rustled at his back. A breeze snaked through the thick stems, making the ripe corn nod. He massaged his sunburned neck, lost in thought, keeping only half an eye on Beth. 'Don't go into the corn,' he said absently.

This holiday was certainly not turning out to be the relaxing idyll he'd hoped for. Though he hadn't expected James to be the first casualty. If Matt experienced a spasm of guilt, it died quickly. He enjoyed finding new ways to vex James. There was an art to it. The skill lay in going undetected as far as possible. Most

154

things could and would be attributed to the carelessness of Matt's personality rather than to vindictiveness. However, it required a certain amount of concentration, a degree of studied focus, to select a joint of meat so marbled with fat or a case of wine so acidic that it was guaranteed to displease James. It had been fun too to fix in place the wooden cross found in the barn, then to remove it, then to replace it again, knowing that James was suffering from the worst case of guilty conscience since Macbeth. Matt knew how the ad man's mind worked. Finally Matt had grown tired of the game, and with no little disgust at his own pettiness he'd hidden the cross where he'd found it in the barn.

Then someone else had put it back again.

But he was more worried about Chrissie than he was about James. Her sleepwalking was beginning to frighten him. Three times he'd woken to find her gone from their bed, and each time he'd discovered her wandering by the pool, naked, talking incoherently, perspiring heavily. He was afraid she might be a danger to herself. Perhaps it was the house, he thought. Perhaps something about the house was disturbing her.

Beth screamed, and Matt was jolted from his reverie. She stood at the edge of the tall jungle of corn, red and yellow poppies scattered at her feet. Matt ran over to her. 'What is it, Beth?'

'There's someone in the corn.'

Instinctively Matt picked her up and turned to peer into the corn. The reed-like stems seemed impenetrable beyond the first few rows: a sterile, airless and lightless space of dry stems and baked, cracked, dusty earth. Matt took a step towards the corn. A breeze shifted the crop, rustling the tall stems, parting the heads like the passage of some animal through the dark interior. 'What did you see?'

'Something.'

'Was it a man?'

'Kind of. Not really.'

Matt turned to the corn again. A teasing rustle came from somewhere within. The light at the top of the corn, where the swollen cobs nodded drowsily, was golden and green. Matt had a bad feeling but he said, 'There's nothing there, sweetheart.'

'Jessie said there are spirits in the corn.'

'Spirits? Who told her that?'

'You did,' said Beth.

Matt lowered her to the ground. 'Come on, pick up your flowers. We're going home.'

Later that afternoon, with the sun a leaking, smudged red blot outside the landing window, Chrissie caught Jessie on the stairs. 'Wanna walk, hey, Jess?' she sang, smiling, face painted by the blood-red light. 'Wanna walk?'

'Yeh! Let me get my shoes on.' She danced away.

Sabine, still brooding on Dominique's words, came out of her room holding some towels. 'Not a good time just now, Jessie.'

'Hours before dinner,' said Chrissie.

'You're not going,' Sabine said to Jessie, avoiding Chrissie's eyes.

Jessie reappeared, face reddening. 'I want to go!'

'I said no.'

Chrissie shrugged at Jessie. 'Your mother said no. That's it.'

Jessie looked furious. Her face seemed to engorge with blood. She swung herself across the banister and clattered down the stairs, leaving Sabine to stare at her towels and Chrissie to stare at Sabine.

'Why not?'

Sabine spoke over her shoulder, retreating to her room. 'She's been getting overexcited lately. I need to calm her down. A little discipline.'

Chrissie followed her. 'That's calming her down? I was just going to take her for a stroll. What could be more calming?'

'Well.'

' "Well"? What does that mean? Now she's primed like a bomb. How does that help?'

'I told you she can't go!' Sabine flashed. 'She's *my* fucking daughter. Why don't you accept it?'

'I do accept it,' Chrissie said quietly. 'I do accept that she's your fucked-up daughter.'

Chrissie turned and bounced down the stairs herself. Hurrying out of the shadows of the house and into the light, she headed towards the pool. As she drew abreast of the barn, she heard Rachel's voice and stopped. In the dark recesses of the barn Rachel was holding Jessie and saying something to her about breathing deeply. Rachel looked up defiantly at Chrissie but continued to murmur in Jessie's ear. Chrissie moved on to the swimming pool, where she stripped off her clothes and dived into the cool, cool water.

29

Thunder is the impulsion of sound waves following a natural
release of electricity. Potential gradient at moment of discharge:
150,000 volts per metre.

30

Denied her walk with Chrissie, Jessie shut herself in her room and concentrated on her reflection in the mirror. She was finding it easier to gaze into her own eyes for longer periods. It was best, she'd discovered, if she closed the shutters so that only a few bars of light penetrated the room and the exercise could be conducted in shadow.

Because in the shadows the room could breathe. A secret life, apparent only while the room swam in semi-darkness, was otherwise paralysed by the sunlight. When the shutters were closed the room relaxed and began to live again. In the shadows mellow old furniture flexed and creaked; dust a century old developed a dull starlight quality; wooden joints in the wardrobe, the dressing-table and the hardbacked chair seemed to expand minutely, almost invisibly but still perceptibly; floorboards swelled and came alive with tiny vibrations. In fact, the entire room seemed to inflate and contract, like a slow-breathing lung, while a barely audible sigh filled it with musty but not unpleasant odours of damp and creeping decay.

Sometimes when Jessie gazed into the mirror she wondered if she were invoking the spirit of the room. But her instructor had told her that there was no spirit there, merely memories trapped in the dust of the room's inaccessible spots. The only spirit, her instructor had told her, was the spirit in the mirror.

Jessie persisted, continuing to gaze as her face evolved through the usual stages of distortion, her face muscles twitching fractionally, as if some unseen being were pinching her cheek or tugging an eyebrow out of shape. Mere visual hallucination, her instructor had told her, tricks of the eye, a laziness of the organ itself. But then the real thing started, which was no hallucination.

A minuscule blue spark.

The spark emerged from her eye: not from the black hole of the pupil but from somewhere in the clouded iris. Her eyes were blue, therefore a blue spark. Green-eyed people saw a green spark, she'd been told, grey-eyed people a grey one and brown-eyed people, inexplicably, a yellow spark. She'd been trained not to follow the trajectory of the blue spark but to continue to gaze into her own reflection. Meanwhile the spark arced to the right, to the three o'clock position, before fading. Then, unmistakably, three more sparks, this time white-hot, a brief, shimmering fountain, dying as quickly as the first.

It was important at this stage – and her instructor had been most explicit – not to lose concentration. This was the point Jessie had reached before, at which moment she usually became afraid and closed down the exercise.

'Remember, Jessie, it's not something coming after you,' she'd been told. 'It's a part of you trying to break free, coming to help you. Don't think of it as something outside you. Think of it as your shadow or, better still, think of it as your angel or your twin sister.'

The first thing Jessie always noted at this time was the clouding of the glass all about the reflected image of herself, as if that part of the mirror not reflecting her own figure was shutting down, pouring light into her instead or at least into the reflection of her. Then the dead, smoked-out part of the mirror crumpled and began to mould, around and behind her, a new shape, like a visual echo, a silhouette of herself draped across her shoulders, plumping in the shadows, darkly humanoid at her back but with the suggestion of oddly curving peaks at each shoulder, an adumbration not unlike wings.

'Then, Jessie, wait. Don't scare it away. Wait until the right moment. Then ask its name.'

One of them, Sabine was convinced, had dug her claws into her husband, and one of them had sunk her talons in her daughter. It was possible that the same woman was responsible in each case. She determined to keep both women in her line of sight.

Right at this moment she knew that Jessie was safely sulking in her bedroom. Through the window she could see Rachel, who was painting a watercolour of the valley, and Chrissie, who was lying flat out by the pool. She'd had to be firm with Chrissie, and that was difficult; and she'd need to adopt the same policy with regard to Rachel. Eventually one of these women would slip up and reveal herself.

She didn't know which offence hurt most: the theft of her husband or the undermining of her influence over her daughter. She did suspect, however, that one was probably connected with the other. If she had to offend an innocent party in the task of unmasking the guilty one, then so be it.

Her suspicions swung wildly between the two. It didn't need perfect vision to see that Chrissie seemed unable to keep her eyes off men in a way that must be an embarrassment to poor Matt. Sabine respected Matt. Surely he could have done better for himself; Chrissie was the kind of woman on whom Matt's finer qualities were lost. Chrissie would always reject the higher things in a relationship in return for short-term excitement. The thrill of an affair, perhaps; under the nose of another woman, perhaps; with a friend of her own husband, maybe. Something about Chrissie rankled, and Sabine wasn't fooled. Rat-like cunning in the woman belied her superficial, almost abstracted charm.

Rachel was more inscrutable. Sabine watched Rachel watching. As a person-watcher herself, she recognized the skills, the cover, the camouflage. Rachel was like a trained spy, scrutinizing people without gazing directly at them by using the periphery of her vision or by pretending to be absorbed in a book or in one of her ghastly daubs. Meanwhile she never missed a trick. She caught every word, she grasped every nuance, Sabine could tell. And she seemed to pay special attention to any interaction between Jessie and her parents, as if she were observing critically, as if she were about to prepare a report to some shadowy agency.

She was also possessed of vulpine intelligence. Sabine wasn't fooled by her Estuary English or her vulgar tattoos. It had taken her some years, but now that Sabine was able to snatch away the fig leaf of the British class system, she approved of it and quickly put it back where she'd found it. The British were appalling but impressive hypocrites. They all claimed to deplore the class system or, even worse, pretended it no longer existed. Perhaps you had to be French, or at least foreign, to detect what nonsense that was and to see the thing working its now fine, now lumbering machinery.

The class system was a tractable but unbreakable protective device. The class system was a means of insulating yourself from the predatory instincts of people who had less to lose than you. The class system was cemented in place to stop people from seizing what you and yours had fought for. The class system existed to stop people of low instincts taking their holidays with your family. Rachel, meanwhile, was someone who was on the make. What she wanted to make, and with whom, and out of whom, Sabine wasn't entirely sure. She only knew she was determined not to let her do it at her own family's expense.

No, from now on she was going to watch Rachel, and Chrissie, very carefully.

Matt delivered Beth and her poppies back to Sabine and told her to say nothing about the man in the corn. Sabine was delighted and whisked Beth away to put the poppies in a jar. Matt wasn't entirely certain why he'd told Beth to remain silent about her fright, other than that he thought Sabine had got enough to worry about already. And, anyway, he knew exactly what it was that Beth had seen.

Beth, Matt knew, had glimpsed a manifestation of everything that was frightening her. She'd seen, in the shadows, the shape of her own anxieties. The tensions in the house were complex enough for an adult to deal with, never mind a seven-year-old kid. Her mother and father operated in a terrible state of unspoken hostility. In some ways it would have been better if they were to have a stand-up, knock-down, spitting and kicking fight on the grass outside the house. James could give Sabine a split lip and Sabine could break a plate over James's head, perhaps slicing off an ear in the process. At least that way some of this smouldering energy would be discharged. Just waiting for something to happen was enough to make anyone jump at shadows.

And kids, of course, pick up tension, like they always do, like they always have done. No, that wasn't true: kids don't pick it up, they *are* it. They experience it, they live it. Especially at the age of seven, with a mother and a father smoking and brooding like deities ready to fulminate in the heavens. Were James and Sabine like this when Jessie was Beth's age? No surprise, then, about Jess.

Matt wondered suddenly when James had last made love to his wife. When he thought about Sabine, he couldn't keep from his mind a longing to put that right. She was a beautiful and sensitive woman who had wasted herself on someone sexually unappreciative and spiritually unworthy. For some reason, he always dreamed of making Sabine sweat. He wanted her to sweat. When he imagined her naked, her lithe, tanned legs and her pretty rump aggressively offered, he pictured a dew on her upper lip, and beads of perspiration gleaming at the nipples of her small breasts, and runlets along her smooth flanks which he savoured with his tongue as he gave her some of the pleasures so obviously denied by James. She was probably the most sexually coiled but frustrated woman he had ever met. James must be mad to do a bunk. The snivelling coward had abandoned this gorgeous, fuckable wife and his two huggable, kissable daughters.

Matt turned his mind from fantasies of Sabine to thoughts of Beth, frightened by the wind in the corn. Yes, what Beth had seen there was her fear for her father, lost in the green-and-gold jungle. Matt knew this because he too had his own man in the corn.

He shuddered.

He found Chrissie on a sunbed. Neither the tinny blasting of her personal stereo nor her wrap-around sunglasses disguised her mood. 'What are you looking so sour about?' he asked. Getting no answer, he sighed, took out his tobacco and pasted a few cigarette papers together. Very soon the air was spiced with the dirty-sweet aroma of grass. Matt waved the joint under Chrissie's nose.

Chrissie took it from him, inhaled briefly, then blew the smoke out quickly as if it wasn't to her taste. She handed the thing back, looking faintly disgusted with Matt for even offering it to her.

Chrissie tended to avoid Matt's grass in the same way she resisted drinking in quantity. Whenever she smoked some of his weed, or drank too much, or stayed up late and became overtired, she had a habit of trancing out. She would disappear, socially speaking. Over the years Matt had learned to recognize the signs. A grey mist formed over her eyes and her head would tilt slightly. You could address her directly and by name and she would fail to respond. It was necessary, at these moments, to touch her to bring her out of her reverie.

'Where do you go?' Matt had asked on more than one occasion.

She would look up, as if the answer was somewhere above her, and then smile and say, 'I don't know.' What's more, he believed her. She didn't know. But he also believed that she didn't want to know.

It was Matt, some time ago, who'd first pointed out that she and Jessie had something in common. 'Jessie does that thing too. She goes away for a moment or two. Especially when someone is saying something she doesn't want to hear.'

'But with Jessie it's not drink or drugs.'

'No. You should get together with her. Maybe you can help her.'

Since that time Chrissie had always felt a special affection for Jessie, which was why she had taken Sabine's rebuff so badly.

Chrissie ripped off her sunglasses. 'I'm not fit, apparently, to take Jessie for a walk now.'

'Says who?'

'Says her mother.'

Matt glanced uneasily back at the house. 'Sabine's having a

difficult time of it. You're not her problem. She's projecting it on to everyone around her.'

'She's a cock-sucking whore is what she is – '

'Hey!' Matt said softly, shocked at Chrissie's vehemence. Chrissie subsided. After a while Matt stubbed out his joint, exhaled a rich plume of smoke and said, 'Beth saw something in the corn today.'

Chrissie sat bolt-upright. 'What do you mean? What do you mean, Beth saw something in the corn?'

'Tell me some more secrets,' Beth said.

They were hiding in the barn. Jessie had found a timbered loft, unknown to the adults. From there they could spy on the grown-ups, when they were in the garden or round the pool, through the cracks in the wood. They could see anyone coming. Jessie thought carefully about what she might tell Beth and what she might leave out. 'You're a blabbermouth, Beth. Anything I tell you goes straight back to them. A blabbermouth.'

'No, I'm not!' Beth protested. 'And I told you about the corn!'

'Shhh! They'll hear us. I'll tell you one more secret. But if you tell anyone else, then that's it. We're finished.'

Beth settled herself into listening position, blue eyes upturned to her sister's.

'There are angels,' said Jessie.

Beth blinked slowly. This wasn't exactly new. 'I know that!'

'Yes, but what you don't know is how to recognize them. They don't look anything like what you would think of as an angel. In fact, they come in lots of different shapes and forms. An angel can come as anything. A bird. A tree. A person. A message on a gravestone. A cave.' Jessie's imagination ran out momentarily. 'A car.'

'A car?' Beth was disgusted.

'I'm not saying an angel does come as a car. I'm saying it might. In disguise. And someone like you wouldn't know it if you saw it.'

165

If this was how angels behaved, Beth looked as though she hadn't got much time for them. 'Can they come as people?'

'I told you they can.'

'Did I see an angel in the corn?'

'No. That was a demon.'

'Who do you like best? Matt, Chrissie or Rachel?'

Jessie knew she had to answer carefully. Even from her young sister this might be a trick question. 'I like them all equally.'

'I like Rachel best. How can you tell the difference between an angel and a demon?'

31

And how could you tell, as Jessie had asked her, the difference between an angel and a demon when sometimes it was like trying to tell the difference between the truth and a lie? She herself forgot, and she forgot often, the gospel of the lie according to Gregory. It was not instinctive to her. She had to train herself. It was an exacting discipline, studying the mirrors in the mirrors.

She discovers Gregory is a user by stumbling on him in the bathroom. His works are all laid out on the closed lid of a battered commode as he taps a muscle on his arm, trying to bring up a vein. 'You're a junky,' she blurts.

Arrested in the act, peering up at her with cloudless blue eyes, he says, 'Good God, no. I'm a diabetic. I have to inject myself with insulin.' He holds the syringe up for her inspection.

Colouring, apologizing profusely for her mistake, she closes the door on him. Back in the room full of mirrors, she thinks about it again, smacks her head. 'Insulin, my arse.'

A lot of things are becoming clear concerning Gregory's behaviour. The remoteness, the mood swings, the occasionally stunned expression, the inability to ejaculate. She's not entirely shocked to discover that he is a drug user. She's seen alcoholics worse than Gregory; has herself snorted powders, popped pills, smoked herbs all the colours of autumn. What really disconcerts her is this astonishing reflex for lying.

Junkies and alcoholics, in her experience, are the most sophisticated and experienced liars and dissemblers on the planet. Addicts have it within their gift to deceive angels. In fact, it isn't the junk, the smack or the booze they insert into their bodies; it is the Gospel of the Lie. In it goes, white as snow, golden as grain – heroin or whisky, it doesn't matter – and out it comes, oozing like tar, an inky sludge of lies, black as the crow.

The effort of continuing with this game offers her a strange and distorted picture of herself. Never having been an especially honest person, it surprises her to discover her own reflex is to tell the truth, naturally. But is it a virtue when a solemn undertaking has been made to do precisely the opposite? Lying, second nature to Gregory, is actually a strain; particularly difficult too to train herself to disbelieve consistently. Now she feels foolish and naïve about Gregory's claim to be a diabetic.

Several times she thinks: *I must stop this now, I must get away from this.* But something happens in those moments when a pure lie passes between her and Gregory. As with the lie about insulin. When their eyes meet after the transmission of a lie, it is as if an appalling secret were shared in that moment, a secret weighing on life itself. With eyes locked they fall, dropping through the fiery abyss towards some terrible and overwhelming revelation.

Later that day Gregory approaches her, proffering a little sachet of white powder. 'I don't want you to have any of this.'

She struggles to control her anger. 'I think it's beautiful and generous and courageous of you to offer it to me. I want you to offer it to me every hour, on the hour.' It is the last time he tries to lay heroin on her. They never discuss his addiction again.

But Gregory has another addiction. The evening in the Père Lachaise is never referred to, but the Edwardian lace-up, spike-heel boots reappear, along with other clothes and cosmetics too. 'It would probably give me no pleasure at all,' Gregory assures her, 'if you were to wear any of these . . .' She shrugs and obliges, always prepared to dress for him. She's still curious about the nature of his needs.

So she whites her face and applies gash-crimson lipstick he hasn't asked her to wear; puts on fish-net stockings and boots that afford him no pleasure; slips into the black, velvet elbow-length gloves he dislikes, the breast-exposing corset he disparages . . .

He lights dozens of candles in his bedroom. Lying naked on his bed, he watches her with dilated pupils, as if he were an animal awaiting immolation. It is difficult to know what he wants. He answers only in the negative, and if she opens her mouth to speak she senses dissatisfaction. So she proceeds by instinct. The first time, she puts his long, thin cock into her mouth and sucks him, but still he seems unable or unwilling to ejaculate. And a refinement is obliquely demanded.

'If you were not to rouge your breasts . . .'

She does.

Then, 'Maybe a cigarette, if you did not have a cigarette . . .' She obliges. 'No, no, an unlit cigarette.' And then, 'Perhaps if you were to take an occasional draw on the cigarette between sucking me, that would not please me.'

Each time a new refinement, a marginal adjustment, a slender modification, before the inevitable moment, at some unavoidable gesture or nuance, when she senses she has somehow disappointed him and the session draws to an unconsummated close. No acrimony, no recrimination, just an unsatisfactory conclusion before trying the next time.

And at each next time the events of the previous occasion have to be repeated exactly, lighting the cigarette in a certain way, inhaling at a certain moment, exhaling as directed, all in a microscopic ritual of uncertain content forever improvised towards its end. 'If you were to take off a glove and nip out one of the candle flames between your thumb and finger, that would not . . .'

This goes on for several weeks. The weather outside becomes worse, curtailing all walks. She reads. Gregory goes out, sometimes remaining away for a day or two at a time. Why does she stay? Because Gregory never asks her to, never demands anything of her. Sexually, other than the disastrous evening in the Père Lachaise, he never even wants to penetrate her. He is a mystery she must see through to the conclusion. And he brings, after all, an angel's covenant, offering guidance, promising revelation. She does not forget that.

But behind all this a bell rings dully in the back of her brain. Dordogne, it tolls, Dordogne. And with the tolling of that bell she remembers her arrested journey. Knows she must get to the Dordogne to see her sister. If only she can remember why.

Then one evening she does remember. It is after Gregory has gone out. A mirror hangs in the sitting-room, its glass bubbled and distorted in a heavy baroque gilt frame, opaque and mottled, an old mirror worn out with looking. She peers at herself as if through a slight mist. It occurs to her that if you stare at your own reflection for long enough – say, for several years – it may become possible to forget which is the real and which the virtual self. Which side are you on? What if you are not a person at all? What if you're only a memory, trying to attain realization? And what happens to forgotten memories? They must go somewhere, since they are recoverable. Perhaps there exists a Purgatory for lost memories. Perhaps this is it. What if our lives are merely memories swimming towards a present moment? What if there is no place called the Dordogne? What if I don't have a sister?

A sudden insight. 'I have been divided from my future,' she tells her reflection.

She stares at herself in the mirror for a long time until it seems she can't tear herself away. Then comes a slight vibration in her cheekbone, a barely detectable twitch of the muscle under one eye. Movements seen but not felt. Happening only in the virtual world of reflection. Then her face slews through a succession of minute distortions, as if being rapidly remoulded by invisible hands. Light around the reflected face darkens, clouds, shadows the face in the mirror. At either side of her staring face long-stemmed golden trumpets form from the cloud or are, perhaps, simply winking images generated by the mirrors of the anterior wall; whatever they are, she fixes her gaze on the face before her, which no longer seems her own. From far off she hears the thin, mournful blast of trumpets. Though her own eyes remain open, the eyelids of her reflection close even as she watches, and the mouth works, speaking in a voice not quite her own. *You are one of the lost.*

'What must I do?' she asks the sightless woman.

Each day is a new landing on the staircase down. You've fallen a long way. He is not an angel. You are.

'I was deceived. What must I do?'

Do? You must kill him.

She hears the soft click of the front door as Gregory returns. Next moment he stands beside her, his face next to hers, looking into the mirror. Her own reflection steadies, reconstitutes itself, opens its eyes as if to deceive him.

'Talking to yourself,' he says, gently thumbing a tear from her cheek. 'But you've been crying.'

'I'm tired.'

'Can I get you something?'

'No, I'm going out for a walk.'

'I'll come with you.'

'No. Please. I have some thinking to do.'

It is the first time she's rejected his company. Gregory looks thoughtful, shrugs. 'It's damp. You'll need a coat.'

Outside, the street is draped in mist, layers of superfine muslin stretched across the pavements and the roads and the lampposts and the parked cars, all beaded with moisture. The Parisian sounds are muted; illumination from the streetlamps is twisted into tight yellow balls; the grey paving underfoot is puddled with faintly nacreous and unwholesome light. She goes to the Père Lachaise because she has nowhere else to go.

But the spirits of the famous graveyard are numbed. Marble statuary struggles for definition in the weak light. Even the cats and the Jim Morrison death-cultists are in hiding. Damp oils the skin, penetrates bone. She turns up her coat collar and wanders the avenues. *You are the angel. You must kill him.*

She comes upon an extraordinary monument there, a life-sized marble wraith of a woman, head hidden by the folds of yards of linen, clinging despondently with one hand to the cell-like sculptured bars of a tomb. It is a preposterous, death-loving effigy, calling attention to its own tragedy, impossibly realistic in the mist, a spectre, a shade, a vampire trying, too late, to return to the tomb before dawn. *Is that me?* she wonders. Nearby a much smaller grave, moss-tangled, inscribed simply with a name and the words *Ma soeur, mon sang.*

Remembering. Remembering why the Dordogne. My sister, my blood.

She returns directly to the apartment. She knows exactly where Gregory keeps his gear, has seen him cut his heroin enough times in order to sell it on. *Fix this, then.* When she has finished tampering with his supply, she is satisfied he won't be able to tell what she's done until too late. *Kill him.* It is critical that nothing should stop her now. She has to get to the Dordogne. Has to get to her sister because her sister needs her help. If only she could remember who her sister is.

32

'You must feel it, Jessie. The temperature has dropped by some degrees. Surely you can feel it?'

Jessie shrugged, feigning boredom. She had other things on her mind besides the weather.

'I think you're pretending. Pretending not to notice this change in the weather. What is it? Has something altered? Have I lost you?'

'It's Mummy. She told me not to spend any more time with you.' Jessie didn't mention how emphatic her mother had been.

'With me?'

'With any of you. Well, at first she said any of you. Then she said Matt was all right. But I'm not supposed to go for walks or drives, or shopping, or anything like that with you.'

'And what do you think of that?'

'It's stupid. I think she's upset because Daddy's gone.' On the other hand, Jessie had sensed that Sabine was in some way relieved that James had disappeared. That worried her. It seemed as if the entire adult foundation on which she based her understanding of the world was beginning to fall apart. She'd always assumed that adults had good reasons for doing what they did, and that what they did was in everyone's best interests. It occurred to her, for the first time in her life, that adults might *not* know what they were doing. That they were making it up as they went along, like children.

Jessie's instructor reached out and stroked her hair. 'You're right. You're a good weatherwatcher after all. You see beyond the obvious. When people are depressed about something they let other thoughts and ideas move them, and then they strike out at the wrong people. You have to be careful when you're with someone who is upset. But, listen, I think your father might come home today.'

'How do you know?'

'Because I'm a weatherwatcher too. I may be wrong but, Jessie, look.' Her instructor lay back and pointed up at a belt of incoming cloud. 'What white-winged outriders have we here? Eight kilometres high, feathered and tailed, portents and significant omens more beautiful than the seraphim, more shining than the cherubim. Messengers bearing crystals of ice. Soaring in the airstreams. Riding the currents. Searching for purchase on the hot, hot earth.'

Jessie tilted her head back and looked. Touched by a late cast of sunlight, the clouds appeared benign, far-off and frail.

'Look at them, Jess. My God, they number in the thousands! Silver wings smeared golden and pink and mauve. And, you know, by morning they'll be lost from view. But what do you think they bring behind them? What do they pull on ropes of crystal, on chains of ice? What, Jess, is tethered in their wake? Listen. Can you hear their voices? Can you? They're busy speaking the names of individual souls far below, in tongues too beautiful to be addressed. All unheard. All unheeded. But listen again. Because here's your father.'

Jessie turned. She heard an unusual sound coming from the house. It was a single ring of the telephone – unusual because in the time they'd been at the house this was the first occasion that the telephone had rung.

'Wouldn't it be funny,' Jessie's instructor said, 'if I was right, and that was your father ringing right now?'

Yes, Jessie thought. *That would be funny.*

'Where?' said Matt, when he answered the phone.

'Where?' said someone else.

'Where?' said another.

Sabine only sighed. 'It doesn't surprise me. Can you look after the children? I'd better start immediately.'

174

'No,' said Matt. 'I'll go. I told him I would. You stay here.'

Sabine pretended to protest but was clearly relieved at not having to drive such a distance. It wasn't yet midday and plainly they could not be back much before midnight.

They all wanted to know what exactly he'd had to say for himself and Matt said not much exactly and Sabine said did you ask him what he was thinking of and Matt said, no, he was too busy writing down directions for where to find him and Rachel said she couldn't believe it and Chrissie said she couldn't believe it either and Sabine started to cry and Chrissie said Matt ought to get going as soon as possible and Rachel thoughtfully offered to prepare some sandwiches for the journey. Then Matt was turning the car on the gravel courtyard in front of the house, and then he was gone, leaving everyone subdued.

'I'm going to make us all a pot of tea,' said Rachel.

In the absence of the men, Jessie sensed a strange change of mood. Very little was said – indeed, nothing at all about James, or where he was, or why he might be where he was, or what was going on in his head. Jessie posed a few questions, as did Beth, but such was the brevity and crispness of the answers received they knew better than to persist.

Jessie took her cues from the adult women. Everyone's tone of voice seemed to have dropped fractionally. Movement around the house was more languid, marginally. In a place where generally seven heartbeats might, so to speak, be heard to pulse at different rates, there was a universal slowing and synchronizing. In the afternoon Rachel, Chrissie, Beth and Jessie wallowed in the pool, hanging on to the side, perspiring in the sticky heat. 'Look at those clouds coming in,' someone said. Low in the west clouds the colour of a fresh bruise were beginning to compress and stack. Sabine lay on a sunbed reading a paperback. Jessie noticed her mother hadn't turned a page in half an hour, but it was Rachel who spoke.

'Come into the pool with us, Sabine.'

Sabine looked up, put her book aside and slipped into the water beside them. Nothing was said. They clung to the lip of the basin, bodies submerged, bobbing only slightly, hiding from the heat, like carp, in the torpor of the pool.

In preparing the evening meal the five females were a model of cooperation; no one had to give orders or instructions. Jessie was amazed when even Beth swung to, helping to find dishes and lay the table. Meanwhile Rachel scrubbed, Chrissie peeled, Sabine chopped; Sabine salted, Chrissie sautéed and Rachel basted. They joked, they laughed. They swapped stories of this and that, and they sat down together to a beautiful candlelit dinner in the absence of men. There was an unspoken sympathy about things unspecified. It was as if they were still in the pool together, sharing an emotional jacuzzi.

Except that at the bottom of the jacuzzi the tiled floor was overheating. Feet were burning, legs were thrashing and the smell of charred flesh was sickening.

'Time you girls were in bed,' said Sabine.

'Can we finish the story?' Beth asked.

'I'll read,' Chrissie volunteered.

There was a moment's silence. Jessie held her breath.

'It's all right,' Sabine said. 'I'll do it.'

'No, really, I don't mind.'

'Stay there. It's my chore.'

The two women looked at each other, galaxies of space in the exchange. 'It shouldn't be a chore –' Chrissie began, but she was interrupted by Rachel.

'Didn't you tell me you were almost at the end of the story, Beth? Mummy can finish that one, and then Chrissie can start the next.'

Chrissie coloured. Sabine followed Beth to the bedroom. Jessie loitered.

'I was trying to be diplomatic,' Jessie heard Rachel say, thinking they were all out of earshot.

'You were right,' Chrissie whispered. 'But she can be such a hard bitch.'

Jessie washed and changed into her nightgown. Before the girls got into bed Sabine sent them back into the kitchen to kiss Rachel and Chrissie goodnight.

By the time Matt parked his car it was raining. He found James drinking coffee in an otherwise empty café by the side of the road. He had three days' beard growth. 'Hi!' James said brightly, standing up and draining his coffee.

'Let's go,' Matt said flatly. They were at a place called Rennes-le-Château in the foothills of the Pyrenees. He didn't know why and he didn't much care.

'Could you pay the bill? I'm out of cash.'

Matt settled and James followed him out. 'The Pyrenees are sensational, aren't they, Matt? Hey, you should have brought the Merc. Do you want me to drive?'

'Just get in. Why should I want to come in your car? I don't want to look like you.'

They drove a kilometre or two in a silence punctuated by the swishing wipers. Then Matt said, 'Right, let's hear it.'

James showed Matt the palms of his hands. 'I don't want to talk about it.' He was acting as if Matt had just picked him up after a difficult game of squash.

Matt stepped on the brake and the car screeched to a halt. The driver immediately behind them leaned on his horn, and James could see him mouth a Gallic curse at them. 'Get out of this car.'

'What?'

'You don't want to talk about it? Get out of my car.'

'Don't be ridiculous.'

Matt leaned across James and opened the passenger door.

'All right, all right.' James closed the door. Matt moved off again. 'You should have come in my car,' James said sulkily. 'You're not going to believe it.'

'No, I'm not going to believe it.'

'Matt, I can't remember a single thing about the last few days.'

'You mean, you lost your memory or something?' Matt kept his eyes on the road.

'That's exactly what happened. One minute I remember being at the house with all of you. Next thing I knew I was sitting in a bar in the Pyrenees. I got hold of a newspaper and somehow three days had passed. I don't want you to tell Sabine this, but I think I've had some kind of breakdown.'

'I've heard of this kind of thing.'

'You never think it's going to happen to you. But when it does, believe me, it's no joke. No joke at all. It's the most frightening thing that's ever happened to me. The last I remember is leaving the house to go for a walk. Then I'm in a bar in Rennes-le-Château.'

'Can't you remember anything about the intervening period?'

James furrowed his brow as if making a great effort to summon the experience to mind. 'It's like a dream. There are fragments at the edge of consciousness. I recall being in a lorry, but then it all goes black. Then I was in the washroom of a bar and I looked in the mirror and remembered where I should be.'

'Except that three days had gone by.'

'Exactly. Three days of almost total amnesia.'

'Lucky you had the phone number. Of the house, I mean.'

'It was in my wallet. What are you doing?'

Matt slowed down, indicating carefully this time, and pulled into a lay-by. He cruised to a halt, put the gearstick into neutral and set the handbrake. Then he let fly a stinging punch to James's mouth, skinning his knuckles on James's teeth. James leapt back in his seat, holding his hand to his mouth. His gums were bleeding. He inspected the blood on his fingertips.

Matt released the handbrake, checked that nothing was coming, indicated to pull out and set off. 'Try again,' he said.

'Who the fuck do you think you are?' James was nursing his mouth.

'That's not for walking out on your wife and your children. That's for making out it's nothing and for telling me such a shitty, stupid story. Now try again.'

'For Christ's sake, what do you want me to say?'

'Think of something.'

'You don't understand any of it, Matt. I just can't do it any more.'

'Can't do what?'

'Any of it. Be the hubby, be the lover, be the daddy, be the boss. I'm ill, Matt. That's not bullshit. It's making me ill. I feel like something's going to blow. I mean it. I feel like I'm being eaten away from the inside, and one day someone in the city is going to find this empty suit of clothes on the pavement, collapsed inwards, this suit and shirt and tie, and I'll be gone from it. Christ I don't know.'

'I don't get you, James. What's the idea of bringing one of your fucking girlfriends on holiday with you? Does that give you a kick? Does that make you feel powerful? Because it's just plain weird.'

'What on earth makes you think – ?'

'Oh, fuck off, James. Even Sabine is on to you.'

James stared morosely out of the window. 'What does she know?'

'I don't care. I just wonder what sort of twisted fuck would want to complicate two weeks in France like that.'

'I wanted people around who care about me. That's all. Sabine doesn't care.'

'God in Heaven! I think I'd rather hear your miserable little lies than all this whining self-pity.'

It was a long drive back in the dark. The rain gave over as they pulled away from the area north of the Pyrenees, but there was a new wind from somewhere. Much of the distance was covered in silence. Matt smoked cigarettes, knowing they would have been prohibited in James's car. James smoked too, sitting in a dis-hevelled huddle, with a swollen lip, bruised and diminished.

When they arrived back at the house only Sabine was waiting up. 'I'll leave you to it,' Matt said, and went upstairs. Chrissie was awake, reading by the dull orange glow of a tiny bedside lamp. Matt took off his boots, and they thumped heavily to the stripped floorboards. He undressed and climbed in beside her.

'Where are they now?' said Chrissie.

'I left them in the kitchen.'

'What did you do to your hand?'

'Skinned my knuckles. It's nothing.' Chrissie switched off the light and lay back, listening in the dark. After a while Matt said, 'Your listening is keeping me awake.'

'I can't hear anything. Nothing's being said.'

'So? Go to sleep.'

'Well, if nothing's being said, that says everything, doesn't it?'

'Goodnight,' said Matt.

33

Jessie surfaced from sleep to realize that someone was sitting on the edge of her bed. Even in the shadows she knew who it was. Before the figure spoke, she recognized the perfume and the smell of skin. She pretended to be asleep. Then she felt cool fingers stroking her brow.

'Can you hear me, Jessie? I had to wake you. No, don't worry about Beth. She's asleep. Everyone's asleep. I had to tell you. They don't want me to talk to you, so I had to come to you now, like this, because we haven't got much time. Something is going to happen, Jessie. I don't know what it is, but there are some things I must tell you while I still have the chance. No, don't say anything. Just listen to me.

'I've told you there are angels and there are demons, you know that, and I've told you that it's difficult sometimes to tell them apart. That's because the demons pretend to be angels, and the angels are not always where we expect them to be. I've come to tell you about the things that are going on between your mother and your father, and the things that are going on in this house, because it is important that you don't think these things have anything to do with you or that you are responsible in any way. You are not responsible, Jessie, not at all, even though you think you are. I know this because I felt the same when I was your age. I felt exactly the same. If your mother and your father are having differences right now, it's not connected with anything you have done.

'Do you know what a vampire is? Of course you do. Everyone does. I want to tell you about a different kind of vampire, one we call a psychic vampire. They don't wear theatrical clothes and they don't sleep in coffins; on the contrary, they look like perfectly ordinary people – or, rather, they are perfectly ordinary people but sick. And they are called psychic vampires because they suck other people's energy from them, just as other vampires suck blood. Energy. Spirit. Delight. Fun. They feed on all the luminous and beautiful things in life; they drain the brilliant rainbow colours from the world and leave everyone feeling exhausted. They do this by being difficult, contrary, provoking pointless arguments and deliberately choosing to be miserable. They poison the well of life. They muddy everyone's pool. Sometimes they don't even know what they're doing. Their vampirism is a form that leaks out of a person and takes shape on the shoulders of one of their friends, or their family, or people in the workplace. It's a little bit like sleepwalking, Jessie. These spirits go sleepwalking but in the daytime, when the people the spirits have climbed out of are wide awake. Yes, wide awake. But nighttime is best for them: they feed in the day but they grow stronger at night. Not everyone has the gift of seeing them. I have. You have, or could have, Jessie. Well, we have one of these psychic vampires in the house, and I'm trying to protect you. I'm going to give you something that will safeguard you, only it won't be garlic or a crucifix or a silver bullet; it will be something else.

'I know what you're wondering. You're wondering why it is that some people are psychic vampires and some are not. Well, let me tell you it's usually because of something that was done to them as a child, when they were very small, something that happened long ago, something that won't let go. When I was a girl . . . when I was a girl like you I, I –

'Never kiss an angel, Jessie. You will become infected. Angelic virus. Never make love to one. Once infected, you begin to see the world the same way they do. The fifth dimension, which is the proper abode of angels, is terrifying. Time does not run like sand, not like here, no, no. It's a world of shadows and black, iridescent light you've never dreamed of, frightening and beautiful. A dimension populated with incubi and succubi and *Doppelgängers*, and no way back –

182

'I kissed an angel once and I –

'I've taught you how to watch for storms, and I've taught you how to watch people for storms. Do you know what happens during a storm? People's faces change. People's bodies change, their blood pressure, their metabolism. The air is filled with angels and demons, released by people. You'll see it. You'll know it when it happens. A storm is coming, a mighty storm. I want you to be ready.

'I lived with a psychic vampire once. He drained me dry. He wanted to take everything I had. It can go on for years. You get weaker and weaker and you just don't know what's happening. Beware of marriage, Jessie; beware of men. Especially those who are eaten from the inside by drink or drugs or power. They fill you full of spunk and they groan and cry and they tell you they love you, but they –

'And you should also know of the incubi. This is how they come to you to feed. Most people think they come at night and sit on your chest and try to fuck you, Jessie. But, believe me, it can happen when you are wide awake. You think you are having a perfectly normal conversation with someone, perhaps eating dinner, perhaps drinking coffee, and their incubus comes out of them, dirty ectoplasm, and it squats on your shoulder or sits on your knee, lapping at your energy with its rough tongue.

'And the succubus, Jessie – that's a female incubus – has two mouths with which to feed. Yes, you can guess which two mouths.

'Do you know where we come from, Jessie? Out of the red earth. That's the Hebrew meaning of the name Adam. Out of the muck. Did you know that everything that grows on this earth is raised out of dung? Are you asleep? It doesn't matter. Did you know that everything that is said to you while you are asleep is heard perfectly? People don't know that. But it's all heard, and stored, and acted upon. That's why people say things to their lovers even though they are asleep. Oh, yes, if there were no dung, there would be no life. We are dung, we are muck, Jessie. But what saves us is the spark. The divine spark. You see it? In the muck, in the blackness, in the smoky cloud of corruption, there floats the tiny spark. Call that God. I've been teaching you how to raise that spark, Jessie. In the mirror. That tiny spark is the beginning of our other selves, our better selves, our higher selves, and beyond that spark everything else is the stench of matter. All corrupt filth. But the spark, Jessie, the spark! It's what teaches us to think, speak, act correctly. It teaches us the tongue of the angels. It lifts us up. It restores us to our place in the clouds.

'Are you asleep, Jessie? Jessie? Don't be afraid. Don't be afraid of anything. I have decided to look after you, to watch over you. You don't have to be afraid of anything. Are you asleep, Jessie? Are you really asleep?'

Jessie heard the figure breathing in the dark, watching her. Then a floorboard creaked, and the bedroom door closed quietly. The figure had gone. Jessie sat up in bed, relieved to see that Beth was still sleeping. She hadn't heard any of it. Jessie pressed her hand to her immature breast, and her heart was hammering, hammering.

34

There are only two types of lightning, fork and ball. That referred to as 'sheet' is merely fork lightning reflected by clouds. Ball lightning is much less frequently observed, yet not so infrequently that it should be described as rare. It is a discharge that rolls itself literally into a ball before either exploding dramatically or simply fading in a loss of energy.

Balls of lightning are playful and have been known to roll along the hallways of houses, entering through the front door and exiting via the rear, or along the aisles of aeroplanes to the consternation of passengers. Fork lightning is less given to games.

35

Some time before dawn Matt was woken by an owl hooting loudly in the night, somewhere quite close. He lifted his head to find Chrissie gone from beside him. The window was open, the shutters were thrown back and a grey, pre-dawn mist hung immobile and spectral below the windowsill, like torn scraps of cloud. Matt got out of bed, pulled on some shorts and dragged a blanket from the bed.

A light burned in the kitchen and the door stood wide open. He stepped on to the patio, nerves pricking against the morning chill of the false dawn. The light was mother-of-pearl, waiting for iridescence, and the mist seemed to muffle and retard even the speed of thought. Still warm from his bed, he stepped off the patio on to the grass, where the cold dew numbed his feet. He paced silently across the grass to the swimming pool, carrying a blanket.

There sat Chrissie, still as a statue, her feet in the water. She was naked, apparently gazing into the pool. Matt said nothing as he drew alongside her, knowing she was asleep. Her eyes were closed, and she wore a distracted smile. Some of the morning moisture had congealed on her shoulders like the bloom on the skin of a grape.

'Do you want to wake up?' Matt said softly.

Chrissie looked up suddenly and appeared to squint at the distant hills without waking. Very tenderly Matt draped the blanket over her shoulders.

'Can we get you back to bed without waking you?' Matt said.

'How many of us are there,' Chrissie was conducting another conversation, 'to fit into the car?'

Matt was about to frame a reply when the owl hooted again,

terrifyingly close. Matt's skin flushed. There was a brief flight of white feathers, so near that for a second it occluded the sky; then there was a scrabbling under the eaves of the house. Chrissie's eyes followed its flight path. 'Bird of omen,' she said, drawing her feet out of the water.

'You're back,' said Matt.

'How long have I been sitting out here like this?'

'Don't know. I woke just a few moments ago. Had a feeling I'd find you in the garden again.'

'I'm cold.'

Matt helped her to her feet and hugged her to him. 'You're icy. Want to go back to bed?'

'I'm wide awake.'

'Let's go inside at least.'

While Matt lit the stove to make a hot drink, Chrissie went upstairs to pull on some clothes. She met Rachel on the landing. 'Everyone's up,' said Chrissie.

'I thought I heard something,' Rachel muttered before disappearing into the bathroom.

'Rachel's about,' Chrissie told Matt. 'We must have woken her. But I thought she was coming out of the girls' room. Why would she be doing that?'

'Here, drink this. Shall we watch the dawn come up through the mist?'

'Do you suppose,' Jessie asked Sabine at breakfast, 'that Daddy is a psychic vampire?'

On her last visit Dominique had left some eggs, and Sabine turned from scrambling them. 'What?'

Beth giggled. Jessie coloured, glanced at Rachel and looked away. 'I'm only thinking aloud.'

'Thinking aloud?' cried Sabine. 'I don't want you to think aloud! Who told you that? Look at me, Jessie. *I said, look at me!* Now, I want to know who put that idea in your head.' Sabine had been poking the eggs around the pan with a wooden spatula. She flung it on to the scrubbed table. Bits of egg splattered Beth and Rachel. '*Now!* I want you to tell me *now*! N O W!'

Her face had become a red, rubberized mask as she stood over Jessie. Beth started whimpering. The eggs were burning in the pan. Rachel got up and turned down the flame.

'Go to your room!' Sabine screamed. 'Don't you dare come out until you are ready to tell me! You hear me! Now *get*!'

Jessie got, and she got quickly. Incandescent with rage, Sabine's eyes burned into Rachel. She stepped out of the kitchen and stood on the patio, arms tightly folded, quivering and smouldering, almost a danger to the tinder-dry grass. Rachel pulled Beth out of her chair and spread her arms around the child. Spotting this, Sabine leapt back inside and dragged Beth out of Rachel's embrace. Any angry words the two women were about to exchange were deflected by the arrival of Matt, sleepy and bestubbled, towelling his hair dry.

'What's going on? What's all the shouting about?'

'Sabine is showing her colours,' Rachel said.

Sabine returned a look of compacted venom. Matt threw down his towel and Sabine allowed him to steer her, by the elbow, out of the kitchen and through the shadowy lounge. From there he propelled her out of the front door and into the harsh sunlight. 'Let's walk.'

'I'm still in my dressing-robe,' Sabine protested weakly.

'There's no one around here. Let's walk up to the church.'

So Sabine, in her slippers and blue silk kimono, and Matt, barefoot, made their way in silence up to the locked church. There they sat on the bench outside the churchyard, opposite the majestic corn and in the full rays of the sun. Sabine's rage retreated, leaving her cheeks and neck flushed. In her kimono and with her hair tousled, Matt thought she looked post-coital and said so.

'Don't tease me, Matt.'

'I'm not. What the hell is happening?'

'I don't know. Everything is falling apart. James has hardly said a word since you brought him back. I don't know how to be with him. He talks as though he's having some kind of breakdown, and yet I don't believe him. It's as if he's playing at it. But then, if he has to play at it, isn't that in itself a kind of breakdown? Isn't it, Matt?'

'Maybe.'

'Then there's Jessie. The things she comes out with, the language, the ideas. Psychic vampires today. She wanted to know if her father is a fucking vampire. I don't know if someone is poisoning her mind or if it's just coming out of her . . . condition, her illness, you know? I feel like a circus performer spinning plates on sticks. If I run to one, then the others begin to topple. They're all going to go, all fall and smash, any day now. That's how I feel.'

'You're not on your own, Sabine.'

'Why do you say that?' She searched his eyes. 'Chrissie? What's the matter with Chrissie?'

'She keeps sleepwalking. I get out of bed and find her in different parts of the house or garden. Sleepwalking. She's not as strong as everyone thinks. Emotionally, I mean. She's frail.'

'Has this only just started?'

'No. Chrissie's sleepwalking has happened before, over the years, but never so frequently.'

'Do you think it's someone in the house, Matt? One of the people in the house causing all this trouble, making everyone behave strangely, making everyone ill? Could it be that?' Sabine was desperate for an answer, however hysterical – so eager to nail someone that Matt knew she felt somehow responsible herself. From far in the distance came the rumour of thunder, like the shifting of furniture in another room. He reached out a hand to smooth her hair, and she narrowed her eyes at him before taking this gesture as a cue to lay her head on his shoulder. Her kimono fell open at the knee, exposing a sallow expanse of thigh. Matt looked back at the house, wondering what James would make of this scene if he were to look out of his window right now, or what Chrissie might think, knowing how vulnerable she was. But

Chrissie, like James, was still in bed, sleeping fitfully, trying to recover from a bad night, and Matt knew that.

Chrissie was dreaming. Vile, corrosive dreams, in which someone was attempting desperately to speak to her on the telephone, but the voice diminished and faded into electronic pipings and whistlings. The failure to communicate was followed by a fierce and terminal argument with an impostor claiming to be Chrissie's twin sister.

'I don't have a twin sister,' Chrissie argued. 'You don't even look anything like me.' And although she knew that this was indeed her twin sister, somehow Chrissie's life depended on being able to deny it and on showing no recognition.

'Why?' her twin raged. 'Why haven't you told anyone about me?'

But the violence of the argument dissolved when the telephone rang again, and Chrissie was flipped back to the beginning of the dream, holding the telephone, crying because she couldn't understand whoever was on the other end of the line.

James too was dreaming. In his dream he was strapped to an institutional bed, and the leather restraints had badly chafed his leg, arms and neck. The room was brilliant-white. No one else was present. An intravenous drip fed into his veins. A plastic hose was fixed into his nostril. A third hose drained bile and blood from his heart. Every hour, on the hour, an alarming electronic buzzer signalled the release of a further 10 cc of black-and-yellow tiger-striped liquid through the drip. The noise of the buzzer was terrifying. His heart squeezed painfully every time it sounded, and the accelerated beating of his heart seemed to pump the liquid. Miraculously, as the liquid proceeded along the tube it retained its black-and-yellow stripes. A nurse came into the room, and James asked her about the liquid. She told him it was required to feed his parasite worm, and if the liquid were not to be administered, then the worm would die.

*

That evening Dominique and Patrice arrived for dinner. On the previous day they had been invited to come whether James was present or not, so they were relieved to find him at the house. They were tactful enough to make a fuss of him without alluding to his disappearance. When Patrice presented him with a demijohn of local wine, James poured himself a glass and had the arrogance to pronounce it excellent. To the French couple, at least, everything seemed back to normal.

Jessie felt nervous for her father, but the meal went well, and Patrice's store of humour kept the occasion light in any language. The evening's atmosphere, however, was unpleasantly sultry. Dominique fanned herself continually throughout dinner. The women wore cotton dresses that stuck to their skins. Everyone was tipping back more wine than was reasonable, in an effort to stay cool rather than to get drunk, but only the second of these effects was assured. Sabine more than once pushed up the hair from the nape of her neck, and each time she did so Matt caught her eyes, briefly. Rachel said little throughout the meal. She was still nursing a huge grievance over her treatment at breakfast. James spoke, in turns in French and English, mainly with Dominique and Patrice. Chrissie, when Patrice wasn't making her laugh about something, seemed almost in a trance induced by the heat and her exhaustion. Jessie ate quietly, as did Beth, both still slightly shamed by their mother's outburst earlier in the day.

'Patrice says there is going to be an almighty storm,' James announced when the conversation was winding down.

'Let it come,' said Matt. 'Today we heard thunder, didn't we, Sabine?'

James looked up. 'Oh?'

'Yes,' Sabine said quickly. 'This morning. Far off. It's coming in.'

Matt changed the subject by jumping up to reveal a surprise he'd prepared for the evening. He orchestrated shifting the table and rearranging the chairs on the patio into an auditorium. The best seats were offered to Jessie and Beth.

'What's he up to?' James slurred, pouring himself another glass of local wine.

'No idea,' Chrissie said dreamily.

'Can we allow the girls a small glass of wine for the occasion?' Matt shouted, answering himself with, 'Yes, I think we can do that. Perhaps you could attend to that, Sabine?'

Jessie was surprised when Sabine obeyed him, handing both her and Beth a half-glass each as if this were perfectly normal behaviour. If Chrissie noticed that Matt could break Sabine's rule about wine for the children, while walking with her was suddenly proscribed, she said nothing. Dominique asked Rachel, and Patrice asked Jessie, and Beth asked Sabine, and everyone giggled and asked everyone else what was going on. Finally Matt produced a large box from the boot of his car. Before opening it he issued orders. 'Patrice, please find me some empty wine bottles. Look under James's bed.'

'Haha,' James said.

'James, fetch me a hammer and a few nails. Please. It's all right, no one is going to steal your wine glass. That's it, good chap. Rachel, a bucket of water, if you please.' Not until everyone had run their errands and reassembled did Matt open the box to reveal a monster collection of fireworks. He got Patrice to set rockets in bottles while he nailed Catherine wheels to the wooden lintel of the old stable.

'I *adore* fireworks!' shrieked Dominique.

Sabine stood over the box. 'It must have cost you a fortune!'

'That's Matt,' said Chrissie. 'Up in smoke.'

Before lighting the first rocket, Matt called for hush. 'Beth, what was the purpose of fireworks displays long, long ago?'

Beth blushed and said, 'To get rid of evil spirits.'

'Correct,' said Matt.

'How did you know that?' Jessie wanted to know.

'Because Matt told me.'

The first rocket punctured the blue-black sky. An ebullient audience offered exaggerated and ironic squeals of appreciation.

Even James joined in, half-heartedly. Jessie studied him closely. He was drinking heavily, somehow diminished by Matt's efforts, strangely sidelined by this display. She felt a fierce stab of loyalty for him.

The display was slightly eccentric. Matt raced around, trying to touch off everything at once, from tiny flares to spectacular pyrotechnic bombs. Catherine wheels stuck and fizzed or fell to the floor still spinning. A hissing rocket snaked and slithered across the ground, igniting the grass. The flames spread rapidly in the tinder-dry conditions, causing a moment of panic before the garden hose was produced to put out the fire. Matt was manic, cackling, carelessly relighting damp squibs and airbombs with his home-rolled cigarette end, projecting rockets at dangerous angles. It was hair-raising, almost hair-scorching, but the display was a great success.

After the event Jessie and Beth kissed everyone goodnight and were shepherded, reluctantly, to bed. Jessie looked back at her father as he sank yet another glass of wine.

While the debris was being cleared away, Sabine cornered Matt. 'The girls loved it, Matt. It was wonderful.'

'There hasn't been much fun for them around here lately.'

'Where did you get the fireworks?'

'Stopped on my way to pick up James.'

Sabine laid her cool, elegant fingers on Matt's tanned forearm. 'Thank you,' she said, before retreating indoors.

Matt looked up and saw Rachel leaning on a sweeping brush, watching him. She twitched her eyebrows at him. He didn't know what the gesture meant, so he twitched back.

The adults settled down for further drinking in the stifling heat of the evening. Even the chorus of crickets dropped rhythm. Matt rolled himself a herbal snout. Patrice said he'd tried it once in Algeria to no effect but was willing to give foolishness a second chance. Dominique declined, as did James, preferring to sink the *vin ordinaire* at an impressive rate. Sabine, by contrast, snatched up Matt's joint and inhaled passionately before handing the thing to Rachel. Chrissie joined the abstainers.

Again there came the scrape of thunder from the far distance, but the remote weather front failed to part the sweltering blanket of local air. Conversation swung from the weather to the girls, from England to France, from childhood holidays to the tyranny of work that lay ahead. Somebody sighed and asked why couldn't it always be like this, and Rachel wondered how many of them would genuinely want that.

After making a serious impression on the demijohn James fell further out of the gaiety and the rounds of conversation, and the others were content to let him slip. Sweating profusely, he was about to get up to replenish his glass when Patrice returned from a visit to the toilet, leading a short, stout, rusticated old man. James assumed it was a neighbouring farmer but was struck by the old man's extreme ugliness. His back was stooped and his large wart-speckled face, like a hen's egg, balanced uncomfortably on his shoulders. He was carrying yet another demijohn of wine. Patrice made no introductions, simply returning to his seat with the others and picking up on the conversation where he'd left off. The newcomer approached James and handed over the demijohn.

James attempted to congratulate him for his instinct in delivering the wine to the right man, when, mashing his words, he realized how drunk he was. 'Certainly picked the right guy.' The man sat beside James but cocked an ear to the conversation of the rest of the group.

'Please yourself,' James said, somewhat offended, pouring himself another glass, spilling it on the lawn, swatting an imaginary mosquito. 'Speak English? *Vous parlez anglais?*'

The old man smiled thinly and shook his head, *non*. His weathered face had the grain of a piece of turned oak and a large polyp fruited above one eyebrow. Again the man turned away from James, as if intent on listening to the others. James, drunk but always urbane, made three further efforts to engage the old man in polite conversation. He commented on the beauty of the region, on the weather, and on the quality of the wine, all in courtly French. The man expressed only impatience with James, as if he

194

was a distraction from the much more interesting conversation going on elsewhere.

James felt rebuffed. He slurped umbrage from his glass. 'Bet you don't, heh-heh. Bet you don't fucking speak English.' As if in answer, the old man smoothed the thin white hair of his head and turned towards James with an air of finality, fixing sad, rheumy eyes on the Englishman.

'Thassa bit more sociable,' James muttered, offering the man the demijohn. It was waved away airily. 'All right. Up your bum. *Santé*.' He let his voice drop – not that anyone else was listening. 'D'you know any of these people?' The others were telling tales, occasionally breaking into gales of laughter. No one was interested in what James had to say to the old man. 'No? Let me introduce you to the circus. *Comprenez?* Starting with that one. *Ma femme*. Froggie, *comme vous*, eh? Worse day my life, marrying a frig. See the fellow sitting next her? Face like a road map? *Les routes nationales?* Probably fucking him stupid, thinks I don't know. Cunt used to work for me. Shows me up, front my children, my girls, few fucking fireworks. Gave him rocket up's arse. That one's his wife: triffic legs, eh? Lives with the fairies, that's the only problem. Twelve francs, you could have her. Haha, only kidding. Same as the other one, Rachel. Used to work for me. Musical type. *Paysanne*, bit of rough, twelve francs. Hey, you're a great conversationalist, anyone ever tell you that? A regular *saloniste*. A true scholar of life. Aw, fuck you.'

Giving up, James poured himself another glass of wine, set it down by his chair leg, stood up, forgot why he'd climbed out of his chair, sat down again and kicked over the glass. Then he fell asleep.

Then Sabine was shaking him by the elbow. 'James. James! Dominique and Patrice are about to leave. They want to say goodnight.'

James jumped out of his chair too quickly, felt a rush of blood to his head. Smacking his lips, he looked around. Dominique and Patrice were indeed about to leave. The old man had already gone. Dominique touched his shoulder. 'Thank you for a pleasant evening,' she said. Patrice pumped his hand.

James had a mouth like glasspaper. 'Where did your friend go?'

Dominique and Patrice looked at him blankly

'Your neighbour. I hope I wasn't too drunk when I was talking to him.'

'What neighbour?'

'The old man who came in with Patrice. He sat there for an hour.'

Now everyone, Chrissie, Matt, Rachel and Sabine, looked at him blankly and then at the chair to which he pointed. 'James . . .' Sabine tried.

'What old man?' Matt asked.

'There was an old man,' James spat. 'A farmer. An old man.'

'We must go,' Dominique said quickly. She spoke very rapidly to Patrice, in a dialect that eluded even Sabine. Everyone moved up the garden, leaving James puzzled and embarrassed in the darkness.

After the visitors had departed Matt said to Sabine, 'What the hell is he talking about now?'

'I don't know,' she said. 'To hell with him.'

They went in, leaving James outside.

36

'Hurry! There's not much time. We have to get them all covered before it starts.'

'Before what starts?'

Events quicken in the mirror. Gregory bustling round the apartment, dragging sheets and blankets from the beds, towels from the bathroom. Blisters of perspiration stipple his brow, oval sweat stains darken the underarms of his white, collarless shirt as he marshals himself from room to room. The collapsed muscles of his face and the poppy-seed dilation of his pupils tell her, if she'd been unable to guess, that he's high. 'The storm. Before the storm starts.'

She has just returned from the bakery with fresh croissants, intent on coffee and a relaxed morning. Gregory clearly has other ideas. 'How do you know there's going to be a storm?'

'Can't you feel it? Can't you, for God's sake?'

'You can feel a storm coming before it arrives? Are you some kind of animal?'

Gregory climbs on a chair, draping a white sheet from the corner of one of his larger mirrors. 'Aren't you human that you can't? I haven't got time to argue. Either help me or leave me to it.'

She picks up a sheet and begins to cover the mirrors on the other side of the room. They work together in hostile silence. 'Would you mind telling me why we're doing this?'

No answer, but she already knows, has heard him describe his phobia before. If a thunderstorm is on its way, there is a good prospect of its bringing lightning; and if lightning were to flash in the night sky over the apartment, there is every possibility it may reflect in one of the apartment's giant or smaller mirrors. He has a phobia about seeing lightning reflected in a mirror. Says it will kill him. Claims, at the very least, it will bring bad luck.

'Bad luck? Ha! What does a fucking junkie care about bad luck?'

Gregory, standing on a chair, is arrested in the middle of hanging yet another sheet. He glares until she continues with the task. Soon all reflecting surfaces in the apartment are covered. Gregory, slightly breathless, pours himself a glass of vodka and says quietly, 'You know you can leave here any time you want. Am I chaining you to the wall? Do I handcuff you to my bed?'

But it isn't as easy as that. She wants to go, but something restrains her. Not chains or handcuffs, something else. It is the violet light. She is afraid of losing the violet light. Leave Gregory, and it will go out of everything.

'Why couldn't we simply close the curtains?'

'Hmm?'

'If you are so afraid of seeing lightning in the mirrors, why not just draw the curtains?'

'But the point is to *watch* the lightning.'

Outside, the sky is the hue of tempered iron. Gregory opens a window. The temperature inside drops instantly as a fresh breeze invades the apartment. He refills his glass, drags a high-winged chair into place before the window, settles back like a man looking forward to an afternoon of televised sport. 'Have you been at my gear?' he says, not taking his eyes from the scene of the gathering storm outside the window. 'I think you've been at my gear.'

'Maybe.'

'So long as I know. I like to know.'

She feels abandoned, superfluous. The sky outside, and the unlit apartment, darken still further. Then comes the first glitter of white light, charging the distant sky. It breaks upon the world like a crack between dimensions, a brief flare of deadly white fibres, a parasite virus fighting for purchase on the land, a desperate climber ramming a finger into a tiny hole in the rock probing for the single-digit grip. White light frosts the sweat breaking on Gregory's face. His breathing deepens, his gaze fixes on the evening sky. For him she is no longer there. He is riding the lightning.

She leaves him. She goes to the kitchen, makes coffee. She drinks the coffee, eats a croissant. The storm picks up pace outside. The lightning fizzes, draws closer. Thunder bangs dramatically, almost overhead. When finally it begins to pass over, she washes her hands of croissant crumbs and returns to the sitting-room.

Gregory is sprawled in his chair. Hazy white light suffuses the room, bleaching everything, a photo negative. The light, she assumes, is a residue of the electrical charge. He has brought it inside, neutralizing all trace of the miraculous violet light that has so softly illuminated him from the moment she first saw him in the graveyard at Père Lachaise. She approaches him cautiously from behind, touching the back of his neck. There is no reaction. She moves in front of him, gently lowering herself to her knees. His empty vodka glass has tumbled to the floor.

His eyes are wide open, still tracking the storm. She prises his right eye open further with finger and thumb, looks deep there. Another brief charge of white lightning is reflected in the dilated black pupil; five seconds later a peel of distant thunder, moving away. He is dead.

In killing him she feels justified. He has tricked and abused her. He has impersonated an angel, and for this cardinal sin no forgiveness is available from archangels, powers or principalities, from cherubim or seraphim.

Now she can proceed to visit her sister in the Dordogne.

37

The following day it was Matt's and Chrissie's turn to make a trip to the supermarket, but by mid-morning Chrissie, like James, was still in bed. She'd had another disturbed night of sleepwalking. In the middle of the night Matt had found her seated at the piano, one finger resting lightly on a black key. He had somehow managed to guide her back to bed without waking her.

'I'll come instead,' Sabine offered. 'We can take the girls.'

'I'm not going to the supermarket,' Jessie said flatly.

Sabine exchanged glances with Rachel, who was sweeping the patio. She'd been very careful over the last couple of days to minimize the girls' contact with both Rachel and Chrissie. 'Come on, darling. It will be an outing.'

For answer, Jessie stepped out of her shoes, stripped off her cotton dress and ran full-tilt towards the pool. There was an impressive splash.

'Come on, Beth, put on your shoes.'

But Beth was having fun making a collection of spent fireworks, ordering them carefully on the grass, blackening her hands. She wanted to scour the field for dead rockets. Sabine tried to dig her way out. 'Perhaps Rachel wouldn't mind going with you, Matt.'

'No fear,' Rachel said. 'I've done my turn. I'll stay here and cause trouble.'

Sabine looked from Rachel to Beth and to Jessie.

'They'll be all right,' Matt said.

In the car Sabine confessed some of her misgivings, at least about Rachel. 'What do you think of her, Matt? Honestly, do you think she's stable?'

'Who the hell is stable?'

'I mean, would you trust your own children with her?'

'Of course I would. You're being over-protective.' Matt couldn't say what he knew: that because Sabine suspected her husband's affair with Rachel she was prepared to impute to the woman the motives and morality of a serial killer. If he so much as hinted at this, it would not only confirm the affair but also demonstrate his knowledge of it. Then no one in the house would get a decent night's sleep.

They drove into the *bastide* town and stopped for coffee before shopping. 'So after I brought him back you got no sense out of him?'

'No.' Sabine pushed her spoon round and round her cup as if there were a meaning in there somewhere. 'He swears he had some kind of blackout. By the way, he asked me not to tell you that he told me that. He thinks it will get back to his workplace, and then his competence might be questioned.'

'You believe him?'

'In a strange way, I do. I think he's falling apart. By which I mean there are so many different people inside him, I don't think he knows who he is. Twelve years of marriage and he's like a stranger to me. And to himself. He doesn't know if he wants to be James the father, the boss, the wine connoisseur, the lazy slob, the free spirit, the husband . . . Do you know how long it's been since he made love to me? My God, since he even kissed me or put his arm around me?'

He looked hard at her. 'Let's go.'

'You should be wary of him, Matt,' she said, as they got up to go. 'He feels you've humiliated him somehow. That elaborate firework show, he keeps talking about it. You took away his role. You showed more care for his children than he did. He won't thank you for that.'

'Fuck him,' said Matt, tipping the waiter.

They completed the shopping quickly and returned via the back roads. Sabine drove and Matt decided to show her where Beth saw someone in the corn. Two kilometres further along the road

Sabine said, 'Isn't that the way to the cave we all went to the other day?' She coasted the car to a halt by the side of the road.

'Shall we take another look?'

Without a word Sabine turned off the ignition and got out of the car.

She unlocked the boot, and Matt's hand shook slightly as he reached in for a torch. Sabine's arms hung uncomfortably at her sides as she led the way along the dusty, white limestone path in the direction of the cave. They walked beside a hedgerow tangled with rampant honeysuckle, and the scent was dizzying. With the rubber torch-grip sweating in his hand he walked behind her, trying to keep his eyes off the tiny veins in the folds at the back of her knees.

Their self-conscious silence amplified the sound of the crickets in the grass. The air was sticky and oppressive. Matt's shirt sucked at his back, and Sabine's skirt shaped itself to her buttocks. They passed alongside a terrace of unharvested grapes. The fruit was already spoiling on the vine, tanging the air with the sharp odour of fermentation, so that it had an almost viscous quality about it. The baked earth seemed tensile, as if something were about to shred in the unremitting heat. Sabine offered a nervous smile across her shoulder before turning away again, too quickly. Matt switched the torch from one hand to the other.

They squeezed through the bushes, a bramble dragging on Sabine's blackberry-coloured hair. Matt's trembling hand freed it for her, and they passed through the bushes to the mouth of the cave. It was there that she turned to him before going in. She pressed a hand against her chest, almost as if she were having trouble breathing. Matt, who was soaked in sweat, noticed tiny pearls of perspiration shining over her upper lip. He was close enough to smell the salt of her.

Something shifted inside the cave. A slight scuffling, like the movement of shale.

Their heads turned to the mouth of the cave, and there came a wheezing sound and further shuffling from the shale floor. Then they heard a low whistle or a gasp of air. Sabine looked at Matt in horror, but he was transfixed by the black, cervix-like opening of the entrance to the cave. She took a step backwards and laid a hand on his arm. The sounds disappeared, though they were straining to hear more.

'Let's not stay,' Sabine urged.

'Listen,' said Matt.

The shale started clicking again, followed by the breathing sounds, again like a low, unformed whistle. Something was approaching the entrance to the cave. A white form began to take shape out of the gloom. It was Beth, her mouth trying to shape a childish whistle. She stopped abruptly on seeing Sabine and Matt.

'Mummy!'

Sabine was almost too stunned to speak. Beth was quickly joined by Jessie and then, a few moments later, by James, who also stopped dead in his tracks and said, 'What are you two doing here?'

With a reflex utterly impressive to Sabine, Matt said, 'We saw you from the road. We were just coming back from shopping.'

'Really!' said James.

'We were creeping up on you,' Matt said, stroking Beth's golden hair. 'We were going to make you jump out of your skins, but you beat us to it.'

'I thought I'd bring the girls here again,' James said. 'Hey, it's really quite chilly in there. You're sweating, darling.'

'I know. It's so uncomfortable. And flies everywhere. Are you coming back in the car?'

'No,' said James, 'we're hunting for the dead, aren't we, Beth?' Beth held up two giant spent rockets they'd found in the fields. He pushed past Matt and through the bushes. The girls followed him. 'You two carry on. Don't worry about us, we're having a great time.'

Sabine looked at Matt before forcing her way through the bushes after them. 'No, I'll come with you.'

'Are you sure, darling? Hadn't you better give Matt the keys?'

She darted back to press the car keys into Matt's hand. He said nothing, and she shook her head briefly at him.

Matt waited at the entrance to the cave until long after they were gone, thinking about what had just happened, about how close it had come. The muscles in his arms and legs had turned to slush. Heat seemed to roll off the rock at his back. A fly buzzed his mouth.

He stepped inside the cave, looking for relief from the blanket heat. The interior was damp and cool. He flashed on his torch and made his way into the recesses of the cave, easily finding the wall painting Patrice had shown them. Matt studied it again. The two main figures were either horned animals or humans dressed in the skins of animals. The skins were decorated with feathers and were maybe those of chamois or some similar creature, and one of the figures was mounting the other – Jessie had been correct about that. The torch flickered as he studied the painting and faded. He tapped it against his palm and the thing came on again, but weakly. Studying the painting, he decided the figures were either dancing or conducting some sex ritual. The brown-ochre paint had faded almost to grey, and in the shadows of the cave it wasn't easy to distinguish the primitive artist's strokes from the crevices and fractures of the cave wall. Then the batteries in his torch failed completely.

Matt drowned in the blackness. He inhaled the mineral damp of the cave floor and tried, but failed, to bring the torch back to life. Orienting himself to what he thought was the way back to the entrance, he reached out a hand for the wall, missed, waved at air. He probed with his right foot, but it fell much further than he expected. Then, in brushing against something in the dark, he disturbed a scent. Again a mineral smell drifted to his nostrils, this time more of a marine odour. He took another blind step in the dark and the mysterious scent began to rise from the cave floor like a smoke, almost an incense, and in the chill of the cave the scent was hot and dry, like an airstream in a microclimate.

But the smell was shockingly human. It was the intoxicating

genital odour of the female, streaming from the rock as if accidentally released by his blind steps. And with the odour came a strange intuition. He sensed that this cave, thousands of years ago, had been a site of ritual in which initiates were led here to experience death and rebirth. The cervix-like entrance to the cave, its damp, womb-shaped interior, the musky, genital odours and the magical wall symbols all betrayed an aura of dangerous sexual adventure. He knew that the transforming ritual of rebirth was possible. More than all of this, the cave reminded him of a promise he had once made to Chrissie. For Matt, the man in the corn and his fear of the cave were one.

Stumbling through the darkness, he found the narrow shaft of light of the cave entrance and raced for it. He panicked and lunged at the crack of light. For one horrible moment it seemed as if the aperture was too narrow for him to get out, but he passed through, panting in the stale heat outside, squinting into the brilliant light.

He looked back only briefly at the slit in the rock before blundering through the bushes. Back behind the wheel of the car, he heard the crumple of remote thunder in the north.

38

'It's coming, Jessie, just like I told you. Isn't it wonderful? Did you feel the temperature drop by another two degrees? Look to the north. Look at it moving in on us, dark, unfurling like a banner lined with celestial light. But you know all that. And the rain is just the ethereal stitching coming loose from the cloud. We've talked about that – ah, that we were given the chance to know such beauty in our brief lives! Now you can believe. Now you can believe in angels – look at them massing there, look at them charging across the heated air, riding the thermals, swarming. Jess, the angels are swarming towards us!

'You know, in the demise of a language, any language, the first skill to be lost is the capacity to write. Next the skill of reading falls away. Finally the ability to speak gradually disappears and that language, wonderfully complex, full of rules and yet infinite in its ability to create new forms, allusions, metaphors and starbursts of pure light, is gone for ever.

'So with the tongue of angels, Jess. Not that it was ever given to mortals to etch on the sky the mysterious cloud-glyphs, but now the secondary reading skill has been lost. It has even become fashionable to deny that the language ever existed. Clouds do not frown, or lour, or threaten or brood, say clever people; they do not fret or sulk. Rain is not tears, it is merely rain.

'There are many dead languages, Jess. But the ability to speak the angelic tongue of clouds, which is to say the ability to be and to live within that language, is not entirely lost. And while earth-bound people argue whether it is sense or nonsense to claim, in life or in art, that the weather reflects the human soul, the custodians of the angelic tongue grieve. I can't tell you how they despair at the arrogance and conceit! They throw up their hands in lamentation, they flex their wings in anguish. How can it be argued that the weather is not a reflection of human concerns, they cry, when it's plain that we are only a pale reflection of the brilliant arc of planetary meteorology – when the weather is not part of us, but we are a small part of the weather?

'But you are not like them, Jess. You know that this is a magical time for all of us. You should know it better than anyone. Your time as a girl is almost over. Hmm? Don't be surprised. I know. I just know. Don't ask me why. It's my job to know these things. Call it a sixth sense, or a scent, or a message inscribed on the wind, but I see it in you, in the rose flush coming and going on your face, in the sheen of your eye. A clear-sighted woman can see these things, with or without the angelic gift of prophecy.

'You are about to bleed. Don't be afraid of, or embarrassed by, the herald trickle. See it as the scarlet banner, the oriflamme of all health and vigour, emblem of a sacred female mystery. Don't listen to those vulgar women who talk of the Curse, don't give them any mind. They are the preterite, the passed-over. You are different, Jessie, one of the chosen. You are like me, and once every month you will be given sight of angels, and the tongue with which to converse. A rare gift, young lady.

'Shall I tell you how it happened with me, my first time? Shall I?'

Jessie nodded because she felt at that moment a nod was required. She felt a long way out of her depth when her instructor was in this kind of mood – when her eyes refused to settle, when they seemed like pools of oil, when she didn't even pause for breath. Jessie watched her instructor's mouth, the lips working quickly, almost as if unable to keep pace with the words uttered, unleashing words like a hail of burning arrows. Her instructor also gave off a strange odour at times like these, metallic and sour, like the taste of Ritalin.

It made Jessie afraid. *Am I responsible for this?* she thought. *Have I triggered this off?* It shocked her that her instructor could so easily behave like two different people. *Am I like her?* she wondered. *Is she like me? Would Ritalin help her?*

39

'Did you get what you went for?' Rachel asked Matt when he got back. James, Sabine and the children were still across the fields, having not yet returned from the cave. Chrissie languished upstairs, hiding from the sultry, sticky heat of the afternoon.

The sky over Rachel's shoulders had turned the colour of an aubergine. She stood within the shadow of the vine canopy, and her eyes seemed to be the same colour as the sky. Matt didn't like the tone of the question. He dumped his carrier bags in the kitchen. Grabbing a beer from the fridge, he pressed the bottle against his forehead. He passed a second bottle to Rachel, and she seemed to accept it only reluctantly. A track of sweat had run from her temple down the side of her face and had stopped under her ear. The nape of her neck glistened where her hair touched it.

'I think so.' Matt collapsed back into a deckchair.

'Ticked them off on your list, did you?'

'My list? I didn't have a list.'

'I think you did. I think you still do have a list.'

Matt was still panting slightly from his exertions with the shopping. Now he was the one with a strange cast to his eye. 'No list,' he said evenly.

'Oh, yes, there is. It's stuck to the door with a dagger. And only some of us can see it.'

'What are you talking about?' said Chrissie, appearing in one of Matt's cotton collarless shirts. She leaned across him, smelling of sleep and perspiration and kissed him slowly and sensuously, swinging her thigh across his legs and lowering herself on to his lap with no regard for Rachel.

'There are people watching,' Matt mumbled through mashed lips.

Chrissie lifted her head and turned to blink sleepily at Rachel before kissing him again. Then she climbed off him and walked down to the pool. They heard a *ploosh*.

'I've been watching you,' Rachel said.

'So, then,' said Matt, 'what's on the list?'

'James. His kids. His wife. The usual.'

'Not his mistress? Shouldn't she be included too?'

'I thought you'd get around to trying that eventually.'

'You flatter yourself. What are you saying? That you're possessive not only of James, but of all his things?'

'Not possessive. Protective.'

'You're a strange one, Rachel, with some odd notions. Well, here's something for you. I've been watching you, too.'

'Why don't you leave Sabine alone? You don't want her.'

'Aren't you in a difficult position to be dispensing moral advice of this kind? Doesn't it feel strange for you to claim to have Sabine's interests at heart? And what exactly are your motives for being here at all?'

'I'm on to you, Matt. I want you to know that. I'm on to you.'

Chrissie came back from the pool draped in a towel. She shivered and looked from Matt to Rachel.

'Rachel's had too much sun,' Matt said. Rachel got up and went indoors.

'What's up?' Chrissie asked.

'She's a spooky one, that Rachel.'

'I've never said it before, but something about her frightens me.'

'I know what you mean,' said Matt.

Within an hour the others returned, and James was still in high spirits. Beth presented a few spent rockets for Matt's inspection. Her daddy had told them they were fallen angels, she proudly reported. Matt sniffed the empty paper cartridges and pronounced them sulphurous enough for that to be true. He looked up. Jessie, hanging on to her father's arm was gazing at him strangely. A debate ensued about the components of fireworks gunpowder, in which one of the men favoured potassium chlorate while the other championed potassium nitrate, after which someone else observed how often people would argue energetically out of ignorance rather than concede that they might be wrong, and that seemed to settle the matter of what went into fireworks.

Matt and Sabine gave each other a wide berth.

'Where's Rachel?' Jessie asked.

'Upstairs, I think,' said Chrissie.

'I'll go and find her,' Jessie said, going indoors.

'No,' Sabine called after her. 'Let her rest.'

Upstairs, meanwhile, Rachel wasn't exactly resting. She was listening attentively to the range of voices from just below the window of Chrissie and Matt's room. As long as she could hear everyone's voice contributing to some preposterous argument about fireworks she knew she wouldn't be discovered. She was making a tidy search through the chest of drawers, turning over Matt's socks, T-shirts and underpants.

So far she hadn't found anything; she didn't know what it was she was hunting for. She was simply looking for something that was not right and would know it only when she saw it. She closed the top drawer and opened the next one. The perfume of Chrissie streamed from the cotton lingerie. She turned the underclothes this way and that, reaching to the back of the drawer, hunting for something, anything, that might have been secreted at the rear. Then she heard Jessie mention her name.

Someone came into the kitchen, and she heard Sabine calling Jessie back. Rachel got out of the room quickly and quietly, closing the door behind her.

Outside, James batted a shuttlecock up and down with a badminton racquet, and Chrissie made some observation about how chipper he seemed. Jessie stopped what she was doing and stared at the ground in order to disguise her interest in what might be said.

'I feel loads better. Anyone want a game?'

'That stroll to the Pyrenees did you some good then,' said Chrissie, but when Sabine coloured, she wished she hadn't.

'Grab a racquet, Chrissie. I like to see your breasts jiggle.'

'Daddy, puh-lease!' Jessie moaned.

'What's the matter? It's what I live for. The thing is,' James becoming serious for a moment, 'I'm giving up drinking.'

'Are you really?' Jessie shouted inappropriately. She rushed to her father, grabbing his sleeve. 'Are you really? Really? Really, really, really?'

James let the shuttlecock fall. Jessie was puce in the face and demanding an answer in a way that astonished him. 'Yes, I think so. At least, after tonight.'

Jessie put her arms around his belly and buried her head in his chest. Now everyone looked sheepish. Beth went to her mother. 'Well, that's a good idea,' Chrissie said lightly, by way of rescue.

Matt and Sabine exchanged a glance. Then Matt stared hard at James. 'Why after tonight?'

'Because tonight,' said James smugly, keeping the shuttlecock in the air, 'is your treat night, Matt.'

'Matt's treat night?' said Sabine.

'Yes. Matt is taking us out to a restaurant. He's treating us all to a meal.'

'Really?' said Sabine. 'Can you afford it, Matt?'

Matt narrowed his eyes at James and took a long time to answer. 'All right,' he said. 'Why not? My treat.'

Chrissie and James had their game of badminton. As they stood at the net panting, Chrissie said, 'What are you up to now?'

'I can't think what you mean.'

Chrissie shrugged. 'As for you going on the wagon, right now I think that's a great idea. Can I ask what brought that on?'

'Let's say I've had a scare, Chrissie. Matt thinks I'm a liar, but I genuinely can't account for most of the time I was away. I remember leaving, I'm not saying I didn't know what I was doing. But the next two days . . . nothing.'

'You think it was the drink?'

'I don't know. Then something happened last night. After the fireworks. Apparently I spent half the evening in conversation with someone who wasn't there. An old man. He really scared me.'

Chrissie blinked at him. 'I don't know if I should tell you this. I saw him too.'

'What?'

'But only for a few seconds.'

'*What?*'

Chrissie didn't get the chance to elaborate. 'Daddy, look! Look, Daddy, look!' Jessie ran to him and grabbed his hand. She was pointing at the horizon, way across the flat plain. Against the sore skyline tiny, branching, febrile darts of lightning flared in glittering sequence, some merely distant, others immensely far off. The fibrous glimmerings were unaccompanied by thunder but for the occasional remote crump. It was a delicate ballet of white light, straining the eyes, accompanied by a sudden drop in temperature and a swooping breeze.

Jessie was strangely energized, dancing, pointing. 'Look, Daddy, they've come! Violet rain, Daddy! Violet rain!'

But Jessie's ebullience was not allowed to endure, and the evening meal at the restaurant was not a success. There were the usual early difficulties when Jessie wanted to travel in Matt's Ka, and if Jessie could, then so must Beth. This created tensions, since it meant Rachel having to ride with James and Sabine. 'I can't for the life of me see what's so fascinating about Matt's damned bubble-car,' James said petulantly.

But Jessie dug her heels in, so Chrissie, Jessie, Beth and Matt in the lead car drew up initially at a modest but cosy-looking roadside restaurant. James pulled alongside them, wound down his window and made a disparaging remark about international tourist menus. He insisted that they follow him. They drove for three-quarters of an hour before James parked outside a hotel offering silver service, crisp linen and a very haughty ambience.

'We can at least choose somewhere where the business of eating is treated seriously,' he said, locking his car and leading the way.

Jessie heard Chrissie whispering, 'Hope you brought your credit cards.' It didn't sound like a joke.

'So do I,' Matt said, rubbing his chin.

Seated, James waved away the waiter's offer of a fixed-price menu. '*A la carte*,' he said. 'Most definitely *à la carte*.'

'Is that all right?' Sabine asked Matt.

'Why are there so many knives and forks?' said Beth.

Matt smiled. 'Have what you like. As James says, it's my treat.' He ordered the wine.

'Good choice,' James congratulated him. 'This will keep us going until we've ordered.'

Jessie watched her father closely. There was a pernicious gleam in his eye.

'I've never *seen* so many knives and forks,' said Beth.

And order they did. James tried to bully Jessie and Beth into trying unfamiliar dishes.

'*Chipirones*? What are they?'

'Baby squid cooked in their own ink,' said Sabine. 'Stop it, James.'

But James ordered them anyway, so that the children could at least try something new. He also thought that between them the company should try lamprey and pickled herrings and brains and pheasant and several other dishes. 'Is that all right, Matt? It's only one fancy dish apiece on top of the main meal.'

'Quite all right,' said Matt.

And there followed further lavish orders, with James bidding well, for soups, hors d'oeuvres, *charcuterie* dishes, poultry and game until the banquet began to take on a medieval quality, the table groaning under the weight of food. After a while James summoned the wine waiter and whispered to him in French. Sabine, however, called the waiter back and wanted to know what had been requested, whereupon she immediately cancelled James's order and sent the waiter away for another bottle of what they'd already had.

'What are you doing?' James said.

'Stop it at once!' Sabine said angrily.

'Stop what? I don't understand you. We're trying to enjoy ourselves!'

'If you are going to order wine at 500 francs a bottle, then you can drink it, and pay for it, yourself.'

Everyone else at the table went silent. 'All right,' said James perfectly reasonably, 'we'll drink this slop all night.'

'It is not slop. It's a perfectly good and rather expensive wine that Matt has selected. Is this a good example to set your children? You're a guest at a friend's table and you throw *his* money around? How dare you humiliate your family like this?'

'Sabine –' Matt tried.

'No, Matt. This is my country, and it's my pride that is being offended here, and I won't tolerate it.'

'You're making something out of nothing,' James said. Jessie noticed other diners looking on. She felt hot. 'I was going to pay for the wine myself anyway.'

'I doubt it,' said Sabine.

'I don't know what you're going on about. This holiday hasn't cost Matt a bean so far.'

'What do you mean?' said Sabine.

'I mean, I paid for Matt and Chrissie to come as our guests. Matt was glad of the chance to put his hand in his pocket tonight.'

Sabine was astonished. 'Is this true?'

Matt set down his wine glass. 'It's true that James wouldn't take anything from us for the holiday.'

Sabine's cheeks flamed. The ground had been cut from under her. She gazed steadily at her husband. 'How very generous of us.'

James looked at the bowed heads of his daughters. 'Eat up, girls,' he said. 'It's nothing but a storm in a teacup.'

But the meal was tainted. After finishing all the dishes, no one, it seemed, had room for dessert or even for coffee – except James who had both, and cheese, and port, and a further bottle of wine. When the waiter came with the bill, Matt produced a credit card and laid it on the folded slip of paper without examination. As the waiter reached to take it up, Sabine placed her hand gently on his forearm. She plucked up the plastic card herself and held it under the table. 'James,' she said.

'Matt's treat,' said James.

'I'm happy to pay,' said Matt. 'Really.'

'James,' said Sabine. James looked away. The waiter shifted his weight from one foot to the other. Jessie watched her parents with horrified fascination. 'Another night we'll go to a restaurant of your choice, Matt, and you will pay. But tonight I'm in such a good mood I've decided that I would like to treat everyone myself. James.'

The waiter smoothed his moustache. Matt pleaded, but Sabine resisted. At last, and with theatrical self-possession, James took out his wallet and skimmed a plastic card across the table. The waiter seized on it as if there was some danger that someone would intercept this card too.

On leaving the restaurant Jessie said, 'Can I go with Matt and Chrissie?'

'No,' James said stiffly. 'You can't.'

On the way home Jessie was sick in the Merc.

40

High-speed cameras show that single (to the human eye) flashes of lightning are actually multiple events of up to forty-two main strokes.

Each stroke within the flash lasts for a duration of 0.0002 seconds. Strokes pulse at intervals of approximately 0.02 seconds.

An average lightning flash lasts for one quarter of a second.

41

The past won't keep still. Events in the instructor's mirror jump like a TV set with a fault in the vertical hold. She looks deep into Gregory's staring eyes again. The storm is subsiding, the lightning in retreat. She sees her own shrunken head twinned in his black pupils. Turning away, she closes the curtains on the night.

Making a scrupulous tour of the apartment's every space, she collects all signs of her residence there, packing her clothes into the bag she came with. Everything else she stuffs into a black plastic bin-liner. It doesn't take long. Gregory was restrictive about what he allowed her to contribute to the gloomy ambience of the place, prohibiting any effort she made to feminize or enhance the décor. Once he told her she could do what she wanted with her own room, but not to 'mess' with the rest of the apartment. Only now does she realize what little impression she made either on the apartment or on Gregory's life.

On the matter of his death, however, she has been most influential.

When Gregory is eventually discovered, there is every possibility his death will be attributed if not to an overdose then to the intravenous injection of contaminated gear. She knows enough about drugs and addicts to guess how much time the police will spend on the corpse of a junkie.

She washes carefully and brushes her teeth. Inspecting her face in the bathroom mirror, she thinks her skin is rather dry. Her main concern is to get to the Dordogne. It is always possible that the streets of Paris may deliver guidance from another angel.

Lying in bed in the silent apartment, she wonders what her sister is doing in the Dordogne. It is going to be a surprise, an emotional reunion. How long since they were together? It's too difficult. Every time she counts back the years, her calculations dissolve in black mist.

But those early holidays in the Dordogne were never obscured by mist. On the contrary, they blazed with golden, biblical light. The faces of her family shone. The green corn was tall and lustrous. Even the dry rocks seemed made of silk rather than stone. Memory itself was like the azure skies, glazed, almost ceramic, apt to crack and break and cut.

And there was Mother and there was Father and there was cousin Melanie. And the dovecote, and the plum tree. And Melanie can have wine. Why can Melanie have wine? Can Mother have wine? Can we all have wine? And Melanie's lips are bleeding. Can we all have –

It is important to forget all that. Gregory remains sprawled in his chair. Returning, naked, from the bathroom, she crosses the apartment to study his body. His dead eyes survey her nakedness. She feels slightly shy before him in a way she never felt when he was alive. To close his eyes would give her away, and anyway she doesn't see the necessity of the rite. Let the dead stare out. It is commonly assumed, is it not, that the souls of the dead fly upwards with the last breath. What if this is a misapprehension? What if the eyes are the egress of the soul? What if the closing of eyes and the penny weights have trapped millions of souls in putrefying corpses?

She touches Gregory's cheek. It has cooled slightly. Some early discoloration of the skin has occurred, where the settling of blood has raised a blue-red tone on the underside of his bare arms and under his chin. Unless she is fooled by the violet light, which, although it still issues from his body, is fading with each passing second.

She returns to her room, sits before the dressing-table mirror and begins to put on her make-up. White face. Delicate black tracks with eye-liner. Pout. Lips deliciously crimson. She rouges the aureoles of her breasts before pulling on stockings and clipping on suspenders. Elbow-length satin gloves. Patent-leather spike-heels. She is ready.

Standing over him, her legs are spread slightly. 'One for the road,' she says, lighting a blue cocktail cigarette and fixing it in a long, elegant holder. Taking occasional puffs, she gazes fixedly at Gregory's dead eyes. She blows smoke into his face.

'Did that help?' she asks him when the cigarette is finished.

She returns to her old hostel, where she lies on the bed staring at the ceiling, allowing her mind to flood with the golden light of the Dordogne. There are games, always games. Queenie-o'koko-who-has-the-ball-io; kingy, thwack, ouch; leapfrog, piggyback, bulldog; and tennis and yo-yo; and invented games and nonsense; and gymnastic headstands handsprings forward-rolls and cart-wheels; and Melanie always wins! Melanie always wins! Melanie, perfect as a string of beads, trim as a pennant on a pole, glowing like a luminous yo-yo. How she wanted to be with Melanie, to go with Melanie, to stay with her. And her father too, always suggesting a new game, fun under the sun, and the holidays stretch on like the winding road to forever.

But, like a stormcloud louring from a short distance, here is Mother's vague disapproval. But brought on by whom? A sourness, but about what? 'Don't be so rough with the girls. Don't play so rough.'

'We're just having fun, aren't we, girls? Aren't we?'

Fun in the sun.

'Hide-and-seek in the corn. Let's play hide-and-seek, girls!'

'Don't!' said Mother. 'Don't go too far into the corn!'

'Why not?'

'Because there are girls who went into the corn' – Father winking at Melanie – 'who never came out again. Counting up to thirty! One, two, three . . .'

And to run and hide on the baked earth, with the light frac-tured by the green-and-golden corn, shrieking and waiting, is wonderful. In the biblical light. Hiding is wonderful, but being found is even better when Daddy grabs you round the waist and swings you screaming almost as high as the corn, panting, breathless.

Mother frowns at the edge of the field. 'They're too old for these silly games.'

Daddy, sadly, seriously, 'Let Mother be a lesson to you, girls. Never get too old. Never get too old to lose your head in the corn.'

And after that whatever is wrong with Mother and Father gets worse. Father stops playing games. At nights, hearing them arguing in their room. Melanie looks across from her bed, listening.

They have their own games, she and Melanie, bolder, more risqué than when Father is around. 'Shall we play Angels?' Melanie suggests.

'How?'

So Melanie leads her deep into the corn. 'We take off our clothes,' says Melanie.

'All of them?'

'Of course! To play Angels.'

When they are both naked, Melanie stretches out her arms. 'Now we spread our wings, like an aeroplane. Each stick of corn is a person's life. And we run through the corn, touching some, bashing down others, as we please, like *this* –' And she follows as Melanie swoops through the corn, brushing the stems, steering around them, bruising this one, breaking that, round and round, the dry stalks whipping against their naked, immature bodies until both collapse in a fit of giggles and exhaustion and Melanie falls on top of her and hugs and kisses her and they lie back on the cracked earth in the green-and-gold light, panting.

Recovering her breath, she asks Melanie, 'Who showed you how to play Angels?'

'Secret.'

'Tell me.'

'Secret.'

'Who?'

Melanie giggles and looks away. 'Your father.'

She stares at Melanie's dust-coated back, certain that Melanie must be lying.

One day Mother, busy in the kitchen, sends her in search of Melanie and her father. Tennis racquets and balls lie abandoned on the grass where the two were playing earlier. They are nowhere to be seen. The sun in the sky is white-hot, the land bleached white. The plum tree frazzles in the heat, a golden-eyed lizard rests immobile under a rock. She leaves the grounds of the villa, crosses the road and enters the corn.

She hears them talking in low voices. Silently, moving with stealth amid the ripe corn, she comes upon them. They can't see her. They are lying on the baked earth. They have been playing Angels, without her.

42

Rachel waited until all the others had gone. She heard the car crunching on the gravel outside the window, paused until the purr of the engine diminished. What if they came back suddenly? What if one of them had forgotten something? She decided to wait for ten minutes before continuing with her search of Matt and Chrissie's room.

Matt's question had got to her. What exactly *was* she doing here? Why exactly had she come along? On the face of it, Matt was right to ask. He knew about her affair with James, though how much he knew was uncertain. She had a feeling he might not even know it was over. If Matt suspected that the affair was still running, then she could guess the thoughts Matt entertained about her. What kind of a person would want to join her adulterous lover's wife and family on holiday?

She buried her face in her hands: what kind of a person would want to go anywhere, in any circumstances, with James and Sabine? Not to mention their kooky friends. Only the desperately lonely.

The saving graces in all of this were Jessie and Beth. Rachel idealized the two children. In many ways she would have liked to make them her own. Spending time with them day by day had made her realize how much she wanted children of her own, and yet that was impossible.

Rachel had tried to conceive, with partners both appropriate and inappropriate. She'd even tried to conceive with James. Her big plan, at the time, was to get pregnant by him, dump him and move on without telling him. She was a self-confessed gene-hunter, quite happy to take the consequences without the baggage. It was a baby she wanted, not a husband. James was her seventh lover taken with this scheme in mind, in a search that had led her from a tepee to here. Those days at his office, when he'd played the wining-and-dining seducer, the office predator, he'd had no idea that he'd been classified, graded, calibrated and finally selected for Rachel's private eugenic programme. When he didn't turn out to be seventh time lucky, Rachel consulted a medical specialist, and her one-woman programme was over.

The worst thing about it was knowing she would make a much better parent than either Sabine or James. She knew she could offer values to a child and not simply abandon her offspring to an arid climate of yuppie self-absorption and greedy complacency. The ironic thing, she reminded herself, was that one of the reasons why she'd come on this holiday was to improve herself. She had had an idea that by associating with sophisticated company she might learn one or two things about style, about maturity, about graceful living.

God save me, she thought, *from style, maturity and graceful living*.

Except for Jessie and Beth, who were terrific kids, despite the worst their self-obsessed parents could do to them. Rachel had a particularly soft spot for Jessie. Her troubles, Rachel had decided, could be solved instantly by lashings of attention. There was nothing wrong with the girl that love and affection couldn't cure. She had tantrums – so what? She went blue in the face occasionally – so what? She took her clothes off in the supermarket – well, Rachel too felt like doing that once in a while. Rachel wanted to propose to James and Sabine that she take Jessie on holiday herself, to give the two of them a break, but she hadn't had the confidence to suggest it. Since the early days of this holiday, and all the weird happenings, Sabine wouldn't even let her and Jessie do the washing-up together. So much for that idea.

Rachel calculated that the others had been gone long enough and that she could expect to proceed uninterrupted with her search. James, in his new-found fit of optimism and energy, had suggested a trip to Sarlat. Because Rachel had cried off, preferring to spend the day alone at the *gîte*, the others had squeezed into one car.

'Please come!' Jessie had begged.

Rachel was heartily sick of the company. 'I'm a bit under the weather,' she said instead.

'Is it a *period*?' Beth asked with horrified fascination.

'Who has she been talking to now?' Sabine remonstrated. In fact, Beth had been talking to Jessie.

'You could say that,' Rachel laughed. Then they were gone.

Rachel pushed open the heavy, varnished door to Matt and Chrissie's room. The shutters were closed. A fan of light broke through the apertures while half the room swam with shadows. There was something about the room Rachel didn't like; nothing she could define exactly, but an aura she'd found distracting when she'd rummaged in the drawers before. The aura wasn't associated with the room necessarily, or with Chrissie or Matt individually. It was something produced by the two of them together. She wasn't sure why, but Rachel felt less uneasy about the couple when they were apart.

Matt she mistrusted. He was altogether too nice, too easy-going, too uncomplicated. It was not fitting in a human being to be relentlessly upbeat. Everyone had their down side, and everyone had their shadow. Where was Matt's dark side? Such people made her nervous. He was like a figure standing before a mirror but with no reflection.

And Chrissie floated too close to the surface of herself. There was something else Rachel sensed – on a purely intuitive level; there was never evidence to back up these prejudices of hers – about the woman. It was danger, a threat. Rachel had noticed some competition in Chrissie for Jessie's attention, and she found herself listening hard whenever Chrissie was talking to the girl. Rachel detected a freakishly irresponsible streak in Chrissie, a deep instability, and she felt protective against her on Jessie's behalf. She understood and sympathized with Sabine's efforts to shield Jessie from her influence.

But it was together that Matt and Chrissie most disturbed Rachel. Together they were a peculiarly irresistible force. Together they could persuade someone like Jessie to tweak the tiger's tail if they thought there was a giggle to be found in it. Neither were others immune to their charm: a mood of either energy or sluggishness could be dictated by the pair without James or Sabine being aware of it. They had a remarkable ability to lead from behind. If Matt spoke up, Chrissie would rhyme and the children would clap along, and then James and Sabine would have to follow. It was odd, given the dynamics existing between them all, but James and Sabine seemed mysteriously in thrall to the other two while the very opposite appeared to be the case.

And they were deeply in thrall to each other. Their intimacy was very close to being a source of provocation. It wasn't just the public embracing and the casual snogging, though that was irritating enough in a couple who'd been together so long. Rachel believed that mature people who mouthed openly like teenagers deserved a tap on the head with a mallet. (Here Rachel checked herself, wondering if she approved more of the model offered by Sabine and James, who never embraced publicly.) But it wasn't the question of their vibrant physicality that troubled her. It was the suggestion of their deep and inseparable entanglement. She wondered if they could manage without each other when individually they seemed to her so weak.

This was why she'd watched Matt's attentions towards Sabine with such interest. She understood what he was going after. He didn't want Sabine. Matt knew what James had done to him, and he had seen a way to get even. What seemed appalling to Rachel was that Chrissie, who must have seen everything too, was in some horrible way colluding with it by letting it happen. It was this, above all things, that convinced Rachel that Chrissie and Matt did not mean well for Sabine and James.

She swung back the shutters, and sunlight spread around the room like a hot flush, probing invasively at its dusty corners. In the creaking, mirrored wardrobe Chrissie's cotton skirts and blouses hung mixed with Matt's shirts. Chrissie's perfume rose from the clothes as Rachel parted the hangers. Uncertain what she was looking for, Rachel smoothed pockets and explored jackets. When she'd finished in the wardrobe, the mirrored door flashed on the dressing-table mirror, revealing a figure behind her, watching her.

Of course, it was only her own reflection in the second mirror, but the surprise made her blood chill. Though there was no one else in the house, she strained to listen. She heard her blood singing in her veins.

Moving from the wardrobe, she went through the chest of drawers again, conducting a tidy search, careful not to disturb the contents in any way. There were no surprises. In Chrissie's lingerie drawer this time she found stockings and suspenders and a contraceptive cap and spermicide. The next drawer contained Matt's socks and boxer shorts, plus a modest bale of grass, cigarette papers and a small metal pipe. The third drawer was stuffed full of dirty laundry waiting to be taken home.

The dressing-table was laden with the futuristic metropolis of women's cosmetics: tubes and bottles of creams and oils. But in the mirror Rachel's eyes fell on a handbag lying inside one of the bedside cabinets.

The bag was almost empty, but in a side pocket Rachel found a photograph of Matt. He was younger, his hair was longer and, amusingly, it was bleach-blond. There was a searching intensity to his dark eyes. In the photograph he stood next to a stone monument or perhaps even a headstone in a graveyard. It wasn't possible to tell the exact location from the photograph, but the inscription on the monument was clear:

> *Though I speak with the tongue of angels,*
> *if I have not love,*
> *I am become as hollow brass.*
> *If I have not love,*
> *I am nothing.*

Rachel thought she recognized the quotation. There was also a photo of Chrissie beside the same monument, her face pale, her make-up exaggerated, her hair jet-black. Rachel wondered how long ago and where the photos had been taken. She put them back where she'd found them.

The bedside cupboards contained a few paperback books but little else. The search had proved disappointing. Rachel looked around the room, ran her hands between the mattress and the base of the bed, opened the twin suitcases that lay under the bed. Nothing. Then, as an afterthought, she went back to the chest of drawers and opened the lowest drawer. She pulled out a pile of dirty T-shirts, underwear and socks, sweeping her hand to the back of the drawer. Her hand closed around a small cardboard box.

The stiff white box was roughly the size of a paperback book. Inside, mounted on a cardboard tray, was a hypodermic syringe. There were also two glass ampoules containing a clear liquid. Rachel held one of the ampoules up to the light. Then she heard tyres crunching on the gravel below the window as a car came to a halt outside.

Rachel became paralysed, still holding the glass ampoule. She heard a car door open and close. Footsteps crunched the gravel. With trembling fingers she fixed the ampoule back in its mounting inside the box, closed the lid and returned the box to the back of the drawer. She heard herself hyperventilating as she stuffed dirty laundry back in the drawer. Then the swollen wood stuck in the runners and the drawer wouldn't close. Rachel pressed her hands to her face. Downstairs, the kitchen door swung open.

Frantic now, she fumbled with the drawer, but the wood wedged obstinately in the runners. The drawer refused to budge forwards or back. Rachel bumped it aggressively, shaking it free of its runners, and laundry spilled across the floor. Hands trembling, she bundled the clothes back into the drawer again. Guiding the drawer on to its swollen runners, she finally closed the thing with a smooth action. Then she remembered the suitcases still open on the bed. She zipped up the cases and slid them under the bed.

The stairs: she heard someone coming up the stairs. Rachel

clattered the wardrobe doors closed and then made a dive for the shutters. She ran out on to the landing and straight into the arms of Dominique.

Dominique was carrying an armful of linen. 'Rachel!' she said. 'I thought the house was empty. Are you all right? You look as if you've seen a ghost!'

Rachel excused herself and returned to her room, leaving Dominique to stare after her.

43

Sarlat was a visitor spot spruced up for tourists, a town of honey-coloured stone and pepper-pot turrets. For James it was definitive France, but Sabine dismissed it as 'designer French'. For a town of ten thousand inhabitants the wash of a million tourists a year had smoothed away any vestige of authenticity, but James could happily potter for hours in its narrow alleys and numerous tiny marketplaces. He liked to chat in French with stallholders and with other tourists too, wilfully oblivious to the fact that many of the latter were English. Most of the tourists would smile back at him with that uniquely English grin fixed in place by the terror of making a *faux pas* in foreign places. It so irritated Sabine that she quickly fell away from his side, leaving him to peruse the sanitized cut-throat alleys. Meanwhile his daughters clung to him as if fearing another desertion.

Matt found Sabine examining leather belts at one of the stalls. 'Here you are.'

'Where's Chrissie?'

He waved an arm airily. 'Somewhere.'

'You know, I hate this place.'

'But it's pretty!'

'Something about it horrifies me. I wish I could understand why.'

'Look, about the other day –'

'What about the other day?' Sabine's nut-brown eyes challenged him to say something which would either incriminate him or clear him for ever.

He changed the subject. 'James is on good form today. Quite a change.'

'He didn't touch a drop last night. I think he's serious. Even though he's dying for a drink.'

'Good.'

'Is it? I really don't care any more.' She moved between stalls selling gay cotton scarves and ceramics. Matt followed. 'You know, in this country style means everything. James showed me that. From how small things are wrapped in a *pâtisserie* to the shape of a motor car. When you grow up with it, you notice if it's not there. James fell in love with that. He's a collector of style. He adores his fine wines; his cheeses have to come in *this* box; his *foie gras* has to come in *that* box.

'You may think it strange, but when I went to England to live with him, I actually enjoyed the escape from style. It was liberating and comical. You don't know how many things you do which perplex French people or make them laugh. But, no, I wasn't allowed to escape. James would be disappointed with me. "Why did you buy that?" he would ask me. "I can't believe you would want to bring such a thing into the house." I was forbidden to take on any aspect of English life in the way he takes on all things French.

'I wanted to assimilate English culture, but he wouldn't let me. He even expressed disappointment when I started to lose my accent. He actually preferred me to say *zis* and *zat* and *ze ozer*. You see, he didn't want me. He wanted the box I came in.'

'Oh, come on!' Matt said.

But Sabine was fired up. 'It's worse than that. I said style is a way of life here. With him it's a way of death. You know, he still wants to choose my clothes. It's taken me a long time to realize it but I'm an accessory. He's just like all these middle-class English tourists who come here. He raids the country for its wines and cheeses out of some facile notion of elegant living. And he found a woman too – what could be better? I'm not loved by him, I'm *touristed* by him. That's how it feels, Matt.'

'I don't know what to say.'

'I tell you, I hate the bloody fucking bastard. By the way, he disapproves of me swearing.'

'But if it's so bad, why stay?'

'Because I'm dependent on my jailer. Then there's the girls, of course. Where am I going to find someone with even half the means to keep them?' She turned, so that her question could search him.

He didn't know if her words were weighted to rule him out of the answer. 'I could never leave Chrissie –'

She stopped his mouth with her fingers. 'You're sweet, Matt. But you're not what I'm looking for. No, I figure I have another ten years or so to serve in my English dungeon, and then I'll leave him.'

They walked on. 'I never realized you hated him so much.'

'Yes, but when I saw you hated him too, I started to worry for him.'

'Me?' said Matt.

'Do you think I'm stupid? You imagine I don't see? And you are his friend. His one and only friend. It was all right for me to hate him, but when I saw you did too, I despaired. His wife and best friend despise him. I wanted to cry and cry and cry. All I could think was, what are we doing with our lives? Why do we go through life living like ghosts, living so indistinctly, acting as if none of it matters?

'I've looked at his face, Matt. I've seen through it, and it makes me afraid. Not for what I see there, but for what I don't see. Because of what I thought was there once. When we first met, I felt heat flowing from me to him and from him to me. We were lifted up. Then, without knowing it, we had reached an equilibrium. Now we're breaking up. Maybe these things have cycles.

'But it's the assembly of faces that terrifies me. The faces he puts on. And the faces I then put on to sustain his faces. And you, Matt, you do the same for him. All of us do it, for him and for each other. Masks of blood and clay. Who are we hiding from? I tell you, sometimes I pray for a storm to come and wash it all away, the cracked clay, the clogged pores, to get down to the child-like skin and bones of what we are.'

Matt nodded thoughtfully. He understood something of what she was talking about.

'I know this,' she continued. 'God will punish us for living so vaguely.'

'This all sounds very serious!' quipped a cheerful voice coming up behind them. It was James. His arms were laden. He carried specimens of *Trappe Echourgnac*, beautifully wrapped, *terrine de canard* and *foie gras* in exciting tins, *pruneaux* in gorgeous vacuum-sealed jars and *noix* in delightful earthenware pots. The children's arms were also laden. 'We've been buying a few things,' he said.

Before leaving the town, Matt had to go in search of Chrissie. She'd become lost somewhere in the interconnecting narrow streets. Finally he found her gazing up at a fourteenth-century house roofed with heavy red-brick tiling. Approaching her from behind he said, 'Time to go.' She appeared not to hear him. 'Chrissie,' he said. 'Chrissie?'

Something had her mesmerized. The sloping, tiled roof began at little more than eye-level. He stepped back to see what she was looking at. There was nothing there. Nothing. The tiles of the roof, though, had buckled and folded marvellously. The passing of centuries had pitched and rolled the tiles so that they sank or lifted like waves on the ocean, one row plummeting to be closed over by another. Faults in the earth. Warps in time.

Matt took her gently by the elbow. 'You're a long way gone.'

She seemed to wake up, startled. 'Was I? Again?'

Matt had seen it all before. 'Come on. Let's go.'

Rachel was playing a Scarlatti sonata in the lounge when James came up behind her and laid a hand on her shoulder. 'Everyone's having a swim. Come and join us?'

'You carry on. I'm fine here.'

'It would be nice if we could all have a splash together.'

Rachel stopped playing. 'That's nice. For almost two weeks you

233

skulk around and lie in your bed, and now you want everyone to play happy families.'

'Why so glum?'

'I shouldn't be here, James. It was a senseless idea to come at all, and I don't know how I let you talk me into it.'

'Shove up.' He squeezed on to the piano stool beside her and tapped at the piano keys. 'I thought you liked being with Jessie and Beth.'

'I do, but have you observed your wife recently? She's red in tooth and claw. She's freezing me out. I'm going to have to leave.'

'Oh, Rachel, there's only a couple of days left to run. Surely it's not that bad. You get on well with Chrissie and Matt, don't you?'

Rachel moved his hand off the piano keys and closed the lid. 'How well do you know those two?'

'Chrissie's a strange one, I admit, but I've known Matt for years. I know him as well as it's possible to know someone. Why do you ask?'

'I think you would be prepared to have him around only as long as he's a failure.'

'That's a vicious thing to say.'

'It was a vicious thing you did. Can you deny it?'

James got off the piano stool. 'Come on. You need a swim.'

'I don't want a fucking swim! I want to be around people who actually care about each other! Not people hand-picked to make you look good!'

'You,' James said nastily, 'wouldn't be here at all if I hadn't paid for you to come.'

'Exactly. And neither would Matt and Chrissie, and you used that fact to sour another evening, didn't you? All of us bought and paid for, to put up with your moods and to be happy when you say so. You know why you wanted us here? Because you couldn't stand to be with yourself and your own. Have you looked at them lately, all these people you pay for? Have you looked at your wife? She hates you. Have you looked at your friends? They hate you. You should be careful, James. Very careful.'

234

The door creaked open. Jessie came into the room. 'Lot of shouting,' she said. 'Are you two coming to the pool?'

'James is,' said Rachel. 'I'm not.'

44

James sat on his bed, focused on the bottle of claret lifted from his special supply. The late-afternoon sun flared on the wonderfully smooth contours of the glass bottle, warming the wine, alchemizing it the colour of spilled blood. He was still smarting after Rachel's attack. He was smarting when he hit the pool where all the others were waiting, and smarting when he came up again. But he splashed, he cavorted, he caught the ball and returned it: he did everything a good man should. He smiled until his cheeks began to squeak.

Because he had wanted to be the new James, the reformed James. It was hard going, but it was nice to be nice. And how his daughters loved it! How they were energized and fascinated and hopeful and adoring of their new model father. He felt shockingly guilty not only about the way he'd allowed himself to spoil the first week or more of their holiday but also about his behaviour towards Matt in the restaurant. Rachel's words had flashed like arrows to the mark. And even if it was true that he'd surrounded himself with people who hated him, he was determined, now, to salvage the final days of the holiday.

The situation was not helped by the movement of the pains in his intestine to his heart. After the night at the restaurant he'd been true to his promise of abstinence. He'd drunk a great deal (as far as he could remember) during his 'missing' days, and had hit Patrice's local wine with a vengeance on returning. He wondered if the mysterious scything, now shifted from his guts, would abate if he were to keep his promise to his girls to stay away from alcohol. James regarded the promises he made to his girls as sacred.

There were disincentives, however, which directed him straight back to the wine rack. He was unable to dispute a single word Rachel had thrown at him earlier. It was all true. And Sabine had been in a filthy mood all the way back from Sarlat, barely responding to him except to snarl.

Impossible! It was impossible! Here he was, genuinely trying to adjust his behaviour, to smile, to motivate, and everyone else had chosen exactly this moment to growl back at him. In these circumstances it was difficult to remain jolly. Relentlessly fucking jolly.

Being miserable was so much easier and a damn sight more enjoyable. You didn't have to work at it, you just relaxed back into the glooping muddy pool. The miserable, he now saw, always held the trump card. If you chose to be positive, optimistic, all they had to do was turn up their lip or twitch an eyebrow. The miserable had gravity on their side. They didn't have to defend the earth's capacity to drag you down. Flight, however, must be maintained by eternal energy and perpetual motion in the face of friction, and at some price.

Enforced jollity was one thing, but delight, genuine, sky-going, silver-winged delight, was quite another. Make one modest leap for delight and the miserable will conspire at once to engineer your fall. They wait, nets spread and lures set, with their bottles and their drugs and their sick fantasies bubbling at you from the depths of the mud pool.

As he sat on the bed in the full glare of the afternoon sun, he touched his forehead and realized he was sweating profusely. Sweating, too, at the back of his neck. Sweating under his arms. He felt deathly. A drink would put everything right.

He was not going to take a drink.

Rachel, Rachel, what was she saying? If only it hadn't all been true.

Worse, it didn't need to be said. He'd been saying it to himself already, and in stronger language than she could muster. The day he got up and walked away from the house, he'd started talking to himself; a voice, not exactly his own voice but one over which he had sovereign charge, had woken in him. He'd marched in time to that voice or, rather, to a whispered command that chased him along the country lanes and down the *autoroutes* until James finally acknowledged what it was he was trying to walk away from.

It felt as though something had climbed out of him to perch on his shoulders for the duration of the three days, speaking in a strange dialect words he barely understood – not beautiful words, not rare words, but an endless and spirited monologue, sometimes abusive, sometimes threatening, often cajoling and just occasionally pleading. He didn't know who was the owner of that voice. He didn't want to know. But he remembered all of what was said.

He'd walked to the mountains of the Pyrenees with a half-angelic, half-demonic spirit on his back. And one of the things it repeated in his ear, over and over, was: *you are sick at heart.*

He remembered sitting by the roadside after getting a lift in a lorry and bursting into tears. He had cried for hours, lung-bursting dry sobs. And after that the spirit was gone from his shoulders, all its words flown, his brain shockingly clear, and all he had left was a monumental self-loathing.

He hated his job and the power that came with it to shift acres of beans, lakes of beer, forests of toilet tissue. The war, in which he was a general directing a scorched-earth policy, of a ravaging and pointless consumerism sickened him. And now he came to assess the material rewards of a good position and an impressive salary, they were for him, as Rachel had pointed out, the capacity to take two weeks in the summer season to surround yourself with a wife who hated you, a lover who despised you, friends who were competitive strangers whom you'd betrayed and with whom you'd kept bad faith, and children who looked at you not with love but with features distorted by pity and fear.

And when he had come home and seen all their faces, after Matt had collected him, all he could do was blot out their blank looks with half a gallon of local wine. That was before the Ugly Spirit had appeared. That toad-like, squat being with the sagging jowls and the facial warts. James knew who that was. It had ridden his back all the way to the mountains.

At first he hadn't recognized it. Then Chrissie had frightened him. After she'd claimed to have seen the man on the night of the firework display, he'd cornered her. 'That man. The ugly man. You say you saw him?'

'Yes.'

'Why didn't you speak up for me?'

'They'd think I was mad. If I told them what I saw, that is.'

'What do you mean? What did you see?'

'That man. He came from inside you. He was hanging on your back. Then he got off your back and sat in the chair next to you. How do you think they would like it if I'd told them that?'

'Ridiculous.'

'It's what I saw.'

'Who was he?'

'I think you know who he was, James.'

He had looked at Chrissie long and hard. He saw, for the first time, something wild, even psychotic, in the defiant cast of her eye. 'What you say, Chrissie, leads me to think that you are not at all well.'

And she'd smiled. She'd smiled! And she'd stroked his cheek and said, 'Poor James. To be diagnosing other people's ills.'

Then she'd pulled away from him, and they hadn't spoken about the matter since. But whatever was happening to him, he knew now that he had poisoned himself with the actions of his own life. He also saw now what was making him ill, what tormented his innards. There was a parasite inside him, but it was not of tropical origin. It was a heart-gnawing worm that he had placed there himself, to roar and to feed and to destroy him. He hated his own guts.

He wanted to change; he really did, but he had a desperate feeling it was far too late. He lifted the bottle of claret from the cabinet and rotated it in the evening sunlight. At least the alcohol defeated the parasite of self-hatred. It was the only thing that would put it to sleep. It was the only thing that stopped the pain.

With perspiration dripping from his brow, James knew he stood at some monumental cross-roads. He had resolved to try, and he had tried. It had taken him only a day to find out that he was not cut out for trying. It was too hard. He preferred to be one of those who dragged other people down rather than one who lifted people up. He looked for his corkscrew.

'I'm the dinner gong,' Beth said, peering round the door.

James almost leapt from the bed. He looked at Beth and a claw of guilt tickled his heart. 'I didn't hear you! Come here, my darling! Come here, dinner gong!' He replaced the bottle on the cabinet and hugged his daughter.

'Bong,' said Beth. 'Bong. Bong. Bong.'

45

Back in the hostel she sleeps in her clothes for sixteen hours. When she wakes the violet light has gone. For the first time since cracking her head on the angel's wing in Highgate Cemetery her vision is clear. She looks in the mirror and her face still bears the white make-up, but behind it there is no violet fog, no sparkling storm, no glimmering of ethereal light. She feels expiated. Clean.

Glancing at the clock, she hurries from her apartment without washing and rides the Métro to Boulevard de Sebastopol. There in the street she sees a man distributing handbills. He gives her a leaflet and makes a remark about the weather. The handbill touts for custom at a disco-nightclub called L'enfer. The man has severely cropped hair, self-inflicted.

'You look like someone I once knew. He was called Gregory.'

'I believe you,' he says. 'You look like a killer.'

'I am. What's your name?'

'I haven't decided.'

'Can I decide for you?'

'Sure. If you give me a cigarette.'

'You won't mind if it's something evangelical?'

'Not at all. If you give me a cigarette.'

Another figure marches aggressively towards them and, under cover of a handbill, he is slipped a small package. The figure marches away.

'That's it,' the crop-haired man says, ceremoniously dumping his leaflets in the nearest bin, 'that's my very last one. Ever. I've discharged all responsibility.' Then he suggests they have coffee together.

She steps back to examine the pile of leaflets among the rubbish.

Leaning into the bin, she flicks a cigarette lighter and sets fire to the pile of paper. The orange flames lick, taking hold. She seems transfixed.

The man takes her arm. 'We'd better go before the whole thing flares up.'

He leads her to a small coffee bar off the main drag. They can't take their eyes off each other. It's as if each is waiting for the other to strike. A waiter arrives with their coffee, looks from one to the other of them, sets down the cups, leaves them to it.

'Do you believe a person can change?' she asks. 'Really change?'

'I do now.'

'I mean, change utterly. Become a different person. Forget everything you have been. Start afresh.'

'I have to believe it's possible.'

She places a hand on his arm. 'There would need to be certain rules to changing one's life.'

'Rules. Yes, rules.'

'One: no lying. I said I'd killed someone and you smiled but in a way that showed me you didn't believe me. When I say no lying, I mean no sophisticated lying either.'

He exhales a thin stream of cigarette smoke, blinks. 'Difficult.'

'But worth it, if the price is salvation. Two: no drugs.'

'It's going to be very hard for me.'

'And for me. Three: no one else.'

'The most difficult of all.'

'Four: no false names, faces, masks, disguises, personae, identities –'

'Four sounds like several.'

'This is the price. And you know the reward: I save you from your demons, you save me from mine.'

From outside they hear the siren of a single fire engine.

'Do you really believe it's possible to become a different person? Tell me the truth.'

'*Though I speak with the tongue of angels, if I have not love, I am become as hollow brass,*' she says. '*If I have not love, I am nothing.*'

'When I look at you now, when I look into your eyes, you seem clear and strong.'

'Who the hell cut your hair?'

'I did.'

They go from the coffee bar back to her place. There they undress hurriedly. Though there is urgency, she asks him to wait while she showers. She wants to scrub her face clean of the make-up. Shower away the very last of the lies. Wash away the last of the old life.

He is astonished when he sees her. He can scarcely believe what is beneath the face-paint. As she lets the towel fall, she is renewed. Her former self slumps like a rubberized suit in the corner of the room. She sits him on the bed, spreading herself before him, undressing him, pushing him back, climbing and lowering herself on to him. He ejaculates inside her almost instantly. Can't control himself. But it doesn't matter because within minutes he's ready for her again.

They are like virgins but without the terror. Urgent, clumsy but tender, as if this really is for the first time. When she comes she says, 'Matthew.' When he ejaculates into her again, he breathes her name.

Later, she asks him to take her from behind and before the mirror so that she can look at his face, which has become angelic, truly angelic, absent of all violet rain and silver storm. This he does, though sometimes, as his measured thrusts buck her from behind, her eyes stray from his to settle, in the dislocated, heart-bursting moments of this love-making, on her own in the mirror before her.

46

Beth tired of her piano exercise and said to Rachel, 'Why is everyone always arguing?'

'They're not,' Rachel said, and then wondered from where came the reflex to lie to children.

'Yes, they are. Mummy and Daddy argue. And Daddy and Matt. And Chrissie and Mummy. And you and Matt. Everyone.'

Rachel sighed. She looked at the piano keyboard and considered an explanation involving chords and harmonic keys but dismissed the idea with a shudder. 'Don't you and Jessie argue sometimes?'

'Yes. But then we forget it. With grown-ups it goes on for ever.'

'Look, Beth, I'll tell you what a wise man once told me. He was a crusty old hippie, from the days when I lived in a tepee. It's like this. Think of a ball of wool. You hold it and pass it on to every person I mention. There's you and Jessie. You may get along nicely or you may fall out one day. That's a relationship, that's what we call it. Then there are all the other relationships you have with everyone else in the house, so pass that ball of wool to me, Mummy, Daddy, Chrissie and Matt. There are six other people in the house – that's six relationships to manage, all going on at the same time. But then there's all my relationships with other people. Another six – or five, not including my relationship with you, which we've already counted. Anyway, if you count them all up, in a group of seven people there are twenty-one relationships.'

Beth looked mystified but interested.

'The point is that any of these can go wrong or get into a mess at any time. That's just for starters. Then you have to count your mother and father as a couple. As a couple they relate to everyone.

That's more relationships with individuals and with other couples. When you count them up, even in a group of only seven people, there are dozens and dozens of relationships, all tangling up that ball of wool. When things are going well, you don't notice them. When they snag, you spend most of your time trying to undo knots in that ball of wool.'

Beth's upper lip twitched slightly.

Rachel thought she should have stuck to the piano-based explanation. That crusty old hippie in the tepee had smoked too many joints, and now, as she looked at Beth, she knew she'd made a pig's ear out of explaining something simple to an anxious little girl. 'Come on,' Rachel said, 'let's play badminton.'

'It's a failure to convert the angelic tongue exactly into earthly forms of language,' Jessie's instructor remarked as they sat before the mirror in the girls' bedroom later that day, 'that we call these types of clouds "thunderclouds". In fact, they are emblematic of the crack between worlds, as you'll see. But all you really need to know is that they produce lightning, the verb of the language of angels, which activates the beings in the mirror.'

Jessie didn't understand any of this. What she did understand was that her instructor's mind was unspooling. She was becoming less aware of Jessie all the time. Sometimes it was as if she was speaking to herself.

'Often I see my lover in the mirror behind me, but not always, even though I know he's always there, in his way, at my back, making love to me. But sometimes I see others, and it is in those, in their faces and in their futures and in their pasts, that I see what I might be.

'And you, Jess, you must learn to see them too. Correction: you must *allow* yourself to see them because they are there even now, and if we were permitted the time together, we would be able to choose a future for you. But time is short. It dilates, it contracts, it bends.'

It was rare now for Jessie and her instructor to find a moment alone together. Sabine had been persuaded by James to drive into town, however, and Beth had been eager to go with them. Jessie had had to display incipient signs of a tantrum in order to stay. She had real tantrums and pretend tantrums, and this had been a pretend tantrum. Then Beth had changed her mind and demanded to stay. Sabine had pleaded in vain, shot a defiant glance at Chrissie and Matt snoozing by the pool, put the evil eye on Rachel, who was wheeling the bicycle from the shed, and finally climbed in the car with James, still protesting.

'I have to tell you this, Jessie, because you are at a time of changing. The first time is when you are seven, when your initial character is determined. And, because the soul migrates every seven years or so, the next time is around your fourteenth birthday; although you are ready to bleed now, you still need a year or so to understand what that means; but then you will be set, and a woman, which is why the age-of-consent thing is so wrong. The next one after that is twenty-one, which used to mean possession of the key of the door but now, I suppose, it just means you are fully cooked by university with a new accent and an assumption that your parents are idiots. Anyway, the pattern is fixed, seven years by seven by seven, and at each cycle you can choose to become a new person – or the choice is made for you.

'This is the problem with your father, who was forty-two over a year ago and failed to take the opportunity to change himself. He should have decided then, but it's probably too late for him, though it may not be too late for your mother. Jessie, I don't say these things to upset you; I say them to try to explain, very briefly, what is happening, which is why I wanted to tell you about your periods and about your bleeding, which is the mark of your new soul emerging. And didn't I promise to tell you about how it happened to me?

'It was in the corn, Jessie, not all that far from here, in another part of the Dordogne where we used to go on our holidays when I was exactly the same age as you are now. We went every year for three years, Mother and Father and me and cousin Melanie, and we had some wonderful times during days that seemed to go on for ever.

'We would run and play inside the corn because of the light, the emerald-and-golden light. We made dens inside the corn, secret places where you could hide from everyone if you wanted to, or you could even get lost, and it was beautiful and frightening. Then one day I found Father and Melanie playing in the corn. They had been playing a game we called Angels, though even in my young mind I must have known there was more to it because I felt so jealous of Melanie.

'I felt she was taking Father away from us, from Mother and me. I knew he liked being with her more than with us. Once I saw him kiss her and hug her in a way he never kissed or hugged us. It *hurt*, Jessie, to see that. You know how a daughter loves a father. How would you feel if someone was taking yours away from you?'

But Jessie wasn't paying attention. *It's all falling apart*, she thought. Her instructor was going over the edge. She *sensed* it. Her mother and father were bent on a course of destructive collision. She *felt* it. For all of them in the house, mere dislike was hardening into hatred. She could *taste* it.

Worse than all of this, she knew she was responsible. She was to blame. Her personality, her derangement, her bad side, had infected everyone. It had spilled across. The more contact the others had with her, the more unstable they became, starting with her instructor. She had polluted what should have been a carefree holiday.

And so she had taken steps to put things right. Steps she was already beginning to regret.

'I had bad thoughts, Jess. I actually thought about killing Melanie. I thought how easy it would be. But I pretended to laugh and play and kiss and hug Melanie because it was what Father did, and by being happy with Melanie I could ensure my father's love. I'd seen Mother's objections, and her misery, and that they only drove him away from her. And then I felt bad because Melanie was sweet and there were so many ways in which I admired and copied everything she did. Then I felt guilty about the bad thoughts I'd had towards her, and I cried in my bed, in the dark, and I hated the bad girl in me who had these terrible thoughts.

'But the bad girl had other bad thoughts. Anything, anything, so as not to lose him. One day when we were sitting in the corn, Melanie, Father and I, I jumped up and shouted, 'Let's all play Angels!' and I ran through the corn. But when I looked back, Melanie and Father hadn't moved, and Father was silent, and he was staring at me. I saw Melanie look at him. I saw Melanie look away. Then he got up and walked out of the corn and back to the house. I asked Melanie why he'd gone but she wouldn't speak to me.

'I used to talk to myself. Close the door and talk to myself in the mirror in our room. The bad girl would answer from the other side of the mirror, like a Bad Sister, making plans to kill Melanie, and I would argue with her, pointing out Melanie's virtues, taking her side. Then the Bad Sister started telling me what she would do to win back Father's love, and I would tell her it was wrong, wrong wrong wrong.

'But the Bad Sister wasn't content to stay in the mirror. She stepped out, and she followed me, trailing behind me, whispering in my ear, suggesting terrible things, telling me what I must do to get rid of Melanie and to win back Father. The Bad Sister told me I must get Father to play Angels with me. Then he wouldn't want Melanie any more.

'We were in the corn. I heard Father coming. I was crouched there, holding my belly, which ached that day. I remember the light flashing through the corn as the breeze parted the stalks for the sun, and the perspiration on my skin was like ultraviolet light. The Bad Sister wouldn't go away. She stuck to my skin, I couldn't get her off me. I couldn't stop her hanging on to me and speaking filthy words in my ear. The light began flashing in the corn, flickering like a brilliant stroboscope, and my head was pounding. I had a pain in my belly, and I felt the trickle inside me.

'Father was coming, coming through the corn. The Bad Sister

told me to strip off my bathing costume. I could hear the corn swishing as Father came nearer, and when he appeared the Bad Sister told me to run to him and hang from his arm and beg him, "Play Angels with me, Father, play Angels with me, play Angels with me," over and over and over. She wanted me to hold him, to hug him, for him to fall down in the dirt and the dust with me, to love me as he loved Melanie, yes, my father.'

The steps Jessie had taken had failed. Her instructor was getting worse, not better. Inching towards the edge. Her thoughts getting further from the ground, lofted by the cold front of her memory pushing in. Jessie wondered whether she had used too much or not enough. She couldn't tell if the behaviour of the others was worse or better. Had she provoked a storm or diverted one? Or merely delayed it? Or made things worse?

At lunchtime that day she had made a soup for everyone in which she had powdered her entire supply of Ritalin, disguised with garlic and seasoning. Now everyone in the house was dosed with Ritalin, and it didn't seem to be helping in the way she'd hoped. Least of all with her instructor, who still spoke dreamily into the mirror.

'But I was saved, Jessie. It never happened. Before he came, I was saved by an angel.

'I remember everything as if it were in slow motion. The brilliant white light was strobing all about me, and there came an angel, Jessie, an angel with a flaming sword, an angel who was no more nor less than a flash of blinding heat and light and who in that instant lowered the sword and parted me from my Bad Sister. The sword passed between us and released me from my Bad Sister.

'When I was able to look again, my Bad Sister was running from us, screaming deeper and deeper into the corn because of her wounds. I put my hand between my legs and there was blood. Then there was a swish of corn and I knew my father was near. When he broke through the corn and saw me naked the smile disappeared from his face. His jaw worked, but no words came out of his mouth. At last he looked at me and said, "You're bleeding. Put your clothes on."

'And I was bleeding from between my legs, where the angel had touched me with his sword, and I could see from my father's face that something had changed for ever. He turned and went out of the corn and back to the house. After that, after we returned home to England, my father went away.

'But the Bad Sister never went away entirely. She would come back to me from time to time, come back through the mirror. Talking. Speaking words at me. She would make me do things. One time she even got me to kill someone.

'But it was all right. I tricked the Bad Sister and made a pact with the man I was going to kill. He came back from the dead. He came back as someone else. Which proves you can be who you want to be, Jessie. You can be anyone you want. You just have to look in the mirror for long enough, and your face will begin to change.

'She's there now, Jessie. Can you see her? My Bad Sister? She's been there a long time. She's been trying to get to me. Coming to find me here in the Dordogne. But it's a long journey from the past. Can you see her? It's just a question of slowing time, which is why I referred to lightning as the verb of the angelic tongue. A single flash to our eye is to the angelic vision – which, of course, operates in relative time and therefore not exactly in this world – up to forty-two strokes of light. Time in the angelic world is therefore forty-two times longer and more dazzling than in the vulgar. Thus visionaries, seers, mystics, those suffering from delirium, mania or temporal-lobe epilepsy, the psychologically distressed and a few other mortals granted moments of angelic vision are offered temporary escape from a vulgar world operating at one forty-second of the intensity of the angelic plane. Madness, for example, is a high-speed camera. The rest of us must rely on the occasional Gnostic spark, strokes of lightning, fork and ball, the sceptre and orb of insight, and are glad to be restored to our own world instantly. Understand?'

But Jessie had stopped listening. She was too afraid. She was backing slowly out of the room without making a sound, trying not to let the ancient floorboards creak, hoping to disappear while Chrissie, her deranged instructor, spoke as if in a dream, a trance, and not to her, Jessie, at all but to the reflection of herself, eyes half-closed, gazing back from the mirror.

As Jessie retreated from the room, she knocked into Beth, who'd been listening at the door.

'What's Chrissie saying?' Beth whispered. 'What's wrong with her?'

Jessie instinctively put a finger to her lips and a protective arm round her sister, and led her quietly away from the storm now passing through their room.

47

It is often said that lightning never strikes in the same place twice: a fallacy. On the contrary, lightning will often strike repeatedly against the same aerial, masthead, weather-vane or tree in a single storm.

Lightning is dangerous, killing many people each year, damaging buildings and starting forest fires.

It also enriches the earth with nitrogen, released from the air by the lightning and carried to the ground by raindrops. The distinctive smell of ozone is also released by a storm.

48

The following morning, a new sound, a distant chatter. It is the noise of the corn-harvesting machinery making slow but relentless progress through the vast, ripened crops. Though it emanates from the invisible distance, it is borne in on the fresh, stiff breeze, along with sinus-irritating dust, the odour of grapes fermenting on the vine and the scent of burst plums from the fields behind the house. The machine starts early, stops abruptly for a long lunch break and picks up again for a couple of hours in the afternoon. Intrusive at first, the monotonous far-off clatter of the machine retreats from consciousness after a while and joins the backdrop hum of a million insects also industrious in the fields.

Then the storm arrives. It rolls in quickly from the north-west, like something that has watched and waited for its moment, swooping in low with wings spread. Compressed, aubergine-coloured clouds darken the land. The corn-harvesting machine chugs to a stop some minutes before the first large drops of rain precede a downpour. Then the lightning comes.

From the house it is possible to watch the lightning across the entire valley. At first it crackles and probes in thunderless tongues of force. Nearby flashes of mercurial light are mimicked by distant, chorus-like displays all across the valley. Then the thunder, but irregular, correlating not at all with the multi-branched bursts of energy. Sometimes it seems that the lightning discharges not from cloud to land but from land to cloud, as if the skyscape were setting up a force-field which threatens at any moment to part the veil of the visible and material plane and offer a doorway into an alternative world. Fracturing and self-replicating, the frazzles of white light are numinous spirits, visiting beings. Impossible, when watching, not to try to guess their purpose, to interpret their message, to view the spillage of light as a sacred alphabet dripping from the sharp quill of almighty power.

'Sit down, Matt!' James cries for the fourth or fifth time. 'You're making everyone nervous!'

Matt prowls. While lightning forks outside he moves from the lounge to the kitchen, back to the lounge, upstairs, downstairs and back to the kitchen again. He slumps and stands up. Sabine blocks the open doorway for a long time, watching the lightning across the land, enjoying the fresh smell of the rain, sniffing the brief vapours. Rachel, also a little afraid of lightning, sits at the piano in the lounge, consoling herself at the keyboard with nocturnes. James plays backgammon against himself, clattering dice and counting blots across the geometric board. The chair opposite him is drawn away from the table as if waiting for another player.

'What are you afraid of anyway?' James wants to know. 'Sit down, for God's sake.'

But Matt can't sit. He goes back upstairs, tries the handle of his bedroom door, finding it locked again. 'Chrissie,' he whispers pathetically, 'Chrissie.' But Chrissie isn't answering. A howitzer-strength bang of thunder sends him back downstairs to the thin comfort of the company of others. More lightning, instantaneous with thunder, making the house tremble, and this time Matt hides himself in the bathroom, trying to disguise the sound of his retching with the toilet flush.

For Matt the thunder comprises a terrible anatomy. At its head a splitting sound, as if the blue-black canvas of the sky is being torn open; and then the main body of the shock, the clap, dumped on their heads, banging on the gates of life; followed by the tail of the thunder, an eerie crumping and creasing, like a splintering; finally a dirty wake, a foul wind rushing to fill a vacuum caused by the beating of supernatural wings. Matt sits on the toilet seat, cowering in the locked bathroom, sweating, trembling, hugging himself, murmuring Chrissie's name.

*

254

Finding a moment alone with him, the storm rolling overhead, Sabine tells James, 'There's something I want to say.'

'Oh?' James looks up from the backgammon board.

'I want us to move back to France. To live. I'd like the girls to be brought up here now. With different values.'

'Don't be absurd.'

'It's not absurd. It's what I want.'

'You think I can get an advertising job in France? You're not living in the real world.'

'Actually, James, I don't care what you say. I intend to bring up the girls here.'

'Over my dead body.'

'It's what I want now. I've thought hard about it.'

'Well,' says James, scattering the dice across the backgammon board. 'You'll just have to think again.'

Jessie and Beth meanwhile have scampered to the barn, where they sit in the front of their father's Mercedes. Jessie eyes her sister furtively. Beth seems slightly drowsy, which may be the effect of the Ritalin soup. The doors of the barn are thrown open so that Jessie can watch the storm at the same time as showing Beth what can be done with a needle and a bottle of blue ink. She is keen to demonstrate to her younger sister how easy it is to prick and ink a tattoo on her lower arm and how she can render an angel out of simple triangles. Outside the lightning flickers and dances about the barn, and the thunder threatens to bring down the roof. 'Do you want one, Beth? Do you want a tattoo?' And Beth says, yes, but doesn't like the pain of the needle, so draws back, whereupon Jessie laughs and begins again upon herself, on the other arm, rendering jagged bolts of lightning behind her angel's wings . . .

And upstairs in her room Chrissie makes her face in the mirror, whitening her cheeks, accentuating the oval of her eyes with delicate coal-black lines, painting her eyelashes, teasing the crescent of her eyebrows, tracing the beautiful, crimson, fruit-like flesh of her lips.

All the while the thunder bangs and lightning flickers briefly, reflected frenetically in the mirror, silhouetting the shoulders of the Bad Sister, arcing within the stormy black holes that are the pupils of her dark eyes; and with each flash of light a fragment of mirror-silver is stripped away, and another year is stripped away, and another tiny distance is bridged between Chrissie and her Gothic history until the dark template of a jagged bolt of lightning itself appears in the mirror, widening, widening, so that the angel/demon of her history is ready and able to step through the mirror, to move through the glass and settle herself in the shape of Chrissie with a sigh almost audible above the clap of thunder.

The storm persists for over an hour. Then it stops, and the clouds pass over. The aerial visitors have gone, leaving the land green, sparkling and steaming, heartened but unsatisfied. It isn't enough. The land wants more: just feeling the passing of celestial armies is not enough. To be ravaged is everything.

'What on earth is *that*?' Sabine demands, grabbing Jessie's arm. The glass tumbler from which Jessie has been drinking falls to the floor and shatters. Sabine wets her fingers with her tongue and tries wiping at the ink on Jessie's right arm. 'You stupid, *stupid* girl,' she shouts, shaking her daughter by the wrist, trying to twist her left arm to see the results of the other storm tattoo. 'You unspeakably stupid girl! Don't you realize? Don't you realize that it won't go away? Don't you?' She shakes Jessie again, hard. 'Answer me, you little fool!'

Beth cowers against the patio wall, relieved she herself hasn't taken up Jessie's generous offer of a needle-and-ink tattoo of her own. But she's never seen her mother so angry, so out of control. Spittle flicks from Sabine's mouth as she shouts. Her eyes are black, bottomless holes; her nostrils flare like an animal's; her entire face seems pumped up with poison. Jessie squeals, trying to break from her mother's grip.

James and Matt come from inside to see what the noise is all about. 'Look at her!' Sabine shrieks. 'Look at your daughter!'

'I wanted to be like Rachel,' Jessie cries. 'That's all. I wanted be like Rachel.'

Rachel, who moments earlier was playing the piano in the lounge, folds her arms, touching her own tattoos with spread fingers.

James crouches beside Jessie and gently takes her arm. All he can think of, as he studies the inked scarification, is how sophisticated and clean are the lines of Jessie's handiwork. 'Is it an angel?'

Jessie moans, nods, still crying. 'From the cave.'

'With a lightning bolt. An angel with lightning. I never realized how artistic you are, Jessie.'

He releases Jessie's arm, stands up and turns to face his wife. The remark, and the expression on his face, only succeed in enraging Sabine further. With a low and strangely dislocated growl issuing from the back of her throat, she launches herself at James, pummelling her fists on his chest, scratching at his neck and trying to fasten her hands around his throat as he forces her fingers away from his windpipe. He can't keep her off him. He grabs a handful of her hair and pulls her head back and away from him as she claws at his throat. They struggle to an impasse where, unmoving, red-faced and ridiculous, they remain locked in a grotesque sculpture. Matt and Rachel stand by, watching stupidly.

'Separate them,' says Rachel. 'Stop them.'

Matt dives in, pushing his arms between Sabine and James. 'Stop it, you two! Your children are watching this!'

'Stay out of it,' James snarls. 'You haven't *earned* the right to interfere. You're paid to speak when I tell you to speak.'

For a moment, James is back at his agency. Mortified, Matt falls back, but his intervention has succeeded in prising the others apart. 'So. Even though you deliberately got me fired, you think I'm still working for you, do you?'

'You were fired because you were fucking useless.'

'What about Rachel? You paid for her to be here too. Is she still working for you?'

Now it's Sabine's turn to be stunned. 'Is it true? You also paid for Rachel to be here? You paid for *all* this wonderful company?' She doesn't need an answer as Rachel turns away. Still panting, Sabine surveys James unsteadily. 'That's it, then. You're satisfied now. Your daughter has scarred herself so that she can look like your tattooed slut.' Sabine jabs a finger under Rachel's nose.

Rachel unfolds her arms. 'That's out of order, lady!'

But Sabine isn't listening to Rachel or to anyone. 'Are you satisfied, now that Jessie also looks like a whore? Like a Parisian tart? Is that what you wanted? Is it?'

'Sabine,' Matt appeals, 'your children.'

'Is that why you brought your slut along with you? So she could be an example to your daughter?'

'The girls . . .' Matt tries again.

Sabine flicks back her straggling locks and turns to collect up her daughters. But they're no longer there. Neither Jessie nor Beth has stayed to watch the conclusion of this latest adults' performance. They have both gone, and no one has seen them go.

49

Both children had disappeared. There was a moment of horrible gratitude, in that this gave the adults an opportunity to flee from the ghastly confrontations taking place on the patio. A truce was enacted as Sabine and James were artificially reunited in the task of searching for their children. Rachel too could step back from her part in the conflict, and Matt could escape from his role as useless bystander in the combat zone.

But after they'd searched the house, the barn, the outbuildings, the cars and the gardens, relief turned to consternation. Sabine and James conducted a second, more careful search of the house, checking the cupboard under the stairs and any other alcove in which the girls might be hiding. Matt remembered the girls' secret hideaway in the barn loft, and Rachel even thought to glance up at the roof, in case Jessie had climbed back up on the tiles; but all to no avail.

'Where's Chrissie?' Sabine asked. 'Is she with Chrissie?'

'I'll go,' said Matt.

With the others searching the outbuildings for a second time, Matt went to his room and tried the handle. The door was locked. He tapped softly. 'Chrissie? It's me. It's Matt. Are you in there?'

There was no answer. He heard a movement from inside.

'Chrissie.'

'Go away.'

He'd been waiting for this, dreading the moment. He'd seen it before. Always it began with her sleepwalking, always it culminated in a similar event. Afraid as he was for her, he knew the best policy was to leave her alone. 'Chrissie, are the girls with you? Just tell me if either of the girls is with you.'

Pause. 'No.'

Matt returned downstairs and reported that he'd checked his and Chrissie's room. James swung open the barn doors and reversed out his car. Sabine struck out across the fields. Matt climbed into his own car, intending to drive in the opposite direction to James. Rachel, about to get in with him, said, 'Chrissie's here if they come back.'

'No,' Matt said, 'she's not well. You'd better stay here.'

'What's the matter with her?' Rachel saw a threatening light in Matt's eye as he closed the passenger door on her.

The house fell uncommonly silent. Rachel dithered on the grass by the swimming pool, considering hiding places that might have been overlooked. She made some tea and took it up to Chrissie, but when she tapped on the door she got no answer. Figuring Chrissie might be sleeping, she left the tray outside the door, went back downstairs and waited for the others to return.

By the time they were all back at the house, dusk was approaching. Consternation was running to deep anxiety. Sabine wanted to telephone the police. She contacted Dominique who, despite trying to reassure her, offered to phone the police herself to apprise them of the situation. By nine o'clock the girls still hadn't appeared. Matt and James went out again in their cars, slowly trawling the lanes, headlamps on full beam. This time Rachel went with Matt. By ten o'clock the house had received a visit from the local police. The officer took off his hat and spoke quietly and calmly with Sabine but had little to suggest beyond volunteering to help by searching in his own car.

After eleven, Dominique and Patrice appeared. Dominique made fresh coffee and tried to console Sabine, who was red-eyed from crying. It was some time around midnight that Patrice had an inspired thought and said something to Dominique. 'Patrice asks if anyone has tried the cave.'

'The cave!' said Matt. 'I'll go.'

'But we can do it,' Dominique protested.

'No, I'll go with Matt,' said Rachel, eager to be doing something rather than sitting around. 'Leave the car, Matt. We'll walk just as they would have done.'

Rachel carried the torch and they set off across fields partially illuminated by a gibbous moon. On reaching the bottom of the hill, they turned and looked back. The house crouched ominously in the dark, silhouetted on the brow of the hill. A sickly yellow light burned on the patio. 'I just had to get out of that house,' Rachel said.

They climbed the incline and passed the outcrop of limestone rock before Matt spoke. 'You're wrong.'

'Oh?'

'It's true I hate James, and over these past few days I've enjoyed seeing him suffer. But I take no pleasure in watching him fight with Sabine, or in observing her unhappiness, or in seeing the children hurt and confused. You're wrong about all that, and you were wrong to accuse me.'

'I'm sorry I made you get between them, but they were fighting like kids in a schoolyard, and you weren't doing anything.'

'I've learned not to intervene.' Matt gave Rachel a hand up on to the grassy trail. 'Plus I've got worries of my own.'

'Is Chrissie all right?'

Matt didn't answer.

'I'm cold,' Beth complained. 'I don't like it here.'

Jessie hugged her. 'It's not for long. It's only until they've stopped fighting.' Jessie guessed they might need a few hours. The ugly scenes on the patio had finally confirmed her worst suspicions: that adults were no more in control of events than children; that in pretending otherwise they were a danger to each other; and that order in the world was only provisional and subject to constant slippage. It was shocking, for an eleven-year-old, to discover that adults lived out their days precariously, on a thin skin stretched over the void.

'Why do they? Why do they do that? We're supposed to love each other,' Beth said.

Jessie said nothing. Her eyes had soon become accustomed to the dark, but now the gloom was thickening around her. She felt there was something in that place with them, some live thing in the shadowy and impenetrable recesses. She decided not to say anything to Beth.

'If they keep fighting, Daddy will run away again,' said Beth.

'No, he won't.'

'He will. What if both of them ran away? Do you think Rachel would look after us?'

'Or Matt and Chrissie.'

'Chrissie is strange. I wouldn't want to be looked after by Chrissie. I like Rachel better. You shouldn't have had a tattoo.'

'Chrissie told me there are angels in the corn.'

'Angels!'

'Shhh!' Jessie hissed sharply. 'We don't want anyone to know we're here. They'll be looking for us.'

'Angels?' Beth whispered.

'Yes. In the corn. You can only see them if you don't look too hard. You have to look for something else, and they come to you.'

'What do they look like?'

'They have swords. Bright, flashing silver swords, and they cut you. Chrissie said they come like a storm getting closer, and you know they are near because of a green-and-golden light and a rushing noise getting nearer and nearer, and they cut you, but that makes everything all right. You mustn't be afraid of them, Chrissie said. Though they scare you, you mustn't be afraid because they make everything all right.'

'Will they make everything all right for us? For all of us?'

A scuffling in the shadows stifled Jessie's answer. Beth stiffened next to her, her wide eyes trying to peer through the dirty light. Then there was silence. Beth started to cry. Jessie hugged her closer and said, 'It's only until they've stopped fighting.'

They made progress along the grassy knoll, and the moon drifted behind a cloud. A slight breeze left behind by the storm nosed at their backs. Cicadas generated an air of frenzy. Rachel looked up at Matt. The furrows of his brow were streaked with shadow.

'Are you all right?'

'I have a foreboding of what we're about to find in this cave, Rachel.'

'I wish you hadn't said that.'

But it was already said. Rachel saw Matt wipe sweat from his brow, though the night was cool. He seemed to drag his feet, reluctant to make progress. Finally they reached the clump of juniper and brambles concealing the crevice of the cave, and they pushed their way through. Matt suddenly put a hand on Rachel's shoulder. 'It's no good,' he hissed. 'I can't go in.'

'Why?'

She shone the torch at him. He bared his teeth at the light, shaking his head. Rachel turned her torch on the narrow fissure in the rock. Painted with moonlight, the jagged crack resembled the imprint or after-image of a lightning flash. 'Wait here.' Squeezing through the slit, she entered the cave. Inside she paused, playing the light around the walls. There was a sob of dripwater at the back of the cave. The night breeze played around the aperture of the cave like an unpractised mouth on a flute. A foul smell emanated from the back of the cave along with mineral odours and the reek of wet limestone.

'Jessie? Beth?' Rachel's call came out as a whisper. She had to crack her voice to raise it. 'Jessie?'

There was nothing. Pressing further in towards the back of the cave, her torchlight settled on a mineral vein in the stone, a strand of glacial black rock reflecting fresh water from the rainstorm like a mirror. Further along she stumbled and grazed her hand. Something shifted at the back of the cave.

Shining her torch around the walls, she found the prehistoric cave painting. The winged creatures. She recognized instantly where Jessie had drawn inspiration for her tattoo. The breeze at the mouth of the cave continued to improvise around two half-formed notes, primitive music. Rachel caught another whiff of something bad inside the cave and shuddered. 'Jessie? Are you in here?'

Rachel heard slow, uncertain footsteps approaching from behind. She turned very slowly, shining the torch. Matt's frightened face appeared in the light. 'Changed your mind?' said Rachel.

'I felt I'd let you down. I don't know what it is, but I hate this place.'

'It's eerie. Listen.'

They stood listening to the breeze in the crevice. It was playing now like a wind instrument, a hollow brass tube half-forming a sound, a not fully realized musical note. Rachel knew that sound. It was a weird descant, the sound to which rocks erode and reform and to which people live and die with aspirations for perfect flight dragged to the ground by feet of clay. It was the sound of nothing changing. She felt a passing moment of black despair and had to stifle a sob of profound sadness.

'They're not here, are they?' asked Matt.

'No.'

'What's that smell?'

Rachel shone her torch on some small creature lying wounded, shifting slightly at the back of the cave, bird or animal, it was difficult to tell. 'They haven't been here. Let's go.'

They were glad to squeeze out of the cave, to see the silver hump-backed moon and the scattering of stars in the night sky. Rachel felt uplifted, but this time it was Matt's turn.

'Matt, what is it?'

'You don't know the half of it, Rachel. Not even the half.'

They retraced their path back to the house. When they arrived, it was apparent from everyone's face that the girls were yet to be found. Dominique and Patrice were still there. Dominique put her fingers to her lips. Sabine was sprawled on the couch in the lounge, covered by a blanket. 'She's exhausted. We filled her full of cognac and she cried herself to sleep.' Patrice made a gesture to indicate he might have mixed something with her cognac. 'James is still driving around the lanes. We're going to go now. We'll be back in the morning.' Dominique came to them and kissed them both with surprising passion. Patrice did the same.

Matt took up the cognac and poured a drink for him and Rachel. He downed his in one. They sat in the lounge, watching Sabine's bosom rise and fall as she slept.

'Want to talk?' said Rachel.

'Not really.'

'I know you're a junkie. Is that your big secret?'

'I knew someone had been snooping.' Matt gave her a wry smile. 'See. You don't know anything about me.'

'I'm coming to the conclusion no one knows anything about anyone.'

'I was a junkie once. In another life. I'm not now. But it's not me I'm worried about. It's Chrissie. I have to take care of her. She lives on the edge. And I owe her everything because she saved my life.'

'How did she save your life?'

'I was living in Paris. I was *playing* at living in Paris. I was *playing* at lifestyles. I was an addict and when you're an addict different people, versions of you, step out of you and offer different lies . . . I mean, different lives. Three people step out of you but you can only follow one, so the other two wither and die right there in front of you. They, I mean the choices you don't make, lie on the floor like suits of clothes, then they're gone – are you with me? Anyway, I was following one of these. He had a different name. He was called Gregory, which is my middle name. Then Chrissie walked into my life and told me she had chosen *me* to save *her*. I was her angel, see, Rachel?

'She was looking for me to be some kind of father-figure. I quickly realized she was manic. I thought it would be amusing to have her around. But as for saving her, how could I? I was a junkie. I did a bit of dealing to support myself, that's how I was living. Then one day – I was looking after an apartment for a friend – she came to me and told me she had decided to kill me. Well, I didn't believe her. But she went right ahead and fixed my gear so

265

that I took an overdose. I almost died. I really believe she intended to kill me. I went into an hallucinatory coma. I could see everything happening in front of me, but I couldn't get out of my chair. I was paralysed.

'And while I was paralysed in my chair an angel came to me disguised as Chrissie and stood over me, blowing smoke in my face. But the smoke broke into words, readable words settling in front of me, like writing on a page. The angel told me I could change my life. That I was being given a second chance. That I could become another person and leave it all behind. Then the angel made an appointment to see me again.

'I thought Chrissie had gone for ever, but she came looking for me and found me on the street. I stared into her eyes and I knew, instantly, that the thing that had possessed her had gone. Passed over like a storm. It had gone from her eyes. And she was clear, lucid. She told me I'd died a symbolic death. She told me she was also ready to change her life and we made a pact to each other, a promise. We stopped lying to each other. This time we fell in love – I mean, really in love. We came back to England together.'

'What about the drugs paraphernalia in your room?'

'The sword of my angel, hanging over me. The ampoules are full of methadone, heroin substitute, and so old I don't know if it's still any good. Some people wouldn't have it in the house, but it was part of Chrissie's terms. She didn't want any sneaking around. She was determined to offer it to me every hour, on the hour. The choice, you see, of which angel to follow. If I wanted it, she said, I should have it, but that our second chance would be death. She stopped offering it after a while, but I kept it to look at every day. The choice makes me strong. It reminds me of the day Gregory died.'

'What about Chrissie? Is she –'

'No, she doesn't use it and never has. Believe me, she doesn't need drugs to see angels. She sometimes sees more angels than she can handle. I told you, she's a manic depressive. These bouts come roughly once a year, lasting from mere days to weeks. Just occasionally they go way beyond my capacity to help, but I never leave her, whatever happens. She's my salvation. I have this fear that if she ever went away, then I really would be dead. Rachel, she represents a chaos I fear in myself. See how we choose our partners?'

'Where is she now?'

'Upstairs. When she's like this I try to keep her away from people, but living so close . . .'

They heard James's car wheels crunching the gravel outside the house. Appearing in the doorway, he looked all in. He didn't need to ask about the cave. His head hung low, he was drained, defeated. Rachel put her arms around him. Matt left them alone and went to bed.

He found the door unlocked. Chrissie was buried under a mound of bedclothes. He whispered to her, and though she didn't reply, he suspected she was wide awake. In the roof he heard the scuffle and scrabble of the owl before he fell asleep.

50

Rachel woke the following morning to the chattering mechanism of the corn-harvester in the field outside her window. Slender shafts of light pierced the shutters. She heard the owl scratching at the rafters in the attic above her room and blinked up at the ceiling. Then she got out of bed, went over to the window and threw back the shutters.

The corn-harvester had made huge progress, cutting giant swathes through the towering corn. She could see the vivid red machine working steadily through the crops a few hundred metres away, reducing everything in its path to rough stubble in the arid soil. Yawning, she leaned out of the window, enjoying the feel of the morning sun on her face. Then something caught her eye. She saw a tiny figure sprinting across the field.

'Beth!' She leaned out of the window and called again, 'Beth!'

The little girl either couldn't hear or was simply ignoring her. She was running very fast, holding her doll and, under her arm, a red blanket. Rachel pulled on a shirt and her shorts and raced downstairs.

Sabine was up, eyes red and bruised, pacing the kitchen. Ignoring her, Rachel dashed outside. She ran barefoot across the grass to where she'd seen the girl. But Beth had disappeared. She could have run off in any direction, through the trees, over the brow of the hill or towards the church on the other side of the house. Rachel sighed and returned to the house.

'I saw Beth.'

'Where?' James too was up.

'Running through the field.'

'Are you certain?' Matt was also about, wearing only his jeans. Chrissie was still in bed.

'Absolutely certain. I was upstairs and I looked out of the window and I saw her running.'

'Which direction?'

'She was running away from the house. She must have been inside all night.' Rachel was thinking. Recalling the moment before she'd looked out of the window, she remembered the scuffling she'd heard above her head. 'Of course!'

She hurried upstairs. Between her own room and the girls' room was a cupboard space. Opening the door, she saw that the cupboard gave on to the attic. Rachel lifted the panel above her head and hoisted herself up. Jessie, with a blanket around her shoulders, blinked sleepily at her.

'I think you'd better come down,' said Rachel.

'Will you tell them not to be mad with me?'

'I'll try. Come on.'

Downstairs, there was too much relief for anger. Sabine hugged her, shouted at her, hugged her a second time. James squeezed her and berated her and made her promise never to do that to them again. 'Now we have to find Beth. Have you really been in the attic all night? Both of you?'

'Yes.'

'Do you realize we told the police? Where is Beth now?'

'I don't know. I saw her get up but I fell back to sleep. I don't know where she's gone.'

'She can't be far,' said Matt. 'She's probably afraid of getting a roasting.'

So it all started again. They combed the outbuildings and the barn, and then scoured the house, all calling Beth's name, this time with Jessie helping. The search was conducted against the background rattle and chatter of the encroaching corn-harvester as it drew ever nearer. After two hours they still hadn't found her. James this time was disinclined to drive round and round country lanes, and Sabine was less than disposed to summon the police. But her anguish got the better of her.

'Where's Chrissie?' she screamed at Matt. 'Why isn't she helping us when we need her?'

Beth meanwhile was comfortable in the den she'd made deep inside the corn. She'd spread her red blanket over the cracked, dry earth and lay back, arms outstretched. With her doll beside her, she awaited the advent of angels. As she gazed up through the stems of the high corn, sunlight fretted the green leaves and oozed like syrup from the heavy golden cobs. She knew that the angels would come. Something in the light reminded her of Bible stories, and high above the corn itself was a sky as blue as Heaven. Looking up through the corn was like staring into a tube. The uppermost tips of the corn shaped a hole through to the sky. Beth thought, for a moment, *what if up was down?* It seemed possible to slither from the earth, to shoot through this narrow tube of corn and to go spinning into the blue itself, where she would fall for ever and for ever amen. For a moment she felt herself slipping, and had to tangle her fingers in the thick stalks of the corn to stop herself tumbling into for ever.

Then a small cloud drifted into the blue space between the nodding heads of corn and Beth wondered if it might be an angel. She tried not to look too hard at the cloud. Jessie had told her that Chrissie had said that if you looked too hard, you would never see an angel, and that to see an angel you had to find it in ordinary things and in ordinary places. Beth squinted at the cloud. She tried looking sideways at it, hoping to discern the face of the angel.

Then she felt the ground vibrating and heard the approaching chatter of the corn-harvester. It was very near, but she knew she must not be afraid. *Green-and-golden light,* Jessie had said, and Chrissie had told her. Here the light was green and golden. *Look for angels in ordinary things.* She was looking, but not too hard, in case the angel should take fright and leave her. But if the angel came to her, everything would be all right. Everyone would stop fighting, and everything would be all right.

The corn-harvester came by, much closer this time, and Beth was afraid. She picked up her doll and hugged it close to her chest. *It can be a person, it can be a cloud, it can be a car.* She could not see but could hear the blades of the harvester going *whop-whop-whop* through the corn. *They come in a rushing noise and in ordinary things.* The machine passed by and moved away from her, retreating down the field before making a turn and coming back again.

Now the small cloud in the sky had expanded, as if spreading its arms in welcome or perhaps opening its wings. Was this what they meant? Was this it? Beth was afraid, but she knew if she waited for the angel, everything would be all right.

The ground trembled as the machine approached, much louder this time. *Though they scare you, you must never be afraid.* But Beth was afraid. Beth hugged her doll in terror and whimpered as the slashing sound came closer and closer. The beat of the cutter through the corn was louder. *Whop-whop-whop.* Like wings thrashing in flight, Beth thought, the wings of angels. The machine hissed and smoked as it bore down on her. This time the machine came close enough for her to see the blades spinning, silver blades flashing in the sunlight. *They have swords. Bright silver swords that cut you without hurting you.* Paralysed, Beth squeezed herself into a tiny ball, hugging herself as the harvester passed by a few paces beyond her blanket. She heard the rushing retreat and the *whop-whop* of the blades diminish as the machine moved away down the field, where eventually it made a turn and prepared to come back.

At the house, recrimination was bloodletting again. With the corn-harvester scything up and down the adjacent field, Sabine turned on James and James responded in kind. Then Sabine blamed Rachel, or rather James and Rachel, who together had frightened the children and filled their heads full of nonsense.

'It wasn't Rachel,' said Matt.

Sabine ignored him. She stepped over to Rachel. 'I've seen you,' she shouted over the chatter of the harvester, 'whispering in their ears, poisoning their minds. I know what you want. You want my husband? Here, take him, with pleasure. But you can't have my children!'

Matt tried again. 'It wasn't her.'

Sabine turned on him. 'Why are you protecting her? What business is it of yours?'

'I'm just telling you you're wrong.'

'What do you mean, wrong?'

'You've got the wrong person.'

'The wrong person? What are you saying? So who was it?'

Matt didn't have to answer. Chrissie emerged like a beam of light from the shadows of the house, stepping from the patio and moving across the grass towards them. Her appearance stunned and silenced them. She wore a long white dress. Her face was whited. Her eyes were made up with heavy black lines, and her lips were painted in a crimson pout. 'Beth,' she said.

Everyone stared in appalled silence. It was Matt who spoke. 'We're looking for her. Are you all right?' He took a step towards her, but she held out a hand, pressing his chest away from her. Then she cocked her head slightly, seeming to listen for a moment before turning and looking directly across the field of corn at the approaching harvester. They watched in astonishment as she walked very quickly towards the cornfield, taking long strides, the hem of her white skirt swishing across the grass. The harvester had made a turn and was approaching the house as Chrissie disappeared into the corn. She seemed to be walking directly into its path.

'What's she doing?' asked Jessie.

Jessie's question broke the trance gripping the others.

'Matt,' Rachel said, 'she's walking towards the machine.'

Matt, staring after her, seemed rooted.

'Is Beth in the corn?' shouted James. His face was puce. Prominent silver-blue veins stood out on his forehead.

His cry galvanized Matt, and the two men plunged into the

field, following the path taken by Chrissie. James outpaced Matt by far. The sound of the harvester grew louder and louder as they smashed their way through the tough stalks. As Matt made up ground, James suddenly appeared to be scythed at the knees. He buckled and went down, gagging now, kneeling in the dirt as Matt outstripped him. Matt left him behind. Within moments the huge machine bore down on Matt, roaring in his ears. The cutting blades flashed in the sunlight only a few feet away. Matt saw something red snatched up from the ground and tossed in the air.

'Chrissie!' His voice was like the shriek of a bird.

He was almost under the blades of the cutter, still screaming when the corn-harvester stopped dead. Its engine was switched off and the driver, shocked and pale, emerged from the corn, unable to speak. Then he began to babble in French. Sabine, Rachel and Jessie had all raced to the machine where Matt was still screaming Chrissie's name.

There was a rustling and the flash of a white dress in the bright sunshine as Chrissie emerged from the corn, carrying a bundle in her arms. The bundle was Beth, shielding her eyes from the fierce sunlight, blinking at them all, afraid and ashamed. Sabine ran to gather the child from Chrissie's arms.

'Here she is,' said Chrissie, handing Beth to her mother. 'You must take better care of these children.'

Chrissie turned and walked back to the house.

'Where's James?' someone said.

51

It was late when Matt got back, but Chrissie and Rachel were sitting out on the patio. Candles were burning. White-winged moths swarmed round the weak yellow electric light on the barn wall. Matt switched off the car engine, and the two women stood up.

'That was a long drive,' he said, throwing the car keys on the table and slumping in a chair. 'A long drive.'

'Can I get you a drink?' Chrissie murmured.

'A beer. No, make that coffee. Hell, anything.'

'You're so late,' Rachel said softly. 'We were getting worried.'

'It was a lot further than I thought. Plus the flight was delayed, and I stayed with them until the last moment.'

'They got off all right, then?' asked Chrissie, handing Matt a cup of coffee.

He slurped his coffee and spilled some of it down his shirt. 'Yes. They got off all right.'

They sat silently for a while, listening to the cicadas, the two women sensing that Matt wasn't ready to talk. Then at last Chrissie said, 'We cleared up and packed while you were gone. We can leave first thing in the morning.'

'The thing is,' said Matt, 'Sabine was incredibly focused. Her mind was on all the practical things. I suppose it's a way of getting through. As for the girls, Jessie was numb but quite grown-up. Beth didn't say a word all the way to the airport. Every time I looked at her in the rear-view mirror, I thought I was going to burst into tears. It's like a dream. I still can't believe it.'

Matt had been the one to go back into the corn to find James. In the race to the corn-harvester, James had fallen to the ground as if felled by an archer and hadn't got up again. He lay on the dry, compacted earth in quivering unconsciousness. His cheeks fluttered with the labour of breathing and his eyes were turned to one side, pupils contracted. When Matt couldn't get James to speak he knew something was seriously wrong. Instinctively he dragged James clear of the corn. Sabine had already taken the girls back inside, but Rachel, Chrissie and the farmer had rushed over to them.

'He's having a seizure,' Rachel had said.

James's skin was flushed and moist with sweat; his lips were blown out. Rachel rolled him on to his side and forced his mouth open. One side of his body seemed entirely paralysed. She looked up with frightened eyes. 'Telephone, Matt! Telephone!'

Matt had raced back to the house and had phoned for an ambulance. When he got back Rachel was giving James mouth-to-mouth ventilation. She stopped and began to compress his chest. 'Is he breathing?' Matt asked, but Rachel didn't answer. She seemed to know what she was doing. Occasionally she stopped alternating between compression and ventilation to feel for the pulse at the neck.

'Go back and keep Sabine and the girls indoors,' is all she said.

The ambulance arrived within half an hour. The paramedics took over and loaded James into the ambulance. Sabine and Matt went with him. Chrissie and Rachel stayed behind to take care of the girls. They watched the ambulance speed away, its sirens blaring pointlessly on the empty road. Chrissie turned to Rachel and said, 'It's no good, is it?'

Rachel looked at her. Then she looked over her shoulder at Jessie and Beth, who were watching from the door.

Chrissie, meanwhile, was something like sane again.

'It's gone, hasn't it?' Matt was to say to her much later.

'Yes.' Her make-up, her face-white, her lipstick had also gone. To the question, put to her by both Rachel and Matt, of how she knew exactly where to find Beth she was unable to find an answer.

She thought it might have been something Jessie had said to her, or she to Jessie, or intuition.

'Was it an angel who told you?' Beth had asked her.

'Probably,' said Chrissie.

'Was it the mirror that told you?' Matt asked her privately.

'Maybe,' said Chrissie. 'There was a moment in the cornfield, when I stood over James's body and looked at his face. I saw the silver blades of the corn-harvester reflected in the pupils of his eyes, and I knew he was dead but that this time there would be no coming back. I'm not afraid of the past any more, Matt. I think the faces in the mirror have gone for ever.'

When the telephone rang, neither of them wanted to answer. Rachel picked up the receiver. It was Matt, telling them what they already knew. James had suffered a massive apoplexy. A stroke. Matt relayed instructions from Sabine that the girls were not to be told. She wanted to tell her daughters herself. Rachel answered in monosyllables, knowing that Jessie and Beth were listening on the stairs. When she replaced the receiver on the cradle she lied and told them that Dominique had telephoned to ask if she could help.

Matt and Sabine didn't return to the house until late that evening. Sabine took the girls into a room. Jessie became hysterical, but they didn't emerge. The following day, despite all the efforts of the previous afternoon and evening, there were further bureaucratic hurdles with police and insurance companies and coroners. This time Sabine took the children with her to the nearest town. Matt offered to help again, but as everything was conducted in French, he wasn't much use. By the following day Sabine had been cleared to fly the body back to England. There was a flight from Bordeaux that evening. Sabine asked Rachel if she would be prepared to drive the car back to England, so that she could go on the plane with the children.

'Of course,' said Rachel.

'And would you drive us to the airport, Matt?'

276

'Anything.'

It was all hideous and framed by enormous practical problems, while the landscape itself and the faces of all involved were twisted by a strange geometry. Before they left, Chrissie asked Sabine if she could take Jessie and Beth for a last walk in the fields. Matt said he would go with them, and Sabine said, yes, they could. The corn-harvester stood abandoned where it had stopped in the middle of the job two days earlier. The driver wouldn't finish the task until after they'd all gone home. Shreds of Beth's red blanket were tangled in the blades. Chrissie stopped and looked at the machine for a long time. Then she turned to the children and said, 'We both love you, Matt and I. Your mother says you may be coming back to France to live, after things have been sorted out. So we may not see much of you in future, but we both love you.'

'Do you still believe in angels?' Jessie asked.

Chrissie said, 'I know this: angels and demons are powers hidden in every man and woman, and you have to be careful when you wake them.'

Matt didn't know what his wife meant, but he saw that Jessie was nodding, as if she did.

At the airport Jessie said to Matt, 'Do you think we'll ever lead a normal life?'

'There's no such thing as a normal life,' Matt told her. 'There's just life.'

'Mummy promised me I wouldn't have to take Ritalin any more.'

Matt blinked, then he seized her and kissed her. After he'd kissed them all, he watched them pass through to the departure lounge, Sabine and her two daughters, diminished and vulnerable, numbed, tired from crying. His heart squeezed. He wanted to call down an angel for each of them, but especially for Jessie, whom he recognized as one of his own kind.

On the patio he drank his coffee and said, 'I don't think I can sleep tonight.'

'Then we'll sit up,' said Chrissie.

'We'll watch for an owl,' said Rachel.

'What will you do?' Matt asked her. 'I mean, when you get back to your job?'

'I'll quit. It's not me. It's important to realize these things as early as possible.'

An owl hooted, and they all heard it.

The morning of departure was marked by cloud, portending a further break in the weather and the turning, somewhere in Nature, of a vast wheel. Dominique and Patrice arrived to bid them farewell. Matt slammed the boot of his car. Dominique and Patrice kissed them solemnly, wished them well and waved them away. They had to prepare the house for a new group of friends who were arriving from England the next day.

Rachel led the way in James's car. They had agreed to drive home in convoy, to share the driving. When Chrissie had stopped waving, she looked up at the sky. 'There's a big change coming in the weather,' she said. 'I can feel it.'

52

Meteorology is the scientific study of the earth's atmosphere. The term derives from Aristotle's *Meteorologia*, the 'study of things lifted high', and includes the examination of day-to-day weather conditions; electrical, optical and other physical characteristics of the weather; climate; and other phenomena.

Micrometeorology is the study of variations in meteorological elements near to the ground over a very small area.

Accuracy in predicting the weather is only partial. More than two thousand years after Aristotle, despite advances in data-collecting technology, meteorology must still be considered an inexact science.

Everything we call weather.

Going round and round in an endless effort to settle and even out that which can never be settled or evened out.

READ MORE IN PENGUIN

In every corner of the world, on every subject under the sun, Penguin represents quality and variety – the very best in publishing today.

For complete information about books available from Penguin – including Puffins, Penguin Classics and Arkana – and how to order them, write to us at the appropriate address below. Please note that for copyright reasons the selection of books varies from country to country.

In the United Kingdom: Please write to *Dept. EP, Penguin Books Ltd, Bath Road, Harmondsworth, West Drayton, Middlesex UB7 0DA*

In the United States: Please write to *Consumer Sales, Penguin Putnam Inc., P.O. Box 999, Dept. 17109, Bergenfield, New Jersey 07621-0120.* VISA and MasterCard holders call 1-800-253-6476 to order Penguin titles

In Canada: Please write to *Penguin Books Canada Ltd, 10 Alcorn Avenue, Suite 300, Toronto, Ontario M4V 3B2*

In Australia: Please write to *Penguin Books Australia Ltd, P.O. Box 257, Ringwood, Victoria 3134*

In New Zealand: Please write to *Penguin Books (NZ) Ltd, Private Bag 102902, North Shore Mail Centre, Auckland 10*

In India: Please write to *Penguin Books India Pvt Ltd, 210 Chiranjiv Tower, 43 Nehru Place, New Delhi 110 019*

In the Netherlands: Please write to *Penguin Books Netherlands bv, Postbus 3507, NL-1001 AH Amsterdam*

In Germany: Please write to *Penguin Books Deutschland GmbH, Metzlerstrasse 26, 60594 Frankfurt am Main*

In Spain: Please write to *Penguin Books S. A., Bravo Murillo 19, 1° B, 28015 Madrid*

In Italy: Please write to *Penguin Italia s.r.l., Via Benedetto Croce 2, 20094 Corsico, Milano*

In France: Please write to *Penguin France, Le Carré Wilson, 62 rue Benjamin Baillaud, 31500 Toulouse*

In Japan: Please write to *Penguin Books Japan Ltd, Kaneko Building, 2-3-25 Koraku, Bunkyo-Ku, Tokyo 112*

In South Africa: Please write to *Penguin Books South Africa (Pty) Ltd, Private Bag X14, Parkview, 2122 Johannesburg*